SELECT PRAISE FOR *A MAN DOWNSTAIRS*

INSTANT NATIONAL BESTSELLER

"A gripping story of troubled relationships, mental illness and buried secrets with a murder at its heart. . . . A clever, twisty and chilling read."

—Shari Lapena, international bestselling author of *She Didn't See It Coming*

"Combining sharp, assured prose with boundless humanity, this deftly plotted novel is a triumph."

—Marissa Stapley, *New York Times* bestselling author of *Lucky*

"Lundrigan expertly weaves a gripping tale about fractured relationships and the secrets swirling around a small community, rocked by a decades-old murder. . . . The prose is poetic in this intensely captivating and unforgettable read."

—Samantha M. Bailey, *USA Today* and national bestselling author of *Hello, Juliet*

"[A] flawlessly written psychological thriller. . . . The dialogue flows naturally, colourfully and masterfully. [*A Man Downstairs*] lifts Lundrigan to an elite level of page turning storyteller."

—*Toronto Times*

SELECT PRAISE FOR *AN UNTHINKABLE THING*

SHORTLISTED FOR THE 2023 CRIME WRITERS OF CANADA AWARD FOR BEST CRIME NOVEL

"From the enticing first pages to the shocking last lines (don't peek!), Nicole Lundrigan's *An Unthinkable Thing* explores the trauma of loneliness and the power of belonging, through the eyes of a tender, unforgettable young narrator. . . . A thoughtful and atmospheric page-turner."

—Ashley Audrain, #1 national bestselling author of *The Push* and *The Whispers*

"Expertly paced, with a voice that's both tender and innocent, this twisted suspense story's jaw-dropping events kept me glued to the pages until the ultimate satisfying surprise. A must read."

—Hannah Mary McKinnon, internationally bestselling author of *A Killer Motive*

"Lundrigan masterfully sets the stage with a nostalgic late-1950s backdrop, then ratchets up the tension as she slowly reveals that nothing is quite what it seems. This slow burn mystery builds to an inferno that will keep readers riveted until the final, satisfying page. Five enthusiastic stars!"

—Nicole Baart, bestselling author of *Where He Left Me*

"A superb read about helplessness, power, wealth, honesty, and truth—nightmarishly compelling." **—*Booklist* (starred review)**

SELECT PRAISE FOR *HIDEAWAY*

SHORTLISTED FOR THE 2020 ARTHUR ELLIS AWARD FOR BEST CRIME NOVEL

"A terrific psychological suspense story hinging on the spellbinding character of Gloria, the mom from hell. . . . Just when you think you have it all figured out, Lundrigan's plot swerves. This book has to be saved for a binge read."

—*The Globe and Mail*

"Haunting, harrowing, and beautifully written, *Hideaway* splendidly showcases the unique talents of Nicole Lundrigan."

—Ian Hamilton, bestselling author of the Ava Lee series

"There are few better at writing familial claustrophobia than Nicole Lundrigan."

—Andrew Pyper, bestselling author of *The Residence*

"A potent exploration of abuse, desperation, coming of age, and broken trust."

—*Quill and Quire*

THE CASE STUDY

ALSO BY NICOLE LUNDRIGAN

A Man Downstairs
An Unthinkable Thing
Hideaway
The Substitute
The Widow Tree
Glass Boys
The Seary Line
Thaw
Unraveling Arva

THE CASE STUDY

NICOLE LUNDRIGAN

VIKING

VIKING
an imprint of Penguin Canada, a division of Penguin Random House Canada Limited

Canada • USA • UK • Ireland • Australia • New Zealand • India • South Africa • China

First published 2026

Viking, an imprint of Penguin Canada
A division of Penguin Random House Canada
320 Front Street West, Suite 1400
Toronto, Ontario, M5V 3B6, Canada
penguinrandomhouse.ca

The authorized representative in the EU for product safety and compliance is Penguin Random House Ireland, Morrison Chambers, 32 Nassau Street, Dublin D02 YH68, Ireland, https://eu-contact.penguin.ie

Publisher's note: This book is a work of fiction. Names, characters, places and incidents either are the product of the author's imagination or are used fictitiously, and any resemblance to actual persons living or dead, events, or locales is entirely coincidental.

LIBRARY AND ARCHIVES CANADA CATALOGUING IN PUBLICATION

Title: The case study : a novel / Nicole Lundrigan.
Names: Lundrigan, Nicole, author.
Identifiers: Canadiana (print) 20250313510 | Canadiana (ebook) 20250313537 |
ISBN 9781037801549 (softcover) | ISBN 9781037801556 (EPUB)
Subjects: LCGFT: Thrillers (Fiction) | LCGFT: Psychological fiction. | LCGFT: Novels.
Classification: LCC PS8573.U5436 C37 2026 | DDC C813/.6—dc23

Book design by Talia Abramson
Typeset in Adobe Garamond Pro by Arthur Dennyson Hamdani and Six Red Marbles
Cover design by Talia Abramson
Cover images: (dock) © Chasing Light - Photography by James Stone james-stone.com / Getty; (lake) © Meike, (shadow) © Cee Gee, (tree line) © Wendy Wei, all Pexels

Printed in Canada

10 9 8 7 6 5 4 3 2 1

For my friend
Daniel Drache

PROLOGUE

July 14, 1996

He is dead.

I'm lying on the dock beside him, staring at the surface of the lake. Minutes, hours, days have passed. What does it matter? The sun won't stop sinking. Zigzags of light melting into the black water. I whisper, Please don't go, *but darkness still arrives, fear pinning me to the wood. My mind twitches with imaginary colors, and behind me, the shadowy pines scratch and crackle. A twig breaks. I hear heavy footsteps, one-TWO, one-TWO. The sounds soon align with my pounding heart.*

I adopt his position. Legs splayed, neck cricked. Dark red palm facing upward. I tell myself I am air. No longer bound to the body that surrounds me. With a single exhale, I leave this awful place. Same as he's done. Floating up and up, past the roof of the cabin where we stayed. Soaking into leaves and insects. Hiding inside the lungs of an angry crow.

I no longer need to think about what happened. How it all went so terribly wrong.

My uncle is dead.

I am dead too.

I've always been capable of that—convincing myself. Of just about anything.

Journal of Abnormal Psychology

June 12, 2003

Cotard's Syndrome: Case Study of a Juvenile

Abstract:

Cotard's (walking corpse) syndrome was first defined by French neurologist Jules Cotard, who used the phrase "le délire de négation" or "the delirium of negation" to describe it. The patient maintains a complete denial of self.

At the age of fourteen years, LK experienced a significant traumatic event—the violent death of her uncle. She was then isolated with the decedent's body for three days in remote wilderness. Later charged with manslaughter, she was deemed unfit for trial and transferred to a secure psychiatric facility. At that time, a comprehensive examination revealed severe dehydration and sun exposure, but no evidence of physical or sexual abuse.

Upon admission, LK presented with unabating delusions, repeatedly claiming she no longer existed and demanding to be brought to a morgue. She also described corporeal decay and olfactory hallucinations of rotting odors. In addition, she exhibited dermatillomania and occasional self-starvation. Catatonia was intermittent. Based on those behaviors, a diagnosis of Cotard's syndrome was confirmed.

Rehabilitation efforts were intensive and multipronged. The initial course of treatment involved body movement therapy, administering of antipsychotics, and twelve sessions of electroconvulsive shock spaced twice weekly. Recovery was spontaneous eleven months after onset, at which point talk therapy (including CBT and DBT) were fully integrated. LK remained at the facility, per court order, until she reached the age of twenty-one.

2023

CHAPTER ONE

Mia

CONTROL WAS ONLY an illusion. Mia understood that, but she couldn't resist tapping the app on her phone. The icon was a stylized green leaf, with the word *Branches* beneath it. Anyone gazing over her shoulder might think it was related to nature or health. Not family monitoring software hidden in plain sight on her home screen. Which was the point, she supposed.

Within milliseconds, she was staring at a map of the city of Callow. The app then zoomed in to her neighborhood, where she noted a blinking blue dot gliding along Main Street. It passed the ice cream shop and then a clothing store. In the app, Mia was considered the tree, and her teenaged daughter was an offshoot. A single branch. Bringing the phone closer to her face, she waited for the dot to veer left into the residential area. That would confirm Elise was heading home.

"What's so captivating?"

Mia glanced up. Her husband was seated at the oversized marble island in their kitchen. She'd already placed a bowl of soup in front of him, plus a slice of crusty sourdough bread.

"Nothing. Skimming an article."

"About?"

"It's not important, Ian," she said, waving the air. "Just silly fashion trends."

"Then you could at least join me. Be good to chat a little."

Chat a little. Such a simple request, though it made Mia's jaw clench.

As Ian gazed at her, she attempted a smile. His face and forearms were tanned and his light brown hair was beginning to gray, especially in his beard. He was wearing his usual tortoiseshell glasses, which gave the impression of both intelligence and boyishness. She used to find that combination disarmingly handsome, and now she wondered if she'd ever feel that way again.

"All good. I'll eat with Elise."

She was about to close the app when the dot stopped. It hovered in position for several seconds, then seemed to slide through a wall. For a moment, it vanished, then reappeared behind the buildings. She knew exactly where that was. A dingy laneway, full of dumpsters and rats. Rickety metal staircases that led to second-floor apartments. A few college students lived there, but it was mostly unsavory men hanging over the railings, smoking weed. The branch had stopped moving.

Quickly she texted. *Where are you?*

Within seconds, her phone dinged: *at cs omw*. C's meaning Chloé's place. Elise's best friend who lived in a beautiful three-story house several blocks south of them. Nowhere near that blue dot.

Dinner's getting cold. HU.

hu??

Hurry up.

lol nt

"Really, Mia. Can't we share a meal together? She's fifteen, and she'll be home when she's home."

Nothing ever fazed Ian. No matter the circumstance, he maintained a continual calm. As though everything was either fine or fixable. That facade had always troubled Mia. He seemed incapable of grasping the dangers a girl might face, or the panic that enveloped a mother when her child disappeared. Even if that simply meant forgetting to text or check in. Mia no longer tried to share her worries with Ian, as he was prone to slipping into "psychiatrist mode." Normalizing Elise's irresponsibility and instead hinting at Mia's "issues."

She put down her phone, then scooped a single ladle of soup into a bowl and placed it on the island. Without sitting down, she leaned forward to take a bite, and a faint odor of sweat tweaked her nose. She was still wearing athletic shorts and a sweat-wicking top from her afternoon run. She wasn't trying. Not like she used to. And while Ian never commented, surely he'd noticed her low-level apathy.

He reached over and placed his warm fingers on top of hers. "This is nice, no? You and me?"

She waited for several seconds. Then eased her hand away. "Mm. Nice." She glanced at her dark screen, itching to check the app again.

"And the house is coming along, isn't it? This area looks great."

"Getting there." She smiled again.

Even though they'd moved four months ago, it still felt chaotic with unopened boxes and mounds of unsorted belongings. Ian was the one who'd insisted they pack up and sell. While they hadn't gone far, the new house was larger and grander. A huge airy open concept. The front contained a formal living-dining area, but she preferred the back of the home. The kitchen, eating nook, and family room were combined into an enormous and functional living space. An ideal spot to create family memories. Ones that weren't tainted by her husband's betrayal.

Ten months ago, she'd learned about his affair. Mia had often suspected cheating; Ian was handsome and flirty, but there was never proof. No racy emails or dinner receipts stashed in a jacket pocket. She'd chocked it up to her own insecurities. Until she noticed a streak of good old-fashioned lipstick on his collar. Almost laughable, if it hadn't shattered some part of her. He would tell her nothing about the woman, but eventually Mia worked up the nerve to ask if he'd brought her into their home. He denied it, but she wondered if they'd had sex in their bed. Or lounged naked on their sofa. Or gotten soapy and slippery in the ensuite shower. Maybe it was all true. Maybe none of it was.

"Oh, I had a bit of good news today," he said. "A request of sorts."

"About?"

"Do you remember that case study I—"

Before he could finish, the front door slammed. "I'm ho-ome!" Elise's voice echoed through the house. Thunk, thunk of her combat boots, and quick steps across the foyer and down the hallway into the kitchen. She was wearing a bright green hoodie that Ian had bought her. Oversized and overpriced. Mia frowned at the skinny white legs sticking out from beneath it. Anyone's guess if there were shorts underneath.

"Have a seat," Ian said, patting the stool beside him.

Elise flumped down. Folded her arms across her chest. "What's that awful smell?"

"Soup," Mia said.

"Seriously? In June?"

"Summer soup. I made it vegetarian for you." She put a bowl in front of her daughter. Then held her breath for two seconds before saying, "So, how was Chloé's?"

"Same." Elise shrugged, picked up a spoon, and poked at bits floating in the broth.

"You went there after school?"

"Yup."

"Huh. That's nice." A sharp cramp of aggravation shot through

Mia's insides. Elise had developed the capacity to lie without so much as a blink. A trait she'd no doubt inherited from her father. "Does Chloé have summer plans?"

Another shrug. "We're figuring stuff out."

"What did you two get up to then?" In general, Mia liked Chloé. She was polite, bright, and worked hard in school, even though it was a struggle. She had a learning disability and attention-deficit. The inattentive kind.

"Seriously, Mom? We hung out, okay? That doesn't mean we, like, did anything."

Mia exhaled loudly. Half of her wanted to yell at her daughter for the snarky tone, while the other half wanted to fold her up and tuck her away. To keep her slender bones and fuzzy hair and freckled face safe from all the perverts and the perils.

Ian nudged Elise's arm. "How about we enjoy dinner?"

Elise sipped from the very tip of her spoon and grimaced. Then let the utensil clatter into her bowl. "Sorry, Mom, but this is just bad. Tastes like licorice. And not the good kind."

"That's a bit harsh, isn't it?" Ian glanced at Mia. "But I get it. Fennel bulb's an acquired taste."

"Well, let it be known I hate fennel ball. Or whatever this is."

The cramp behind Mia's ribs intensified, and she brought her hand to her sternum. As each year passed, it was becoming harder to accept the utter monotony of her life. Wife to an unfaithful husband. Mother to an entitled teenager. Not to mention that since the pandemic, her career had stagnated, and her friendships evaporated.

"You don't have to eat it," she said.

"Phew!" Elise blew out air and then grinned at Mia. "And no offense, okay, Mom? I appreciate you making it." Then she slid off her stool and drifted downstairs. She'd begged to have the nanny suite on the lower level, and Ian had agreed. He thought the arrangement offered the right amount of privacy for everyone.

"Guess we learned something new about our daughter tonight." He chuckled with an annoying lightness.

"I guess." She took another mouthful of her soup, then asked, "So, you mentioned someone needs a favor?"

"Not a favor, no. More of a proposal." Folding his cloth napkin, Ian placed it beside his empty bowl. "Do you recall the case study that was a feature piece some years back?"

"How would I? I mean, you've published so much."

"It was in the *Journal of Abnormal Psychology*. The one where the patient had Cotard's syndrome."

Mia hesitated before she spoke. "Was it a young woman? Something happened, and she developed a weird delusion?"

"Good memory."

"Rings a vague bell." Which was a fib, as she'd remembered instantly. Back then, she'd been both fascinated and unsettled by the case, and if she were completely honest, more than a little caught up with it all. The subject of the study had lived right there in Callow, and as a young teen, had attacked and killed a relative on a seemingly carefree summer vacation. She was then trapped in the woods for days with a decomposing corpse. The property owner eventually discovered them, and when questioned, the girl made the outlandish claim that she, too, was dead. A breathing ghost. Her psychosis was so rare, summaries of the journal article Ian had written were printed in national newspapers and magazines. Even made the cover of *People*, which was where Mia first read about the unusual delusion.

"The editors are compiling an anniversary edition and want to include a selection of pivotal studies from the past. That particular case being one of them."

"So reprinting it?"

"Not quite. I'll need to review and recapture it through a modern lens. Evaluate the analysis and treatment using current psychiatric paradigms." He scraped the handle of his spoon back and forth over the lip of the bowl. "I was considering adding an addendum."

"Like an update? As in, how she's doing today?"

"Essentially, yes."

Mia leaned forward, the cold edge of the countertop pressing against her hip bones. "I'm confused. How could you even reach her?" Ian had treated her at Albethey Psychiatric Institute, a facility about forty minutes outside Callow. But she'd been released, of course, and after all those years, could be anywhere. Have any name or occupation.

"That won't be too difficult," he said, tugging at his ear. "I'm sure."

She noticed her palms were clammy against the marble. "Have you kept in touch? Do doctors even do that? Stay connected with former patients?" Not just former; decades had passed.

His face changed then into unreadable blankness. "I can't discuss details, Mia."

"Sorry. I know." Perhaps Albethey kept track of former patients, especially when criminal conduct was involved. Using a softer tone, she said, "And if she agrees to talk, how might that work? Am I allowed to ask?"

A firm nod. "Of course. Likely over video. But who knows if she'll say yes. Who knows if I'll even go that route. The deadline's months away, so I've got time to decide."

Then Mia uttered the words she was supposed to from the start. "That's fantastic news, Ian. Being one of the experts included in this special edition. Must feel good."

"It does feel good." He pushed back his stool and stood up. "Well, I've got some review to do, darling."

"About her?"

"Yes. I should dig out the files at least." When he reached the bottom of the staircase, he stopped. Then said, "I do worry about you, you know. You just seem . . . distracted. Even mildly depressed, I would say."

"Me? I'm totally fine. Bit tired is all." Which was mostly true?

He nodded grimly, then floated, almost effortlessly, up the stairs to his office.

CHAPTER TWO

Mia

SITTING ON THE hardwood floor of her walk-in closet, Mia peeled the tape off a box labeled Keepsakes and folded back the cardboard flaps. Inside she found Elise's childhood artwork, plus handfuls of old birthday cards and letters. A pair of leather baby shoes that were barely worn. At the very bottom, she located an old copy of *People*. From June 23, 2003.

Discovering the article was completely random. She'd been at the dentist's office and plucked up a magazine from the tall pile in the waiting area. The tiny inset in the top left corner showed the blurred profile of a female and the headline "Meet the Girl Who Believes She's Dead." There was no actual "meeting," though, as the patient remained anonymous, and was only referred to as LK. But there was an in-depth interview with the attending psychiatrist, Dr. Ian Morrison. Not only were the circumstances of the entire thing creepy and bizarre, but Mia was shocked to discover the murder had occurred just outside of her own city. She'd opened her purse and shoved the copy inside.

Pulling it from the box, she placed the magazine on her lap. When she leafed through the pages, it fell open to the article. The upper third of the first page was a stock image of an ominous cabin surrounded by dark water and looming pine trees. In the middle, the back of a young girl in shorts and a striped tank top, her blond hair covering tanned shoulder blades. On the opposite page, a professional photograph of Ian. Unsmiling but still somehow playful. Mia grazed the headshot with a fingertip. He looked so young.

In the text, Ian outlined his years of treating LK. The extreme rarity of the syndrome, especially in a child. How her manifestation was not connected to schizophrenia, as was most common, but instead a derealization brought on by the deadly assault of her uncle and the resulting isolation. Whether or not her actions were premeditated was undetermined. At Albethey, her therapy and treatment were handled exclusively by Ian. He was a new psychiatrist on the institute's team, barely finished his residency. In his interview, he described how she believed her blood was no longer moving through her body. Her pulse was an artifact. Her mirrored reflection, a frightening illusion. She was also convinced that she was rotting and would wash repeatedly to mask the nonexistent odor of her own decay.

Mia had kept the magazine all these years, in part because it was how she'd met Ian. When she learned he taught at Callow College, she'd decided to take a course. Theories of Personality. She audited it, to be specific; marketing was her major. So she wasn't exactly his student when she approached him at the end of a lecture, gripping the magazine to her chest like a groupie desperate for a signature. She shyly asked if he was open to answering a few questions. Though she understood he was limited in what he could share, she was intrigued by the case. The girl.

Later that evening, they met at a dimly lit bar on the other side of town. She drank cosmopolitans, while he sipped vodka sodas. Within two weeks, she was sleeping with him, and after a month, they were staying over at each other's places.

She dropped the course. Kept the textbook. He flooded her waking thoughts and infiltrated her dreams. Her body practically feverish, and parts continually damp. Mia recalled once when he'd left his sweater behind. How she'd inhaled the smell of him. Awed by the tiny pills in the fabric, as it proved his arm had once been inside that sleeve. The sheer joy in knowing he was alive. *This is it*, she'd thought. *This is love.*

Reflecting on it, instead of softness toward her youthful self, she felt a hot flush of embarrassment. How silly she'd been, pretending to be sophisticated, mysterious. Believing that having a sexual affair with a man thirteen years her senior was somehow risqué. Now, even her choice of cocktail seemed idiotic. A garish red drink in a martini glass.

"Hey, Mom. What's with all the mess?"

Mia lifted her head. She hadn't heard her daughter approaching. Elise was standing in the doorway to the closet.

"Being productive, I suppose. Trying to get another box out of the way."

"That's not what your face is saying. You look like you've got the ick."

"What?"

"Like, repulsed, I mean."

"Oh." She reached up and touched her mouth.

"I can help a bit tomorrow if you like?"

"Really? That'd be super. Do something together."

"Right?" Elise smiled. She'd straightened her hair and had doe-like lashes glued to her eyelids. Her lips were coated in a high-sheen gloss. "Anyway. Wanted to let you know I'm heading out."

Mia glanced up at the skylight. Nothing but blackness pressing against the glass. "Um, no. You're not heading out."

"What? Why not?"

"Because it's a school night."

"You're joking."

"Nope."

"But Mom. Literally nobody's at school tomorrow. Exams are over." She stared hard at Mia. "It's just a stupid year-end assembly. Then parent-teacher stuff. We're all going to Chloé's to swim."

"When it's pitch-dark out?"

"Her pool has lights, Mom. And Chloé and me are both certified lifeguards." She sniffed. "If you forgot."

Without all the makeup, Elise looked identical to Mia at that age. So much so, Mia found it alarming. The desire to protect her child was almost feral. She could feel it in her jaw, her teeth. It bordered on pathological, Ian had once said.

"Still." She envisioned the blinking blue dot and the questions she could not ask. *Why were you in that laneway? Who were you with?* "I'm not going to change my mind."

Elise whipped up the hood on her sweatshirt. Heart-shaped face once again concealed in shadow. "You're awful, you know that? Out of all my friends, I got the worst mother." She turned on her heel and stomped across the hallway. Stomped on every step, as well. Two full flights of stairs. Then the sound that was becoming increasingly familiar. A door slam.

Ian appeared seconds later. "What was that fuss?" The disagreement had pulled him away from his work.

"More of the usual," Mia said softly. "I hope she doesn't do permanent damage to her heel bones." She flipped the magazine over, covering it. "Do you still have much to do?"

"Nearly finished. Just some notes. Want to join me for a scotch on the back deck?"

She faked a yawn. "Sorry, I'm wiped. But you go ahead."

"Sure. Another time."

Yes, maybe. Another time.

Once Ian went back to his office, Mia replaced the items in the box and pushed it to the back of the closet. Then went to the ensuite bathroom and washed her face with a steaming hot cloth. After slathering on moisturizer, she slipped into a long nightdress with short fluttery sleeves. The color on the tag read *cocoon*. Another gift from Ian. He was trying so hard to fix things. Told her he wished she wouldn't keep clinging to the past. "Be honest with yourself, Mia. Is that serving you?"

The house was quiet as she climbed under the cool sheets. She turned out the bedside lamp, then checked the Branches app one last time. Reassuring herself that the blue dot was blinking over the rectangular outline that represented their home.

She was sleepy but at the same time felt out of sorts. Wired, almost. From the hallway came a faint click-click—Ian's fingertips on his keyboard. She guessed he was summarizing his old notes about LK. Though he was nonchalant during dinner, Mia was certain he would make every effort to reconnect. After the case study was initially published, it led to a huge jump in his career. The academic circuit, the talk shows, the news radio. He was a keynote speaker at multiple conferences and a guest lecturer at prominent colleges. He was even given a promotion at work. But in the years that followed, the invitations had dried up, and there was an inevitable decline toward normalcy. His later publications garnered much lighter interest. Just last week he'd complained about poor enrollment numbers in his courses. "Even my waiting list used to be full."

Mia knew exactly what Ian was thinking. This might be his chance. To recapture that professional stardom. To reinvigorate his career. But what if he found the woman and things weren't fine? What if she was still troubled? Had relapsed or hurt someone else. Did Ian even recall the letter? An unhinged diatribe in slanted handwriting, which LK had mailed to Albethey shortly after her release. Mia had discovered it in a box of papers just after she'd moved into his apartment. She couldn't recall the exact details, and though nothing had come of her threats, the truth was plain: LK had been in love with Ian. Believed he'd abandoned her when she needed him most. And she'd planned to teach him a lesson.

CHAPTER THREE

Lainey

AN UNCOMFORTABLE TENSION was spreading through my body. I crossed my legs, squeezed my thighs together, and tried to dissect the feeling. It was always the same. Desire comingled with disgust.

I was in a moderately priced hotel room, seated on a velour chair. A man I'd never met before was in the matching chair beside me. We were both watching our respective mates, who were naked and writhing on a king-sized bed. No phones or cameras allowed.

"Tiff" was currently splayed on her back. My partner, Andrew, had his head between her legs. For a moment, he paused and turned toward me. Even in the dim lighting, his mouth and chin appeared wet, shiny. I offered him the classic expression of want. Bottom lip pulled in, top teeth gently biting down. He grinned, then worked his hands beneath the woman's backside, positioned her thighs over his shoulders.

"Woah, they're into it." "Tim" was likely in his late fifties with some serious middle-age spread and a gullet that quivered when he spoke. He leaned forward, gripping his knees as Tiff brought Andrew's hands to her breasts. I could see the implant scars. Lines so thick, it could've been a back-alley plastic surgeon.

"Seems so," I replied. Though I could tell Tiff wasn't *really* into it. Her moans were high-pitched and fake. I was experiencing a shard of discomfort and realized her tone reminded me of my mother's. When I was three or four years old, she'd often leave me alone at night, and I'd be woken hours later to her rasps outside the bedroom door. "Give me a sec to straighten up, hon." Then she'd rush in, nudge me from the warm bed. Pupils dilated, index finger pressed to her painted lips, she'd whisper, *I found him, sweetheart. I've found a good one for us.*

The bottom drawer of the dresser was kept empty for such occasions. Those evenings when she was convinced of love and had snuck some loser into the women-only residence. I would lie inside, wood scraping over skin, my polyester nightdress hitching on the pressboard. A sparkly fear that my stomach might dare to growl.

Eventually I would hear her. A string of controlled and pathetic whimpers. Never of pleasure but of accommodation. Perhaps even of hope? Not that any man could ever tell. Or rather, ever cared. None of it mattered anyway. Though I did find it curious that her voice still echoed inside the darkness of my head.

Tiff's moans were beginning to grate on me. So was the sight of her skin, translucent, crisscrossed with blue veins. I had the impression that, unlike Tim, she ate poorly. Wasn't getting enough vitamins and minerals. Her mouse-colored hair was limp, and she had cheap highlights, as if she'd tied a plastic bag to her head and hooked the strands out herself.

I could not see a connection to the man beside me. His casual pants were neatly creased. From the dry cleaner or a meticulous wife. His pale yellow shirt looked brand-new; skin deeply tanned, and fingernails manicured. He looked like money. Smelled like it too. It was blatantly obvious they did not belong together.

Perhaps someone might say the same about me and Andrew, though we'd been a couple for nearly three years. On a frigid day, he'd joined my steamy ashtanga class at Om Bliss, the yoga studio where I taught. I could still recall his smirk as I made minor adjustments to his downward dog. Later, we bumped into each other at the café down the street. He asked if he could buy me a hot chocolate, which caused bile to rise in my throat. "The one drink I despise," I said. "How unlucky for you," he'd replied, and we popped next door to a juice bar. I had a smoothie with a double shot of chlorophyll. When I told him it was my fortieth birthday, he asked me out for dinner. A tasting menu at his friend's restaurant. He was slender, dark-haired, face still plump with youth.

I've often wondered why I caught the attention of a twenty-nine-year-old. Maybe he viewed me as a woman in control. Drifting about the studio, speaking affirmations. He never noticed the hum of agitation gluing me together, even when we started dating regularly. I met his friends and went with him to visit his family. Within a year, I moved into his condo. A corner unit with uninterrupted views.

And now our relationship was fairly mundane. Dull even, if I excluded the random hookups with strangers. Deciding about meals or what movies to stream or his work dilemmas (corporate security specialist by day and occasional DJ by night). But our dynamic was functional. I had a home. A dinner companion. Decent sex when I needed it. Andrew never wanted or expected more. He was a man who would happily slide his fingers into every part of me, except my past.

"Good god." A strangled sound erupted from Tim's throat.

I tried to stealth-monitor Tim in my peripheral vision. He was a skip-n-jump from senior citizenship and had edged forward in his seat. His meaty palm pushed into his gut. I wondered if the old guy was feeling pure exhilaration. Or having actual pain. It was tough to tell. I just hoped he wouldn't topple off his chair.

I'd found Tim and Tiff on an app. Not my best procurement, if I was honest, but not all matches were winners. They said they were kink-friendly, looking for fun. Profile was generic and not offensive. No images, just a cutesy cartoon shark with a gag ball in its mouth. I swiped, and of course there was a match. A handful of texts volleyed back and forth between us. He said he and his wife had been married for fifteen years. *Uh-huh.* They both enjoyed adventurous activities from ziplining to popping MDMA. *Eye roll.* In the past couple of years, they'd begun to explore a swingers' lifestyle. "Indulging each other's whims" was how Tim gently phrased it.

When I asked what he specifically wanted, he explained he had a fantasy about his wife being "ravaged" by another man. He wanted to witness that, up close, then reclaim her for his own. Which hypothetically aligned with my own situation, I suppose. Andrew enjoyed being the spectacle. With me, his dedicated observer.

The actions on the bed were moving toward Act II. Or was it Act III? White arms and legs shifting, repositioning. Then full-on rutting. It was always the same routine. Oral her, oral him, then some variations of copulation. Nothing remotely intimate. When Tiff bent over, I caught the glimmer of a plug. A cheap turquoise gem. She must have been wearing it all along.

"Yeah, baby," Tim breathed. "Yeah." He swiped a hand across his shiny forehead.

As I was stifling a yawn, I sensed the vibration of my phone in the back pocket of my jeans. A short buzz, then a longer buzz, which meant an email. I had the urge to peek. I glanced at Andrew. He was lying flat on his back, and the woman was throwing her leg over his hips. She reached down, gripping his erection and guiding it inside her. Then began bouncing in a farcical way. Skin slapping skin. The odor of their sex overwhelming the citrus room spray.

Andrew moaned loudly and said, "Ohh, fuck." He arced his head, revealing his narrow palate. It was the only unattractive part of his body.

My toe tapped the air. I knew I shouldn't look. But Andrew had his eyes squeezed closed. He wouldn't notice my momentary distraction.

Shifting in my chair, I withdrew my phone. Expecting a spam email or some online store announcing a sale: *New In!* But it wasn't either of those things. When I read the notification on my home screen, my stomach lurched.

Sender: Dr. I. Morrison

Topic: Follow-up on your health

I pressed three times with my shaking thumb to unlock my home screen, and then I tapped the message. Scanned it quickly. "Hope this note finds you well." He mentioned reevaluating his previous case study. "Would you be willing to have a preliminary discussion?" "With potential for some sessions together, with you setting the parameters?" "I'd be grateful for your time."

A concise message. Professional and courteous.

I slid my phone beneath my leg. Tried to slow my breathing, but my heart would not stop skittering. As though a rodent, huddled inside the cavity of my chest, had suddenly been revealed by a spotlight.

To this day, I could remember seeing my former psychiatrist for the first time. Inside a beige room at Albethey. The walls were void of any decoration. Metal chairs and table both bolted to the ground. He'd simply appeared, as though he'd oozed into the space. Had the door even opened? I'd watched him closely. Not from my seat, but from above. Gazing down from the upper corner of the room. At that time, there was a great chasm between me and myself. We were attached to one another by the weakest of threads.

He smiled at the me who was sitting there. "Hello, Lainey," he'd said, as though I was real. When I was nothing more than a heap of bones disguised by oversized loungewear and slip-on shoes. I immediately sensed he was some sort of predator, and I was trapped in his cage. I did not respond.

At first.

"Babe?"

When I lifted my head, Andrew was already dressed. Tim was standing at the door. He jammed the ball cap back on his head, while Tiff tightened the belt on a cheap trench coat. Her hair was disheveled, and a pinkish stain encircled her mouth. Smeared lipstick.

"Sorry," I said and stood up. They'd finished. I hadn't been paying attention.

"It's been a slice, kiddos," Tim said, grinning. "Happy to stay in touch."

"Sure," Andrew said. "Let's do that."

They stepped out of the room. I always found that once the lust had disintegrated, parting ways was usually hurried and awkward. No sweet sorrow there.

"So, that was pretty hot," I said after the door closed. I stepped toward him and tickled my fingertips along his forearm.

Andrew and I often stayed in the room overnight, but he tossed the key card on the rumpled comforter. "I saw you. On your phone."

"Oh, that. I had to check something."

"It couldn't wait?"

"I'm sorry. I got lost in my head for a bit." I'd missed Tiff's fake orgasm. Missed Andrew's real one.

"You were supposed to be focused on me. That's the whole point."

"I was. I was doing both."

"Didn't seem like it." His tone was sulky. "What was so important?"

"Um, the studio. Someone was asking if I offered private yoga lessons."

"If you're not enjoying it, what we do, just let me know." He bent to haul on his sneakers. "Cool?"

I glanced at a smear of fluid on the bedspread. While it invariably made me feel aroused, I also did not enjoy it. Watching my lover lick another woman. Hearing him cry out as she rode him. I would never understand the pull of that lifestyle. As far back as I could remember, all I ever wanted was one person, male or female, who was wholly dedicated to me.

CHAPTER FOUR

Lainey

I FELT AS though I was breaking the rules. Sneaking away to see another man without telling Andrew. Not that he knew anything about my former relationship with Dr. Morrison. Or those shitty years of my life. He'd never be able to comprehend the complexity of it, or how it had shaped me in ways I couldn't begin to untangle. And I certainly did not have the desire to try to explain.

Campus was much quieter than I'd expected, even for summer semester. I noticed a few clusters of students sitting beneath leafy trees. Others loitering on the stone steps of buildings. Everyone had books and coffee, wore shorts and vintage tees. The scene made me agitated, how young and uninhibited they all appeared. Having normal experiences. Not confined to a nuthouse getting "multi-pronged treatment" simply for being broken.

I quickly stepped inside a building. The cramped hallway was dimly lit, had skinny windows and a musty odor that was uncomfortably familiar. Fitting for a place that studied the recesses of unsound minds. Like my own. Or how mine used to be. Though perhaps I was being generous with my self-perception.

Lowering my ball cap, I eased open the door of the lecture hall and slipped inside. Took a seat near the very back. The room was cool enough to make my bare arms prickle. Once my eyes adjusted, I saw that there were only about twenty students scattered among the seats. The room's capacity was easily over a hundred.

Dr. Morrison stood at the front, left elbow balanced on a lectern. He had to be in his mid-fifties by now. His hair was the same shaggy brown, and his body was still slim but definitely thicker around the middle. He was wearing a crisp white shirt with the top two buttons undone. Giving the impression he was relaxed, but not trying to entice his mostly female audience.

As he moved about, organizing his papers, I sensed there was something different about him. His shoulders were no longer square. His back had the slightest curve. Overall, he looked like an average older man. During the long nights at Albethey, I often slipped my hands inside my underwear while thinking about him. Willing him to come to my room at night and press himself on top of me. It never happened, of course, and I could be forgiven for such childish fantasies. It was slim pickings at the asylum.

"I'm sure you'd all prefer to be outside on this gorgeous day," Dr. Morrison said. "Instead of sitting in the dark discussing perversion."

A ripple of giggles. Then he opened his laptop, pressed a few buttons, and huge black text appeared on the massive screen behind him: *Paraphilic Disorders*.

Clicker locked in his fist, he began moving through slides. Defining the various behaviors that were considered deviations from society's norm. *Voyeurism. Exhibitionism. Fetishism.* "Studies are ongoing to identify the etiology and underlying physiology associated with these disorders. Some investigations indicate a biological root cause." Then he shifted gears. Discussed how cultural constraints have influenced psychiatry's perception of sexuality. Explaining that healthy individuals may engage in activities that are acceptable within particular subcultures. "So, if that's the case, would they still be defined as deviant?" Hands shot up.

I had to smile. After last night's hotel room with Tim and Tiff, the irony of this specific lecture was not lost on me.

A stream of lively chatter ensued between several students and Dr. Morrison. Some comments were just plain stupid, but he was never dismissive. Instead he offered counterpoints, provocative questions, subtly shifting their understanding. Observing how he managed the room, altering others' thinking in such sneaky ways, I found it quite clever. I'm sure he had done the same with me back when we were a team.

My early days at Albethey were a painful blur. Even now I found it difficult to articulate my experience during those initial months. Other than I was nothing but also everything. Limited and limitless. I felt neither comfort nor pain. Joy nor sorrow. Hunger nor thirst. At times I could communicate, but there were also moments when panic surged. Especially when I hyperfocused on the body that surrounded me. Examining myself, I would see a gnarled hand. A veiny leg. A limp strand of dirty hair. I was convinced I was spoiling, flesh falling away from my own bones, and those sights sparked such acute fear, I would completely shut down.

But over the days and months, the delusions receded. It wasn't an instant recovery, more so a gradual ebbing. I doubted I ever required the strong drugs or shock treatments. I simply responded to warmth and encouragement. Dr. Morrison's presence, his exploration into my distorted thought patterns, even his tone of voice all gave me a sense of security. I developed what I would consider a mild preoccupation with him. Psychiatrists use the term *enmeshment*, which meant blurred boundaries. On my side, at least. But who could blame me? Inside the utter tedium of that institution, he became the face of my existence.

After I was released, I struggled to acclimate to life on my own, and my adoration soon disintegrated into loathing. First, Dr. Morrison's availability decreased. Our appointments petered out to only once per month. The final straw was when my "story" appeared everywhere. Likely I'd given permission, as I'd signed every document he'd plopped in front of me. Or perhaps nothing was required from me at all. And so there I was. Entirely alone, while sordid details about my life and my breakdown were all over the place.

Even though my identity was kept secret, I still felt exposed, and I spent several years trying to hide. It took me a while to get my head straight. To unscrew what he'd screwed over. But eventually I realized I didn't need Dr. Morrison. I was able to look upward and, like everyone else, see only a godless sky.

As I was the sole beneficiary in my uncle's will, I had the financial means to care for myself. I inherited his estate, which included all his belongings and investments. The "Slayer's Act" did not apply to me. I was never convicted of murder. Never even formally charged, though that important detail was often omitted in salacious write-ups.

Long after people had forgotten about me, I began to weave myself back into society. I completed an undergraduate degree in business. To my chagrin, I was unable to work a regular job. Interactions with my peers were often fraught, and any sort of stress seemed to mess up my thought processes. HR dubbed me "unpredictably reactive." Afterward, I turned to intense fitness, drinking up the temporary endorphin rush of CrossFit and Ironman. When that faded, I landed on yoga, believing it held the secret to wholeness. I trained as an instructor and began to teach a few classes each day. I learned to ground, to stretch, to breathe. To hide the revulsion I felt toward my own existence. How I'd always been nothing more than a fucking board game that others played. That was how I'd viewed it, anyway. Mostly still do.

"Okay, okay." Dr. Morrison's deep voice sliced through the animated chirping. "Let's get back on track here." The next slide appeared. Some statistics. A couple of no-brainer statements. One: Paraphilia was almost exclusively identified in men. And two: Masochism was the exception, which was twenty times more prevalent in women. His eager students typed furiously on their laptops.

As I watched my former psychiatrist work the room, I tried to sift through the sensations in my chest. A tightness. Or a tremulousness? This was a tough one, but the challenge was not new to me. I'd always had difficulty identifying and labeling my inner states. Emotions seemed infinitely complicated. Apparently, it was a legit shortcoming, though the medical name escaped me now. One in ten people, Dr. Morrison once explained, had no words for their feelings.

Perhaps I needed to take a step back and instead consider the internal shift I'd noted since receiving his email. Maybe the emotion was *furious longing*. Or *incensed wistfulness*. Two couplings that kind of made sense, given the situation. I'd made plenty of mistakes when I was young. Though, in all honesty, it hadn't been my intention to sideline my life. I was simply convinced it was the right decision. I accepted that the suffering I'd endured at Albethey was deserved. I had it coming. But now, with the benefit of many years in the rearview, I wasn't so sure.

All day I'd been having these curious and unsettling thoughts. What if the dark things from my past could be set straight? I'd survived the ordeal of youth. But also had not survived. I lived each moment pulsing with covert rage. My mind trying to both protect me and destroy me. What sort of life was that? I might as well have stayed dead.

And the primary question that tickled the base of my throat: *What if I could be different?*

I pulled out my phone and opened his email again. Him contacting me that way was certainly a breach of privacy. Yet the whiff of desperation was appealing. I composed a quick reply and, without thinking any further, clicked Send.

He glanced at the lectern and then put up his hand. "Sorry, sorry. I need to check this."

Picking up his phone, he tapped his screen. And in the moments before I left the lecture hall, I saw a grin spread over his face.

CHAPTER FIVE

Mia

MIA WAS PERCHED on a plastic chair outside Elise's classroom. Behind the milky glass door, another mother was having her ten-minute meeting with the homeroom teacher. They'd already gone well over their time, and she tried to ignore their strained voices. It reminded her of her own high school years, waiting in the office while her mother spoke to the principal. Mia could still remember some of what she'd overheard. "Poor social integration." "No capacity to weave and bob." "Making herself a target with her peers." Her mother had flown out of the office in a huff.

Leaning her head back against the wall, Mia was tempted to close her eyes. Even though she'd already had two cups of coffee, the caffeine hadn't dampened the fatigue. All night, sleep had eluded her, and she'd found herself brooding. Initially over Ian's affair. But eventually her mind settled on his patient from the case study. When Ian reconnected with her, what was he going to find? How could a person ever manage to detach from that devastating history and grow into someone normal?

The house was silent when she'd snuck downstairs to the couch in the family room. She'd brought her laptop. Though Ian was unaware, she'd long known that the patient's full name was Lainey Kemper. Google offered nothing, only pages of results that seemed unrelated. As expected, there was nothing about LK either, beyond some old articles. Mia tried entering a string of keywords: *Uncle + cabin + teenager + murder + 1996.* That produced a few random hits, a woman gone missing on her honeymoon, a mother drowning her newborn in a lake, but none of it was connected.

She also searched for Albethey. Partway through the second page, she found an article that reviewed the history of the institution. A photo essay with images taken in the 1930s. The sights were disturbing. Women lying in oversized bathtubs, canvas covering them so only their heads were exposed. Others in straitjackets and flouncy skirts they might have worn to a dance. So many of the patients had identical posture. Their spines with the bend of a sickle. As though an invisible weight was balanced between their shoulder blades. Thankfully, care had markedly improved by the time Ian started working there.

The door opened abruptly, and the other mother brushed past in a hurry. Ms. Jacobs appeared behind her, face flushed. When she noticed Mia, she smiled widely and said, "Well, I clearly don't need to ask your child's name. The resemblance is striking."

Mia laughed lightly over the remark, then stood and entered the classroom. She slid into a student desk, and Ms. Jacobs placed a sheet of paper in front of her. Elise's report card.

"Dad's not joining?"

"No, not today." Had Ian ever attended a school meeting? A concert or a play? Mia couldn't recall, though she was certain if she asked, he'd claim to be highly involved. Highly invested.

"As you can see," Ms. Jacobs said, "your daughter's done very well. Elise is a high achiever. Not only are her marks excellent, but her class participation is measured and insightful."

"All good news," Mia replied.

"Certainly is. She's well-adjusted, confident, and demonstrates empathy toward others. Especially in group work. She has a strong circle of friends. And her reading buddy from first grade absolutely adores her."

"Sounds like a great year overall. To be honest, she doesn't share so much anymore."

"If it's any consolation, I hear that from nearly every parent. But I really don't have any concerns, Mrs. Morrison. Elise is a joy to teach." She shuddered slightly. "I wish all these kids were so easy."

With such a positive assessment, why had the pain in Mia's chest expanded? Guilt, perhaps. Elise had barely spoken that morning, beyond asking for pizza money for her and Chloé. Clearly, she was still upset over Mia's refusal to let her go out last night. Had it been unreasonable? Perhaps Ian was right: School was nearly finished, and Elise only wanted to go swimming at her friend's house. Mia could have confirmed her location with the Branches app. She knew she had to ease up. Not let go, exactly, but she was beginning to realize the tighter she tried to hold on, the harder Elise fought to get away.

As she came out of the classroom, she heard someone calling to her. "Mia! Mia Morrison?" Just down the hallway, a cluster of women was gathered. She recognized one of her former coworkers. They'd both been employed at Callow College in the marketing department and worked together on digital campaigns to encourage donations for mental health initiatives. Mia had started part-time when Elise was in kindergarten, and later worked full-time, but when the position became entirely remote, she decided to step away.

The woman scooped the air with her arm, and Mia had no choice but to join their little circle.

"Where have you been? We thought you vanished."

We? As though they were a collective.

"Well, still here!" she replied cheerily. "I moved, so that's been eating up a lot of my time."

"Oh, that's right. I heard."

Mia wanted the linoleum flooring to crack open and swallow her. At work, there had been a steady stream of gossipy chatter, and she could only imagine what else the woman had heard. About Ian. About her marriage. She'd always believed her relationship was enviable, but after the affair, everything flip-flopped. She'd morphed into a fraud.

"We're going to grab a bite to eat. Care to join?"

She blinked. "Um." What could she say? Though the woman had always been friendly enough, they'd never clicked one on one. And she could already guess the scene. A lunch of salad and wine spritzers while discussing facial treatments and vacation plans.

Her phone buzzed, and she pulled it from her purse, glanced at the screen. A text. *Are you home? I'm on my way over!!*

Mia took a breath of relief as an excuse appeared out of nowhere. "Can I take a raincheck? I have to meet my mother."

"Any time," she said with a bright smile. "Family first, right?"

•

"Finally! I'm on the verge of fainting here."

When Mia arrived home, Faye was already seated on the front steps. Her shoes were off, and with fabric pinched in her fingers, she was puffing the front of her linen dress.

"Why didn't you knock, Mom? Ian's home."

An instant scowl. "You've answered your own question."

Mia was too tired to respond. She said nothing, unlocked the door, and stepped inside the air-conditioned foyer, her mother padding along behind her in a cloud of patchouli.

When they reached the kitchen, Faye began rifling through the cupboards. "When will you get these organized? You know what they say: cluttered home, cluttered mind."

"It's on my list."

"Do you have green tea? You really should switch, you know. A much healthier choice."

"I don't know, Mom." Mia sat down on a stool. All she wanted was another coffee. "Maybe I will."

"No maybes. Your skin looks dull, my darling. I promise it'll help."

Though the comment was rude, she once again held her tongue. Only a couple of years had passed since they'd fully reconciled, and the relationship with her mother was still delicate. A rift had developed when Faye discovered Mia and Ian were dating. She'd been quite vocal about her objections. Droning on about the minor age difference and power imbalance. And when they eloped, Faye was livid. Understandable to a degree, as Mia was establishing boundaries and her mother no doubt felt excluded. But there were deeper issues, as after the marriage, Faye barely spoke to Mia for years. Sometimes Mia would receive a random postcard from some random place, but never with a return address. The estrangement had hurt. When Faye returned to Callow, both agreed not to speak of the past. Though, of course, Mia still thought about it. The oddness of her mother's behavior. She could never full grasp what she'd done that was so terribly wrong.

"Did you know green tea has anti-inflammatory properties too?" Faye dropped a tea bag into a mug. "Might help you with that puffiness." She was wearing a butter-colored dress that nearly touched the floor, and her loose hair waved over her shoulders. A green stone, wrapped in thin leather cord, hung around her neck.

Since she was a child, Mia had witnessed many versions of her mother, but this latest transformation had to be the most irritating.

The previous incarnation was much better: overalls and trendy tees, canvas lace-up sneakers. A woman dedicated to her *Stardew* farm and excited over her crop yields. Now all Faye talked about was health and healing. Nothing credible, just energies and vibrations, holistic arts and cleansings. She wore organic fabrics and carried various crystals in her pockets, some even tucked inside her bra. Obsidian. Labradorite. Mia could not remember the reasoning, though Faye had explained everything in depth.

One evening, after a couple of glasses of wine, she'd complained to Ian about it. "Why can't she just be one person?"

"Your mother's perfectly fine," he'd insisted. "True, her sense of self is ever-evolving, but that's not unusual at her life stage."

"Let's hope I don't turn into that. Though there's probably a gem to ward it off."

His expression was stern. "To be honest, Mia, what's more concerning is the degree of vitriol you're expressing."

She'd gone quiet then. Mostly she'd been joking, a superficial grievance. All she'd wanted was for Ian to have agreed or at least laughed along.

Faye leaned in closer. "I assume your spouse is in his office?" Her tone was icy.

When Faye first moved back, she and Ian had been cordial with each other. Warm even. But that changed as soon as Mia told her about the affair. Now her mother displayed a pointed frostiness toward her husband.

Before Mia could reply, Ian strolled into the kitchen. "Oh, Faye. Nice to see you so . . . so randomly."

"You as well, Ian." A clipped reply.

At first, sharing with her mother had felt good, but relief had quickly been replaced with regret.

"No offense to you," was Faye's initial response, "but that was obvious, dear." She claimed her awareness was proof of a "burgeoning intuition." Her "mediumship." Thanks to recently completing a master's of metaphysics through an online college. "I'm not at all surprised he strayed."

The response had stung. As far as Mia knew, she and Ian had always been a united team. While he treated patients, taught, and did research, she'd worked, raised Elise, and looked after their home.

"And all those girls in his courses," Faye continued. "Most of them aren't there for the knowledge, you know."

"They're women, Mom. Not girls. And his courses are degree requirements."

She frowned. "Please don't be naive, Mia. There are laws associated with attraction. And abundance too. It's basic physics. Have you seen the comments on Rate My Professors? I looked him up on a lark when I was researching my own profs."

Mia bit down on the inside of her lower lip. It'd be too easy to say something sarcastic about her mother's "profs." Doubtful they would even be on that website.

"And a good deal of them are hyperfocused on his appearance. They give him chili peppers in their comments. Incredibly inappropriate. I flagged them, of course, but my little complaints simply fly off into the ether." She swiped the air with the back of her hand.

"I don't want to hear anymore." Mia's worst fear was that Ian had slept with a student.

"Of course, not another peep out of me!" Tips of two fingers pressed to her mouth, a twist to lock it closed.

Mia knew she'd leaned too heavily on her mother, and all the support had created an uncomfortable emotional debt. When Faye acted entitled to updates, Mia did not know how to shift the topic.

Or to once again establish privacy. There was no way to roll up what she'd already unfurled.

"Are you seeing patients this afternoon?" Mia asked Ian.

"No, at the college. Class goes till four." He gave her a dry kiss on the cheek. "And remember, I'll be a little late this evening. Meeting with the property manager."

Mia had forgotten about that. Years ago, she and Ian had purchased an investment property, and the latest tenant had been a major headache. His rent was several months in arrears, and though they'd served him with an eviction notice, he seemed in no hurry to vacate.

"Another mess to deal with, I suppose."

"Nothing we can't handle, Faye." He plucked up his thermos full of hot coffee. "But thanks for your concern."

"Well, then," she grumbled as she loudly slurped her tea, "I wish you a light-filled day."

Once Ian was gone, Faye wandered toward the oversized windows in the family room and stared out at the back garden. After several moments, she sighed and said, "So much of a person's life is luck, isn't it? The two of us aren't so different, you know, but somehow you've mostly managed to avoid hardship."

"What are you talking about?"

"It's just I sense the universe is teaching you a lesson." Faye turned around then. "Which is not a bad thing, Mia, though I know it's not easy either. That's when the growth happens."

"Mom, can we not. Please?"

"Yes, of course. Me and my ridiculous musings. Maybe I should dart back later with some sage? The vibration in here is unsettled."

"That's because we *are* unsettled. We're still unpacking."

"No, it's not that." She placed her mug on the coffee table, then wiggled her fingers. "There's something more sinister."

Mia rolled her eyes. "It's called stress, Mom."

"No need to be snippy. I'm only trying to help."

Another wave of guilt washed over Mia. She *was* being snippy. While her mother had no filter, and certainly could be thoughtless, for the most part, she meant well. It wasn't Faye's fault that Mia was upset. As if a strained marriage, a house move, pervasive loneliness, and a snarly teenaged daughter were not enough, now she was concerned about Ian's latest endeavor. Seeking out an unstable woman with a history of violence and delusion.

Faye came away from the window and breezed toward Mia. She leaned in close and cupped Mia's face with both her hands. "You need a change, my dear. Go and get yourself cleaned up. I'm going to arrange a small surprise."

CHAPTER SIX

Mia

MIA PRESSED HER face into the padded slit of the massage table. Six feet to her left, her mother lay in a similar position. The room was softly lit, and the gentle sounds of a burbling spring were playing on a speaker hidden behind a plant. A lady had placed hot stones along both their spines and, without a whisper, exited the room.

Faye sighed. "Doesn't this simply transport you, Mia?"

Not quite, but it was pleasant. The warmth radiated through the muscles of her back and neck. Knots of tension melting.

"It's definitely helping. Thank you."

She'd needed the break. Over the past months, her brain would not shut off. It seemed to constantly recycle thoughts of pain. Catastrophizing, when reasonably she knew lots of couples had gone through similar situations and recovered. Strange to consider that the wanderings of her own mind were her biggest hardship. Or that was how Ian framed it, at least.

"So," Faye mumbled. "Big day coming up."

"What day?"

"Ian's birthday, of course. Tell me all your plans."

"Nothing much, actually." The date had crept up on her. Or perhaps she'd forgotten it on purpose.

"Come now. You're holding out."

Was there a slight edge in her mother's voice? Perhaps Faye was really asking, Are you having a cocktail party? Prepping dinner for a dozen? Things Mia had done before but had zero desire to do this year.

"Ian and I agreed the house is in too much upheaval to entertain. I've reserved a table at that French bistro on Main. Same place we went last year for your birthday."

"A lovely choice." She sniffed. "I suppose I should get him a little something. So as not to make a statement. I'll drop it off on your step."

This time, the tone was undeniable. Disappointment. "You don't need to do that, Mom. You're welcome at the house any time."

"Good to know, my darling. I never want to impose." After a few seconds, she continued. "Ian certainly seemed chipper this morning."

"Did he?"

"Yes. Like he had a tiny feather in his cap."

Mia hadn't noticed anything other than veiled irritation emanating from her husband. Perhaps Faye actually had developed some sort of intuition. "He did share some good news last night. Related to his work."

"Promotion?"

"No, a publication. They've asked him to revisit . . . well, a case study."

"You sound almost concerned."

"Do I?"

"The energy in here shifted immediately."

Mia hesitated. She knew sharing details about Ian's work was a terrible idea. Especially given how absorbed she'd been with the case when it was publicized. Still, she wanted to talk about it. To say it out loud. "Do you remember LK?"

"Who?"

"It's a pseudonym, Mom."

"You've still lost me, dear."

"That girl who killed her uncle in the woods and then developed that weird syndrome. Where she literally thought she was dead? She was Ian's patient."

Several seconds passed before Mia heard a tongue clicking.

"Yes," Faye said, "it's come back to me now. That . . . that young woman from the news? I don't know why your husband's investing more time into a psychopath."

"Ian never labeled her a psychopath."

"And that matters? No matter how you slice it, it's incredibly unsafe."

With the heat, the cotton towel beneath Mia's body had grown damp with sweat. "Anyway, it's a prestigious journal. And it might reinvigorate his career."

"Oh, that's right. His precious career. Well, I do hope you don't get all wrapped up again."

Mia shifted, felt the stones edging sideways. "I wasn't *that* wrapped up."

"Are you kidding me? That's all you talked about. Like you couldn't get enough information on some sick girl's misery." Her mother must have lifted her head, as her words were no longer muffled. "It was a weird phase for you. I thought you were quite unwell, if I'm honest, and last thing you need to do is invite that negativity into your life again."

"You're not being fair, Mom." She wasn't inviting anything. How many women desperately loved true crime? Watched documentaries, listened to podcasts, read books, followed court proceedings. Some even spent their lives pouring over minutiae, trying to solve cold cases themselves. Perhaps initially Mia had been overly invested, but so were umpteen other true-crime enthusiasts. Plus, she was no longer that way. The curiosity had abated, and now her overriding sensation was deep uneasiness.

She remembered one aspect of the case that no article ever mentioned. Ian had written a formal plea in 2003 and presented it to the board of Albethey, shortly before his patient's twenty-first birthday. Mia had found the document in the same box as LK's letter.

In it, Ian detailed the mental state of his patient. Even with years of treatment, he described lingering delusions of death and decay. The alarming ease with which LK dissociated. He said that she'd expressed a "steadfast unwillingness" to shift her care to another psychiatrist and stated her intention to discontinue antipsychotics. Ian had recommended she not be released. In his professional opinion, she remained a threat to herself. And to others.

Mia sat up, the warm stones tumbling from her back and clattering on the floor. "Let's just enjoy our afternoon, okay? I shouldn't have mentioned it at all."

CHAPTER SEVEN

Lainey

PLEASE WAIT FOR *the host to start this meeting.*

Beneath the desk, my knee jerked up and down. Seven minutes had already passed, and Dr. Morrison still had not joined our "preliminary discussion." I recalled him as punctual, anally so, but perhaps I was misremembering.

The computer camera was working, and I was reflected in a tiny window. It was impossible not to check and recheck my look. Was it obvious I'd just gotten chocolate highlights and bleached my teeth? Was my makeup okay? Minimal enough but still providing the right amount of allure? And my blouse? With a deep V-neck, was I basically inviting him to peek? I adjusted the lighting, then the position of my chair. A little closer. A little farther away. Would he instantly know I was overthinking?

A flicker of my laptop screen, and finally the man appeared. He was wearing thick tortoiseshell glasses and a pink cotton shirt. His sleeves were rolled up, like he was ready to dig clams on a beach. For a moment, I wondered if he'd done the same as I had. Made specific choices, evaluated his appearance before logging in.

His mouth was moving, but I couldn't hear him.

"I think you're muted?" I said and touched my ear.

Leaning forward, he examined his screen, then slapped a hand to his forehead. I watched closely as he slid his finger along the trackpad, his tongue softly touching his upper lip. Finally he smiled. "—ciate your patience, Lainey. I'm useless with technology."

I took a moment to breathe. Subtly, so he wouldn't note a marked rise and fall of my chest. Though we were separated by physical distance, this encounter was undeniably intimate. After I sent the email during his lecture, I received a reply within the hour. Asking about my schedule this week. He wanted to have a "quick chat" to update me on everything. So that I was "fully informed."

"All good, Dr. Morrison." Glancing down, I saw that most of the polish was already gone from my thumbnail.

"Were you waiting long? The program did an automatic update. It took forever."

"No. I just logged in that second."

He hadn't blurred his background, and I had a clear view of the room. I couldn't see his desk, but both the walls and filing cabinets were white. The only item with color was a large abstract canvas, but even that was in muted tones. Delicate twirls of gray and blue that were likely meant to be relaxing. It reminded me of an oncoming storm.

"So. How have you been doing?"

"Alright. Yeah. I'm good."

As I examined his space, I developed a sudden tingly discomfort, as though a phantom charge was skittering between my temples. Was I nervous? Petrified? Indignant?

No. I recognized the sensation then. *Helplessness.* Dr. Morrison was seated in his office at Albethey.

"Coping well?"

"Sure. Using all the regular vices to stay sane. Alcohol, sex, online shopping." I grinned automatically, then forced my face to relax. I hadn't fully decided how I was going to present myself, but "flirty girlie" wasn't an option I'd been weighing.

"Ah, I see." Dr. Morrison smiled. "Before we start, just a little housekeeping, okay? To confirm, you've reviewed and signed the e-document I sent?"

"I did." Though I hadn't bothered to even skim it. Multiple pages outlining his responsibilities as a psychiatrist. And my rights as an adult interacting with him. Nothing new there.

"And as I mentioned, if we proceed, I'll be recording our sessions. For accuracy when I review. The files will be encrypted and, of course, strictly confidential. Do you give your consent?"

My hands slid back and forth over the armrests of my chair. Did I give consent? To be recorded? There were countless videos of me and Andrew screwing. In his condo, at hotels, in restaurant bathrooms. Even a sizzly one up against an oak tree during a woodsy hike. Though that was my body. Not really me at all. Capturing my words and thoughts on video seemed like leveling up. "No problem," I finally said. "Record away." I was screen-capturing as well, though didn't feel the need to announce it.

"Excellent." He leaned back in his chair, gazed at me. Like we were estranged pals having a tender reunion. "It's been awhile, hasn't it?"

"It has." I shifted again. I knew he was evaluating me. No doubt noting my posture or the multiple times I'd cleared my throat.

"It's very good to see you."

Another tiny cough. "You, too, Dr. Morrison."

He sighed, but in a pleasing way. "As I described in my initial correspondence, there's been renewed interest in my work."

"Related to me?"

"Exactly." He picked up a pen, clicked the top in and out. "Sharing your journey and exceptional progress with the psychiatric community was vital."

"And everyone else, right? I mean, it was all over."

"True, it did take on a life of its own. Which, of course, was out of my control." *Click. Click. Click.* "But your identity was carefully concealed. Protecting you was my primary focus."

"Of course." I nodded. Clearly neither of us was above a little distortion.

"Now, getting to the bones of it, I'd like to include present-day data."

"And I would be the data."

His mannerisms exuded warmth, confidence. "Yes, Lainey. Basically. Your participation would add a longitudinal element to my study."

"I get it. But I don't understand why anyone would still care?"

"The unusualness of it, I would say." He ran his fingertips through his beard. The hair thick and dark, and not unappealing. "Plus your condition was—and is—quite rare."

My condition. Cotard's syndrome. I'd read everything I could about it. Partly in an effort to understand what had happened to me. But mostly to prevent it from ever happening again. "It just seems weird."

"I understand why you'd feel that way. And if you choose to move forward, it would be entirely voluntary. Any identifying details would be altered. Same as before. At any time, you can withdraw from our communications. I want to be very clear about this, Lainey. You have full control."

Inside, I giggled. In my world, that meant something slightly different. Ropes and switches. A little PVC, maybe. Once or twice, a gag ball. Role-playing that was all in good fun.

"Gotcha," I said again.

"Do you have anything to ask me? Anything at all?"

In his tone, I sensed his eagerness for me to play along. A subtle prodding so that he could produce an article that brought him further recognition, further respect. And even though I knew what he was doing, my body still reacted to his wishes. Or maybe reacted to his handsome face. The deadness inside me trying to glisten.

Focus. Focus!

I pushed out my single question. "Would our conversations be like therapy?" I'd once tried to talk to my family physician. But the woman's kindness made me almost nauseous. Conversely, Dr. Morrison's curiosity, a little dirty, seemed a safer environment.

"Well, that depends."

"On?" I'd assumed the answer would be a resounding yes.

"On you, really. We could narrow in on where you are today, but if you'd like to take the direction of our conversations elsewhere, that's your prerogative."

"I-I don't know," I stammered. "I'm not sure." What was the right reply?

I saw an unmistakable flicker around his mouth. Consternation, perhaps. But he did not alter his tone.

"Understandable. We may be dredging up difficult periods."

"Yes." What he meant was bludgeoning my uncle. Could I still use the term *allegedly* if I was institutionalized because of the incident? I certainly liked to think so.

"These are things you've perhaps managed to navigate, but there's still a risk that our communication might spark regression. I'm here to help you, in whatever way you deem—"

"Regression? Do you mean relapse? Is that even possible?" My underarms were suddenly slick.

Click-click-click went his pen. "Have you experienced another episode since our time together?"

"No." Firm no. While I was certainly able to detach and compartmentalize during periods of stress, I'd never vanished from myself again.

"Then I'd say the chances are exceedingly low. We can take things step by step, okay? You will be safe, Lainey."

Safe was a curious word to toss out. And a guarantee of it. I wouldn't bet on it, but I'd already decided I was going to try. "I do want help, Dr. Morrison. Genuinely. But it's just . . ." There was one more tiny point to address. I'd thought I'd be able to look him squarely in the face. But fessing up was tougher than I'd imagined.

"If you can articulate your concerns?" There it was again. Barely detectable, but still a sweet note of desperation in the mix.

"Well . . ." I needed to just spit it out. "Basically . . . I didn't exactly tell you the truth."

Once my delusions had lost their grip, Dr. Morrison and I began therapy five times per week. During those hour-long sessions, I took some creative license. I wove a complex (and mostly manufactured) tale of familial relations, sidelined friendships, and internal conflict. Eventually I told him that I'd injured my uncle in a state of emotional dysregulation for a dull and senseless reason. Dr. Morrison never questioned anything and mostly swallowed my stories like crunchy-shelled M&M's.

But his face was betraying him now. Pleasantness dissolved. He'd worked with me for years. Trying a range of treatments, from the pointless to the torturous, to help me "heal." At the end of it all, my hot mess had made him a hot ticket, and now I was telling him his careful research was built on fiction. His analysis, a sham. Articles all bullshit. In a sense I'd fooled him, manipulated him. (With some degree of ease, I might add.) But I had good reason. Or so I believed at the time.

"I'm sorry? What does that mean—you didn't tell me the truth?"

"Bad things happened in the woods, Dr. Morrison. Bad things happened before too."

His Adam's apple bobbed as he swallowed. "Might you be comfortable elaborating?"

Lowering my eyes, I purposefully let the tip of my tongue touch my upper lip. Then said, "Elaborate how?" I spoke steadily, but my head was buzzing. Like I'd stabbed a hornet's nest inside my skull. "Maybe I told you what you wanted to hear? But I'm ready to share my story now."

Even the very worst parts.

CHAPTER EIGHT

Lainey

AFTER THE VIDEO call ended, I paced around the condo. My body felt itchy with no obvious place to scratch. Dr. Morrison was leaving things in my hands, he'd said, and had "kindly requested" that I reach out in a day or two to let him know what I'd decided. I was welcome to contact him at any time if I had further questions or wanted clarification. "Absolutely no pressure," he said, as he leaned forward in his chair, staring straight into my eyes.

If I was honest, there was an intoxicating power in that. An almost tipsiness, knowing that I was in possession of something he craved. A valuable narrative that resided exclusively inside my mind. But this time, I would resist the desire to play games. I genuinely wanted to get better. What was the point in existing if it simply hurt?

I stepped onto the condo balcony and leaned against the metal railing. Andrew's two-bedroom was on the eleventh floor and overlooked a park. Grass, trees, and a paved pathway that circled Callow's most famous landmark—a clock tower. In winter, I watched people entering through the black gates and strolling the loop. But now that everything was a sea of healthy green, I couldn't see much. A woman with multiple dogs leashed to her belt. Several teenagers clutching bright red drinks. Two men nuzzling on a wooden bench. I searched, wanting to witness something else. An act of aggression, perhaps. Or some harmless property destruction. Why did normalcy create a hum inside me. Was it revulsion? Or maybe sorrow? I couldn't tell the difference.

Each time I blinked, I caught flashes of my uncle. Like a series of stills from a home movie. We were waiting on the veranda of a rustic cabin, pine trees looming in the background. A still lake. And then we were both waving. At someone.

There were images of swimming, paddleboating, roasting marshmallows over a crackling fire. Several wet swimsuits drying on a hook. Bowls of popcorn, a spilled Boggle game, a pile of moldy comic books.

As each summery scene shifted to the next, we drew closer to the end. Those last moments when we were together on the newly built dock. A glittery spray of broken glass. A single white incisor. His mouth with an ugly gash. Thick red liquid seeping between the boards and striking the surface of the lake. *Plunk. Plunk. Plunk plunk plunk.*

I shuddered and moved back inside the condo. Even though the unit was spacious, the walls were shrinking, and I needed to get out. To breathe. I grabbed Andrew's keys from the hook by the door and took the elevator to the lower-level garage. A drive would clear my head. I would find some country road where I could stamp my foot on the gas pedal and watch a cloud of dust billow in my rearview mirror. I would pretend I was free. Pretend I was happy.

I never intended to go back to Albethey. As it was so far outside the city, it wasn't a difficult place to avoid. But that was where I ended up. Idling my car in the lot just outside the secured doors to the psychiatric wing. I crouched down in my seat and waited an entire hour.

The historic building was red brick, with dormers and a steep roof tiled in slate. There were old turrets and several sleek extensions. Made me realize housing psychos was a lucrative business. From the outside, the place had a romantic vibe. The padded rooms, locked doors, and pervasive smell of rubbing alcohol were all neatly disguised. I felt no notable physical sensations while I sat there. No agitation or increased respiration. Clearly the sight of that place was not triggering. Then again, why would it be? The only time I'd viewed the front was the day I left.

A man came through the double doors. He was wearing a ball cap, royal blue with an iconic yellow swoosh. I wouldn't have paid him much mind but for the shirt. I locked onto the pink color as he made his way down the stone steps. Was I imagining a pop in his gait? Were his lips whistling? With an even pace, he walked toward the Reserved section and compressed his frame into a ridiculously tiny Audi.

I gripped the steering wheel tighter. I really should get back to Andrew's. I'd whip up a creamy pasta for dinner and act like I was a normal person. Having normal thoughts. Instead of stalking my former doctor at the madhouse I used to called home-sweet-home. But as Dr. Morrison left the parking lot, I did as well. Staying one or two cars behind him. Trailing was not an issue, as his sports car was an offensive seafoam green. Definite demerit points for that, though it made it easy to spot as he moved between lanes.

How many hours had I spent imagining his life outside Albethey? When I was young, I'd created an entire world for him. Not that I could remember much of those imaginings now, other than the void I'd left in his life. His niggling desire for us to be united. As though we were lost lovers. "How can emptiness be so heavy?" he used to whisper inside my head. The thought now made me chuckle, though

I'd deemed it practically poetic at the time. Perhaps I was slightly preoccupied when I was fresh out of the bin. But it was totally harmless, of course.

Suddenly I wanted to know where he lived. What sort of property he owned. What area he'd chosen to call home. And why not indulge myself? The video call hadn't been easy, and perhaps I deserved a small reward for taking the first step.

Without using an indicator, he pulled off the road and into a corner store's lot. I detected entitlement in the way he parked next to the front door. Blocking other vehicles. He jogged in and minutes later emerged with a carton of milk locked in his fist. When he tossed it on the passenger seat, I knew he was married. Or at least had a significant other. A single man wouldn't stop to run such an errand on his way home.

I continued following him. He took a left into a residential neighborhood. Cramped bungalows and overgrown trees. Rolling through several stop signs, he finally slowed, but instead of pulling into a driveway, he parked at the curb. I was surprised by the location. I'd expected a fancy estate, a flagstone driveway. Sprinklers popping up to water a picture-perfect lawn.

When he climbed out, he had no milk in hand. He slammed his door harder than required and took long purposeful strides. Heavy on the heels.

This wasn't his home. He had other business here.

I stopped several cars behind his. He was approaching a shabby single-story dwelling, mustard-yellow door that had leaden glass windows on either side. An overgrown crab apple tree dominated the postage-stamp yard, and kitschy plastic flowers on metal sticks were stuck in the ground. The kind a little kid might blow and marvel at the spinning.

He was on the stoop now. Raked his fingers through his hair and adjusted his glasses. Then his hand formed a fist, and he banged on the front door. Only a few seconds passed before he banged again. I experienced a thread of exhilaration that someone was making him impatient. *Not very nice, Lainey. Not very nice.*

I could not see who finally answered, but I had the distinct sense it was a woman.

I tapped the gas, the car easing forward. Ever so slightly. If I moved up, just beyond that flowering shrub, I could—

My phone buzzed. I jumped. Pressed the brake. A text from Andrew. *Where r u?*

I stared at the screen. That was a very good question. Where exactly was I? On some random street in Callow. Doing what? Trailing a man who was basically a stranger. Why? I had no idea. It hadn't taken long to realize my constructed version of him was much more appealing.

omw, I texted back. Then after a second, I followed up with *had to grab milk*. After all, I, too, was part of a couple, and that was an errand I might logically do.

I drove home in a bit of a daze. Before I knew it, the door to the underground garage was lifting in front of me. I considered then that I should have noted the street name. Or the house number. I could have looked it up to see who lived there. Not that I'd know the person, but there was nothing wrong with being inquisitive. It was a sign, I often told my yoga students, of a healthy mind.

Or perhaps I didn't notice on purpose. My psyche whispering once again, *Focus!* To remember what I'd decided. The only reason I was interested in Dr. Morrison was free therapy. And yeah. How badly I needed it.

•

"Where's the milk?"

As I came out of the elevator, Andrew was standing in the hallway, holding open the condo door.

"Milk?" I brushed past him. Then remembered my idiotic lie. "Shit. Totally slipped my mind."

"Hm," he said.

I kicked off my shoes and followed him into the kitchen. He unknotted a white plastic bag. Lifted out Styrofoam containers. Placed them on the table.

"What'd you get?" I sidled over. Through his cotton polo, I tickled the small of his back.

"Just pad Thai and vegetables. Hungry?"

"Famished." My encounter with Dr. Morrison must have given me an appetite.

As we ate, I tried to maintain the guise of dedicated listener. He was describing, in numbing detail, a hiccup on his latest project. The building was entirely refurbished, everything state-of-the-art, but they were attempting to "cheap out on security." His team was having an issue with the hardware and software. Getting the camera systems to communicate with the computer program. "But," he said, "they seem unfazed by the issues, and only focused on their deadline to open." I struggled to maintain interest in his work, like a good partner should, but at least I suppressed my yawns.

"Enough about me," he finally said. "How was your day?"

Of course I didn't mention my psychiatrist and instead told him about the class I'd started teaching at Om Bliss. Vinyasa flow. Which was where I'd met my new favorite student, a young dude whose yoga short-shorts were so skimpy, I now knew he was a dedicated waxer. Or laser-er. "Crow pose was not his friend."

Andrew snickered. "Should I be jealous?"

"Oh, totally." When he tilted his head, his expression made me brace. So I said, "You know I'm not serious, right?"

"Of course." He wiped his mouth with a cheap serviette. "Though, Lainey, I've got to ask. What's going on with you?"

"With me? How do you mean?"

"I don't know. Lately, you seem kind of . . . spacey?"

Since that night in the hotel room, he'd been unusually attentive. As though he'd detected a shift in me. And he was right. A knot was growing in my head, and I was struggling to find the right strand to pull. But really, if I was going to tell my psychiatrist the truth, any strand would do, wouldn't it? It didn't matter where I began, it would all unravel in the end.

"Just my classes, actually." An easy redirect. "And the people there. I guess I don't really gel with any of them." I hadn't intended for that grim confession to slip out. That I considered none of my coworkers a friend, even though they were all genuinely decent. I couldn't bring myself to really relax around them. To share any elements of my life, either past or present. On the whole, working in a yoga studio created a surprising amount of stress. Acting healthy and balanced took tremendous effort.

"Well, maybe they're not your crowd."

"Yeah. Maybe." But if they weren't, who was? I did not have a crowd. Besides Andrew, I did not have a single person.

He was quiet, then finally said, "You know you can quit if you want to."

"Quit the studio?" I laughed. "And what? Go back to my old job, which drove me completely cra—which wasn't a good fit."

"No, that's not what I mean. Do whatever you want. Instead of something that's draining you."

"I might be a bit moody, but I'm not drained."

"I'll support you, Lainey. I want you to be happy. Whether you believe me or not."

What was this confusing overture?

I sighed. Audibly. While Andrew was usually sweet and naive, this dinner conversation was making me feel . . . off-kilter? Would that be considered an emotion? Over the past couple of days, I'd found myself wondering why I'd chosen him. Out of all the men who'd flirted, asked me out, tried to entrap me in a courtship of monotony, how come I was locked in with this guy? At first, I assumed I stuck around due to my low expectations. Or his total lack of interest in who I really was. Or even the unlimited exploration of all things erotic, which had its high points. But then, during my Zoom session, I realized something. My boyfriend of three years bore a striking resemblance to Dr. Morrison. Similar stature, similar physique, same sharply cut cheekbones and dark curly hair. A younger version, obviously. But standing side by side, the pair could be father and son.

I couldn't tell if my inner wobbliness was related to this new awareness. But I did know I was entertained by it. My subconscious had been making choices, leaving me in the dark.

Pulling his clean plate closer, I piled it on mine. Then brought the dirty dishes to the sink. As I was rinsing the remnants down the drain, he came up behind me. His abdomen pressing into my back. He wormed one hand around my waist, the other gripping my hair and sweeping it sideways. My neck exposed for his mouth.

He breathed in my ear. "Don't make any plans for next Saturday night."

"Oh?"

"There's a little gathering in the west end. We should check it out."

I knew what he meant. He'd heard about a play party. I could feel his excitement against my left glute.

He unbuttoned my jeans and tugged until they were a clump of fabric around my ankles. Fumbled with his pants. Yanked my panties to the side, the band of black lace cutting into my thigh. I leaned forward, bracing my palms against the bottom of the stainless-steel sink. Within seconds he was inside me, thrusting.

My hip bones grated against the countertop, and steaming hot water sloshed over my fingers, wrists. Plates. Forks. Shiny knives. I barely noticed. I was thinking about Dr. Morrison. The movements of his lips, hidden behind those whiskers. A smattering of gray at his temples. I imagined it was his hands gripping my shoulders, and I squeezed my eyes closed. Panted. I was one of those rare and lucky birds who could get off on penetration alone.

After Andrew groaned, he slumped against me. "I needed that."

"Me too," I replied, shuffling my feet so I turned toward him. I touched his cheek, smoothed his hair. The man I'd selected was exceedingly handsome. I wondered what he might look like in a pair of tortoiseshell glasses. Or even a beard.

CHAPTER NINE

Mia

MIA WAS UPSTAIRS sorting dirty laundry, a chore she now despised. Since the affair, she'd gotten into the shameful habit of inspecting her husband's clothing. His collars and cuffs. Even his underwear. Though she didn't expect to discover anything, it still made her anxious.

As she pressed the button to start the load, Ian popped his head through the door. He'd opted to work from home for a few hours, as he needed to sort through a pile of documents. Mia understood it was paperwork related to LK.

"Where's Elise?" he asked.

"At Chloé's." According to the blue dot, at least. Mia was relieved that over the past couple of days there had been no further visits to that filthy laneway. Perhaps Elise had thought it was a shortcut after school. Or a GPS error in the app.

"I'll need to have a word with her. I know the girls have some top-secret summer project, but she's clearly rifled through my office drawers for supplies."

"*Summer project?* When did she start that?"

"I don't know. She mentioned it yesterday, maybe?"

Mia faked a smile and said, "Well, that's nice." Elise hadn't shared anything with her. Not a word. "Oh, I forgot to ask," she continued, "how did things go with the property manager the other night?"

Ian clapped his hands together. "Our tenant vacated, though he left the place in a state. Stiffed us three months' rent too. But at least that little headache has resolved itself."

"That's good news."

"And even better news. Remember the case study review? I obviously can't share much, but I've made contact, and she's open to discussion."

"Already? I thought you were taking time to consider things."

"I did. And decided to jump in with both feet."

Mia paused. She was curious about the woman's reaction to Ian reaching out and wanted to ask, but thought better of it. "Smart thinking. Less stress later, I guess?"

"Speaking of stress, Mia, can we talk about Faye for a moment?" He shuffled his feet. "I recognize I was the one who was entirely in the wrong with my . . . behavior, and I don't fault you for sharing with your mother. But her nonstop commentary. It's gotten, I don't know, corrosive? Even this morning."

Mia knew exactly what he was referring to. Earlier that day, Faye had "dropped by" yet again. Third time that week. She claimed she was desperate for a good coffee, and her ancient drip machine wasn't cutting it. When Mia asked, "What about green tea?" Faye vigorously shook her head. "The fishy undertone is so unpleasant. I can't see how you stomach it."

As soon as Ian came downstairs, she began commenting on Mia's stud earrings. Asking if they were new. And when Mia had replied yes, Faye shrugged and said, "My goodness, guilt can be pricey." Next she took an extraordinary amount of time preparing a latte for herself, and every time Ian had tried to speak, she lifted the steamer stick from the foaming milk to obscure his words.

Small things. Almost insignificant. But it only amplified the tension in Mia's marriage.

"I see it too. I'm just not sure what to do."

"Of course. I get it, she's your mom. But you and I are all about repair, right? Rebuilding. And she's using every opportunity to be divisive. Not overtly, but you recognize the tone."

Repair. Rebuilding. Yes. "I've noticed. And I'm sorry."

"No apology needed, okay? But do you think you could get her to lighten up? We all need to get along here."

"That makes sense," she said. "And I'll address it. Soon." When she could think of a way.

"But don't bring me into it, of course. You know your mom a whole lot better than I do, and we don't want to risk a harsh reaction." Then he smiled and stroked her arm. "Maybe frame it as a favor to you. Just say you'd prefer if she eased up, as it's causing you unnecessary strain."

He was doing it again. Planting words in her head. Guiding her in the most inoffensive way. As though it were a kindness, and she should appreciate the guidance. When underneath it all, she was beginning to realize, the pervasive message was that she was incapable of thinking for herself.

Mia closed her eyes and shook her head. Once again, she was in overanalyze mode, reading intention into everything. Ian was just trying to help. Every marriage had hardship. Everyone made painful errors in judgment. But at the end of the day, they were still a family. They had to be.

"I will. I'll sort it out with her."

•

When Ian finally left for campus, Mia flumped down on the sofa in the family room, listening to the empty house. No creak of floorboards. No rustle of summery wind. Not even a grunt from the fridge, ice cubes knocking into a storage tray.

How was it she had no one to call? Other than Faye, of course, which she wasn't keen to do. Over the course of her adult life, she'd had plenty of friendships. With neighbors. Or other young mothers she'd met on the playground. Even some of the women she'd worked with at the college. Easy connections, but all of them seemed to have disintegrated. Take the woman who lived two doors down from their last house. She and Mia got along instantly. Things progressed to family dinners, with husbands and kids. But about a year ago, there was an unexplainable retreat. No response to Mia's invitations or texts of *Are you okay?* At first she wondered if she was just not cut out for close female friendships. No different than being in high school. But lately, a new possibility had occurred to her. Perhaps those lost connections had something to do with Ian. Mia wondered if he'd sent signals that she'd missed. Had he made her friends uncomfortable? Had that lady been the other party in the affair?

Plucking her MacBook from the side table, she positioned it on her lap. There were two profile options available on her locked home screen: P and Other. P was her personal laptop. Other was a mirrored version of Ian's.

He didn't know about the software, of course. She'd installed it shortly after discovering his affair. It took a little maneuvering, as he guarded his passwords, citing confidentiality requirements. So she'd sent him a personal email that appeared to be from a trusted colleague. "Blast from the past" was the subject line, and it included a link to a years-old *Psychology Today* article where Ian was quoted extensively. He clicked the ego-stroking link, which then activated the installation. A few hundred dollars later, and the program was buried deeply among his directory files.

At the time, she'd thought it would improve her trust. Being able to read every conversation he had or check every website he visited. For the most part, it was an exercise in boredom. Nothing untoward or illuminating. After a while, she couldn't even bother to keep up with the email summaries she received. It felt like work. There were a couple of interesting moments. When he googled *How to get my wife to forgive me* and *How to stop my MIL from making me insane.* And when he visited a Reddit thread: *When your wife leaves you, and it fucks your career.* In recent weeks, she'd considered removing the software. Now she was glad she hadn't.

She clicked Other, and his homepage background appeared. A childhood image of Elise. Right under the tip of her pixelated nose, a folder labeled LK.

Mia tugged at a hangnail on the side of her thumb. While she'd managed to justify monitoring his online activity, she'd never looked at his professional files before. Well . . . except that one time. Years earlier, she'd read Lainey Kemper's therapy notes. Of course she knew it was an invasion of privacy, but she'd reasoned it was already in the past. The doctor-patient relationship had ended. Case closed. So it hadn't seemed *that* bad. But if she watched a video session shortly after it was recorded? There was no gray area there. It was unethical. And probably illegal too.

She shouldn't do it. Being curious was not reason enough. But the woman was dangerous, was she not? Also she'd been in love with Ian, even though that had been a lifetime ago. And now she was roaming the world with no restrictions, no limitations. Nothing preventing her from walking up to Ian on Callow's campus and saying hello. Could this patient be a threat to both him and his family? As a wife and mother, didn't Mia have a right to information? Surely, she did.

Surely . . . she did not.

All the mental volleying was making her skull ache. She closed the laptop and two seconds later flipped it open again. Ian always told her she had to stop dissecting everything: "Do stuff for yourself, Mia. Whatever you want." Maybe it was fine, and nobody would care if she took a quick glimpse. Besides, who'd ever know?

Sliding her finger over the trackpad, she double-clicked. The folder was not password-protected. Inside, a solitary MP4. Another double-click, and the icon wiggled. So much for any sort of security.

Mia leaned closer as the recording of Ian and LK's first Zoom session began to play.

"I appreciate your patience, Lainey. I'm useless with technology."

The woman's appearance surprised Mia. She'd anticipated someone drained, doughy-faced, clothing and hair disheveled. Even hesitant and jittery, as though the world had trampled her. Instead, LK was the picture of beauty, calm, and poise. She had dark brown hair, sharply chopped at the shoulders. Her skin flawless, her cheekbones naturally pronounced. Her lips were stained a subtle orange red.

Neither of them had disguised their backgrounds. Ian was in his office at Albethey. Likely scheduling the call between seeing his patients there. And was the woman in her home? There were two oversized windows, fabric shades blocking the light. The floor-to-ceiling shelving was jammed with books, though the spines were too far away to read. And on a pedestal table, a glass vase full of gladiolas.

The two of them were chatting so casually, she appeared almost . . . ordinary?

"If you can articulate your concerns?"

"Well . . ." The woman shrugged. Shifted in her chair. "Basically . . . I didn't exactly tell you the truth."

Mia leaned closer to the screen.

"I'm sorry? What does that mean—you didn't tell me the truth?"

Mia sensed a shivery anticipation building. As though she were slowly turning the crank on a real-life jack-in-the-box. And somehow Lainey Kemper was going to burst from the laptop screen.

"Bad things happened in the woods, Dr. Morrison. Bad things happened before too."

Then the undeniable prick. A rusty hook piercing Mia's rib cage. She needed to know. She needed to know everything.

CHAPTER TEN

Mia

OVER THE PAST couple of days, Mia had noticed a burgeoning flush of affection for Ian. While she wanted to believe it was due to the compassion he'd displayed for his patient, she suspected it was because of her own behavior. The spying was clearly wrong, but every marriage had a scale of deceit. And by engaging in reprehensible behavior behind his back, perhaps she was bringing a degree of balance to their equation. Which then caused some of her bitterness to recede.

She'd been lying in bed for an hour. Beside her, Ian was still sleeping. She inched closer to him and placed her hand on his chest, moved her fingers through the graying hair. Today was his birthday. He was fifty-five years old. She'd purposefully opted not to buy him a present, even though there'd been plenty of opportunity. She'd wanted him to notice her neglect. Though now, in this moment of warmth, she regretted her choice. Of course, she reasoned, a gift doesn't necessarily need to come from a store. There were other surprises she could offer.

She moved her palm down over his stomach, then cupped him between the legs. He stirred slightly as she slid her head beneath the covers. Curling her fingertips over the band of his loose cotton underwear, she lowered the front. She refused to consider that the other woman had done the same. Had been where she was now. That thought made her feel good, even though it might be a lie. With soft suction, she pulled him in, and immediately he hardened. His hips shifting even before he was fully awake. Then a throaty "Ohhh. Oh god."

"Happy birthday, you," she whispered when she emerged from the covers.

"Happy birthday, me!" he replied, wide grin.

They climbed out of bed and showered together. Then, hair still damp, descended to the kitchen. By some small blessing, Faye had stayed away that morning, and Elise was still asleep. So she and Ian were alone for breakfast, side by side at the island, sipping coffee. Neither of them spoke. Just cast shy glances at each other. For the first time in ages, things were pleasant.

•

At the restaurant, they were seated at a table near the front windows. Mia, Ian, and Elise. Plus Chloé. Elise had asked to invite her friend, and knowing at some point her daughter might balk at dining out with her parents, Mia had agreed.

Crisp white linen covered the table. In the center, a single candle glowed, and off to the side, a bottle of champagne waited in an ice bucket. Mia was wearing a floral midi dress with a soft frill at the shoulder. She'd even gotten her nails done in a fire-truck red.

The server brought a plate of oysters with champagne vinegar and fresh herbs, and for the girls, stuffed mushrooms and warm baguette. As Ian noisily slurped, he stared at her over the rim of his glasses. Maybe she was misreading, but his gaze did not seem particularly affectionate. Was he bothered about the seating? Did he not like the tarragon? For a split second, her stomach dropped. Maybe he'd caught her. He knew what she'd done. Not only had she watched the video twice, but she'd scanned the pages of his appointment book for any mention of LK.

"All good?" she managed.

"Thank you," he said, tossing an empty shell on the ice. "This is exactly how I wanted to celebrate."

Relief rinsed through her. "I thought so. Just us. Finding our way." Beneath the tablecloth, she stroked the inside of his thigh.

When Chloé reached for her third hunk of bread, she mumbled, "Sorry. When my Addy wears off, I'm, like, totally starved."

"Eat up." Mia nudged the basket in Chloé's direction. "They'll bring more." She'd often heard Chloé complain about the side effects of her medication. How she wanted to stop the pills, but her mother refused to allow it. "So," Mia continued, "what have you two been up to? Anything to report?"

A casual question, though inside she urgently wanted an answer. The blue dot had been in the laneway again that afternoon, remaining motionless for seventeen whole minutes.

"Actually yes!" Elise straightened her spine. "We're—"

"Starting a business," Chloé chimed in.

"What?" Mia leaned forward. "What sort of business?"

"Swim school. With Chloé's pool. We did all the marketing this week and put flyers up everywhere. Went door to door with leaflets. Lessons can be daily or weekly. Swimming and water safety stuff."

"And we've already got seven customers! The moms can chill on a lawn chair. We'll even have complimentary kombucha in a cooler."

"Chloé's mom helped a ton with all the design stuff. And printed everything for free."

"Plus she's buying the kombucha." Chloé laughed. "So it doesn't cut into our profits."

"That's fantastic," Mia said. While she was proud of her daughter for taking such initiative, she couldn't deny there was also a shard of jealousy. Couldn't Elise have asked her for help as well? Even for an opinion? She also had a background in marketing.

"Cheers to two of Callow's newest entrepreneurs," Ian said. "That's really something."

Mia and Ian lifted their coupes of champagne, and the girls raised pale pink mocktails. All of them clinking.

When they lowered their glasses, the sound of clinking continued. Turning in her seat, Mia saw Faye standing outside on the sidewalk. Tapping excitedly on the restaurant window. Then she brought both hands to her cheeks, and her face morphed into a look of utter surprise.

"How random is this?" She was out of breath by the time she arrived at their table. "An evening stroll, and the cosmos led me right here."

"Mom, I—"

"It was your nails, dear. That garish color. I'd have moseyed on by if they hadn't screamed at me."

Ian's jaw clenched. "Nice to see you, Faye."

"I won't stay," she said. "I really won't." Her dress billowed as she rapidly waved at the server.

He hurried over. "Should I bring another place setting?"

"I mean, if you insist." When she finally settled into her chair, she said, "And I'll have the steak frites. I haven't eaten a crumb all day."

"Yes, ma'am."

"But can you make sure the frites are fresh? Last time I was here, they were . . . kind of limp."

"Mom. I don't—"

"How lovely it is to see everyone. Mia. Elise. And . . . "

"I'm Chloé. We met before at—"

"Yes, yes." She plunked her oversized boho bag on the table and began rummaging through it. "And not to mention, our celebrant of the evening. I'd like to offer my best birthday wishes to my dear son-in-law." Her hand emerged clutching a velvet pouch. She pushed it across the table. "A tiny token that's from the heart."

Ian slowly loosened the drawstring that was cinching the top. Then tipped the contents into his palm. A large blue stone, marbled with yellow and black. Holding it up to the light, he examined it and finally said, "That's thoughtful of you, Faye. You shouldn't have."

"Not at all. It's lapis lazuli. Something you need."

"I need? And why might that be?"

Mia winced. Ian had stepped into the trap.

"Well," Faye said. "For starters, it's supposed to bring harmony to your love life, Ian. And truth. Figured you could use a bit of that."

"I see," he said, sliding it back into the pouch. "We could all use a little, I suppose."

"Just make sure to keep it on your person at all times."

"Mom, please, can you—"

Ian touched Mia's hand. "It's okay, honey." Then to Faye, "Without a doubt. I'll keep it taped to my chest."

The girls were giggling, while Ian's knee was jerking up and down. Though his face gave nothing away, Mia was certain he was aggravated. And she couldn't blame him. A family dinner had become yet another platform for Faye to highlight Ian's indiscretion. It was her own fault. She shouldn't have told her mother about the affair. She shouldn't have shared her worries. She shouldn't have even shared the birthday plans.

During the rest of the meal, Mia tiptoed through the conversation as though there were a sinkhole hidden up ahead. She pushed the girls to share every detail of their upcoming swim school. Then prattled on about the sump pump in their basement and a summer cocktail she'd seen on Instagram. Any neutral topic to pass a few minutes.

Faye gobbled her dinner and drank the Chardonnay she'd ordered for the table. When she was two-thirds through the bottle, she focused on Ian and slurred, "So. My daughter mentioned you'll be reexamining an old case?"

Blood drained from Mia's head. Ian had surely told her that bit of information in confidence, and instead of safeguarding it, she'd immediately spilled it. And what if Faye decided to reveal Mia's former preoccupation with his patient? While Ian was certainly aware she'd had a vague interest—after all, she'd initially approached him with questions—he likely hadn't grasped the degree. It would be one more thing for him to twist.

"Yes," he replied calmly. "The journal has made a professional request. I'm considering how to proceed."

"But didn't she kill some poor man? And then the whole thing went . . . viral? Isn't that what the kids call it?"

Elise and Chloé giggled, but Faye didn't seem to notice.

"Mom, perhaps this isn't appropriate dinner conversation?"

"And why not? It's the current state of humanity, Mia." Faye gulped from her glass. "Our world is burdened with nutcases. Screwballs. Right, Ian?"

"Those are not terms we use, Faye. When people become unwell, they need help. Plain as that."

"Sure, sure. I just don't know why you insist on working with criminals. Aren't there any regular unwell people around?"

"Thank you, but I'm quite ca—"

"Anyway, it's not my place to speak up. But I will say it has got me thinking." Faye gripped the beads around her neck. "About my own past, and all. How it can lock us in place."

"Anyone still have room?" Mia asked quickly. "Should we check out the dessert menu?"

"It made me realize that my energy is stuck, and I refuse to accept that any longer." She reached over and stroked Elise's arm. "It's like a pipe, my darling. It can flow, or be stodgy, or completely blocked."

Elise smiled brightly. "And is yours blocked, Grandma?"

"That it is, dear. I need a"—hands thrust into the air—"a celestial plunger."

"Really, Mom. Can you keep your voice down?"

"Oh, like the sword in the stone?" Chloé offered. "But instead you want, like, a thing for the toilet?"

"It's sticking out. And only you can release it, Grandma. With your powers."

Both girls fell into each other, snorting.

"Have your fun, but I did my research, and lo and behold, a higher being has taken the wheel. I'd actually like to run my idea by Ian. If he'll indulge me?"

"Of course I'll indulge you, Faye. When have I not?"

"Might be good to have a professional's opinion."

"I can certainly recommend someone, if you want to explore therapy."

She laughed. "Oh, no, no, no. I don't need that. Just a clear eye."

Ian took an audible breath and exhaled through flared nostrils. His patience was gone. "My eye is nothing but clear."

"I'm sorry," Mia whispered in his ear, when he finally paid the bill. "I'm so very sorry for this."

CHAPTER ELEVEN

Lainey

WHEN I LOGGED in for my second session, there was no virtual waiting room. He was poised at his desk, pen in hand, eyes alight with boyish keenness. This time, the sight of him didn't freak me out. His face had quickly regained a degree of familiarity.

After a few general questions about my post-Albethey period, he said, "If you'll indulge me, Lainey, I'd like to narrow our focus for today."

"Sure." I shrugged. "You're the professional, right?"

He gently asked if we could review some of his original notes. If I had to guess, telling him I'd been untruthful had put him on edge, and he needed clarification.

First we went through my recollections of my mental health at Albethey. I did my best to answer his questions with accuracy and sincerity. Every aspect of my experience with Cotard's syndrome was terrifying. When he was satisfied with my replies, we moved on to our therapy sessions. That was where I'd introduced a degree of deception. Granted, the narrative I'd created contained just enough honesty to make the bullshit believable.

"To summarize, you shared a close bond with your mother?"

"Um. Correct?"

"And after her death, you were taken in by your uncle."

"Hundred percent true."

"You consistently described him as good-natured, soft-spoken, and focused on establishing stability."

"Yes." I paused for a moment, then said, "But also no."

Dr. Morrison frowned slightly. "As a teenager, you claimed to have a debilitating fear of being alone. Would you say that was truthful?"

I bristled slightly. "Yeah. Probably accurate."

"Based on my notes, that fear eventually led to the death of your uncle."

As he read a portion of his summary aloud, I realized that I'd painted quite the idyllic picture. A warm and supportive homelife. My uncle and I cooking together, doing homework together, going on nature hikes together. We took weekend trips to museums and art galleries, and on occasion, he let me loose in the mall with his credit card.

"I mean, elements of that are accurate. We did do those things." In certain ways, my uncle was good to me.

But then I blurred reality. Apparently, I'd told Dr. Morrison that something changed when I became a teenager. No matter how perfect my father figure was, none of it had the desired effect on me. My mood was often sullen, and I frequently yelled at him. Or destroyed things just to witness his reaction. I stole his belongings without remorse and snuck out whenever I felt like it. Even though I sensed my uncle was growing weary of my combative nature, I'd been unable to curb my caustic behaviors.

Our last summer together, he took me to a lakeside cabin for a vacation. The place was so breathtaking that I promised myself I was going to do better, try harder. But it was too late. He delivered devastating news: He'd been offered a new job which required him to travel, and with reluctance, he'd accepted the position. I would be placed in a boarding school. Left alone in an unfamiliar town with strangers. The news, I'd explained, flooded me with a glittery rage. And I attacked him.

"Did I really say those things?" When I tried to recall all the lies I'd manufactured at Albethey, my mind was a riddle of holes. Possibly a side effect of the shock treatments. Or the antipsychotics that had circulated in my system. "All that last bit? None of it's true, Dr. Morrison. Not one word."

•

Several days passed before I arranged our third session. For no other reason than that I'd promised absolute openness and I wanted to build a little anticipation.

"What should we discuss now?"

"Whatever seems right for you, Lainey."

"First memories, maybe?"

"If those are important to you, then yes, that's a very good place."

Even though his demeanor was nonchalant, I knew he was furiously yanking that little wire on the bus, saying, "Yes, yes! Let's step off here." Rooting around in the pivotal years of childhood—wasn't that every therapist's wet dream?

He was in a different location this time and, once again, hadn't blurred his background. Behind him was a dark wood credenza that matched his expansive desk. A coffee mug was casually perched on a pile of hardcover books. On the wall above that, an arrangement of sixteen miniature artworks framed in black shadow boxes. One was a blue-green blob; another a chaotic snarl of colorful squiggles. The bottom right was a bird with stick legs and spirally eyes. Right next to that, a large E with a floppy ear growing from its spine.

It was his home office. And Dr. Morrison had a child.

"Boy or girl?"

A moment passed, then he glanced over his shoulder. Realizing what I saw, he said, "Girl."

"What's her name?"

Quick smile, and he tapped the tip of his pen on the leather blotter. "As I recall, you were born in a facility? Your mother was incarcerated?"

A clunky redirection. Maybe his daughter was still a toddler. Sometimes that was a thing for old-ish men. Snagging and shagging a barely legal, who'd then squirt out an heir. Or maybe the cutesy art display was years old. If she was on socials, how hard would it be to find her?

I was getting distracted. *Focus, Lainey! Think: Mother. Think: Facility.* "Sort of," I replied. "But she wasn't incarcerated. It was more of a group home for offensive women." Or girls, rather. My mother was young.

"How might they qualify as offensive?"

He sounded so earnest, I knew he was being sucked in. Iron filings to a magnet. "*Troubled* might be a better word."

"But they kept the two of you together?"

"They sure did." I tried for peppiness. "Maintained the sanctity of that mother-child bond."

He tilted his head, then scribbled on his notepad. Clearly, I'd overpepped.

"How long did you remain in the group home?"

"Until I was four."

"Any recollections of your time there?"

"Not many, to be honest." And I was being honest. "I remember it smelled like a deep fryer. And also no one liked my mother." Except me, of course. I loved her with a level of desperation only a child could attain.

"Why might that be?"

"Because they were shitty, I suppose. She was the only one with a kid, so they gave her a single room. All the others shared rooms with bunk beds."

I forced myself to tell him about the nights I'd wake up. Alone in the bed with a scratchy blanket and a grimy-faced Cabbage Patch. "She never abandoned me. That's not what I'm saying. She was always back by sunrise." If she returned alone, I'd pretend to be sleeping while she stripped off her damp clothes. Through a squinting eye, I'd watch her standing naked in the early light. Hot red scores marring the skin on her belly.

"How did she get those injuries?"

"Did it to herself. Dragging her body over the barbed wire on top of the chain-link fence." A chick desperate to fly the coop. Then just as desperate to return. To me, I was certain.

Dr. Morrison had papers splayed on the desk before him. I watched him jotting stuff in the margins. When he was finished, he looked up at me. "Did you feel safe in those situations, Lainey?"

I paused. I'd never given it a single thought. "I don't recall being scared. So yeah, let's say I did."

"Do you believe that being unafraid and feeling safe are the same thing?"

Was this therapy or a pop quiz? "I don't know, Dr. Morrison."

"I do think it's important to explore the distinction."

Whatever. "Next question."

"Of course." He glanced at his notes. "You mentioned you were there until you were four?"

"Yep."

"And where did you go after that?"

"Don't you already know?"

He nodded. "I do. These sorts of details are well-documented. But I want to leave space for you to tell me your story, Lainey."

"Fine, then. Some sort of halfway house. Transitional living. Or whatever they call it."

"And?"

"I don't know. It wasn't so bad. I was fed. My hair was brushed. My mother had a job, and she walked me to kindergarten in the mornings."

As those words left my mouth, I suddenly began to feel weary. A fatigue lapping over my muscles, my bones. My eyes oddly gritty and wanting to close.

"Do you recall what sort of employment?"

Bartending. Which required the heavy application of lipstick. Ass-cheeks hanging out of Daisy Dukes. Some occasional whoring. My mother had been certain that was the way forward. Her primary goal? To locate a man who wanted to save the both of us. So we could be a proper family.

"She worked at the library. Shelving books."

Obviously a bold-faced lie. But I was finding our conversation to be physically depleting. Like his mouth had leeched on to me, and he was sucking. Not in a good way.

"Do you know how long she maintained that position?"

Position. If I wasn't so tired, I would have chuckled. "A good long time, Dr. Morrison." Would I have time to nap before Andrew got home? I wanted to doze for an hour. Maybe two. To recalibrate.

"Lainey?"

"Sorry. What was that? I lost track for a second."

"Perfectly okay. I was just asking about your early school experiences?"

"Mostly positive," I said. Which was true on those days I could focus. I liked to believe my mother did her best, but she lacked common sense. In her defense, I knew very little of her upbringing, and perhaps it was more feral than mine. Though even as a child, I understood I wasn't meant to have sips of coffee to offset the previous night's cough syrup. "School was easy. They said I was smart."

"Not surprising. Your intelligence scores at Albethey were quite remarkable."

"Were they?" That tidbit was a shot of sunlight on an otherwise gray day. I couldn't recall ever taking a test. Or being told the results. And certainly, nobody ever used the word *remarkable*. Though I guess everything I did back then was a measurement of some sort. An evaluation of my stability.

"Did you and your mother have any routines?"

"Does the playground count? Every Sunday afternoon."

"Sure it does. That's a healthy habit."

"Oh, totally. It was like clockwork. I always looked forward to it."

I was lying again. But seeing as these were early days in my therapy journey, I had to give myself a little grace. I wasn't going to be perfect from the jump. No need to outline the very minor incident in first grade. I'd foolishly been caught telling classmates about the mechanics of sex. A concerned parent complained, so I ended up with a case number. My mother feared losing me, and when the social worker arrived, she wore a blouse buttoned up to the neck. She managed to convince the woman I was a precocious reader who'd dipped into a medical textbook. Contents well beyond my age or comprehension.

To demonstrate dedication, she brought me to the park every week. While I played by myself, she sat under an oak tree. One arm belted across her chest, the other moving only to bring a cigarette to her lips. None of the other mothers ever spoke to her. None of the other children ever spoke to me. We were alike in that way, my mother and me. We were other.

"So there were positive developments then?"

"Absolutely. Things did improve."

As I spoke, my brain spat out a memory. Like a cat with a hairball. I was five or six. My mother and I were walking back to our apartment, and we met a man on the sidewalk. "Hey Janet," he'd said. "Who's the little lady?" She introduced me, and he took both my hands, stretched them out wide. As he sized me up, his roving eyes made me squirm, though I didn't know why. "Hell, she's already a looker, this one. If you need a hand with her, give me a shout." He laughed, but it was a joke I didn't understand. When I glanced up at my mother, I knew she didn't get it either. Her expression was strange.

That evening, she cut my hair into a pageboy, and kept saying, "You will thank me for this. You will thank me."

As wavy strands tickled down over my shoulders, I did not experience gratitude. My emotions were a mystery to me, even at that age. Instead I kneeled on that bathroom floor, fixating on a cracked tile. It was damaged, but it still had something surrounding it. Stained grout holding it in place.

"Lainey? Would you say you learned anything from your mother."

"Learned anything?" I felt heat erupt in my core. "I don't know. Never to rely on anyone else? Don't get attached?"

He made a note, and I realized my reaction was stronger than the information I'd provided. A reformed baddie who'd morphed into a park-going librarian. I had been much better at controlling a narrative when I was younger.

"So you had to be self-sufficient while your mother worked? Granted, at far too young."

"Sure. That's how I'm constructed, I guess."

He scratched his jaw with the end of his pen. "*Constructed.* That's an interesting term you chose."

Ugh. More bullshit. All I wanted to do was crawl under a blanket and block out the world for a while. But instead of revealing that, I maintained a cordial tone. "How so, Dr. Morrison?"

"Well, it suggests a worldview. That you believe you were shaped by external forces."

"Aren't we all shaped by external forces?"

"Certainly. To a degree. But I'd venture to say most are unaware."

The heat had moved from my core to my throat. Morphed into a hard pulse at the side of my neck. I'd had enough of this mindless interaction. Him gaping at me while I picked through my thoughts.

"I'm done," I said.

"Understandable, Lainey. I know this has been diff—"

I clicked the Leave Meeting button. Then stood up too quickly. The den began to fade, and I gripped the edge of the table until the static subsided. I shouldn't have been so abrupt. Hanging up like that demonstrated impulsivity. But it was getting next-level stupid. Sure, I was constructed. No different from every other person. Little cruelties forming a shell, only allowing expansion within a particular shape.

Anyway, none of it mattered now. I could do whatever I wanted. Which was probably the reason I was so lost.

CHAPTER TWELVE

Lainey

I HOPED THE evening's activities would soften the tension from yesterday afternoon. Since talking to Dr. Morrison, I'd been out of sorts. As though my mother had emerged from my mouth, and now the memories of her had a same-day freshness. Her feeble attempts at mothering, her profound inadequacies. But mostly my blind adoration, and then the inevitable pain.

At 11 p.m., Andrew and I took a taxi to the address provided. He was in full go-go mode and chatted nonstop the entire drive. About some "moron from work." About his next DJ gig. It wasn't nervous energy though. I was certain of that. His glee was practically puppy-like in its intensity.

We pulled up in front of a mega-mansion with a stucco facade and an expanse of lawn. Andrew slammed the car door, startling me. "Sorry," he said. "Why so jumpy?

I shrugged. "Double espresso?"

"Clever girl." He tapped his temple.

We walked up the flagstone path hand in hand, past boxwood and sprays of petunia. There was even a miniature lamppost beside the front steps. All the blinds were closed, and I was certain we'd messed up the location. Or the date.

When Andrew swung open the wooden front door, I hesitated, and he tugged me forward. I expected to see a gray-haired couple in recliners. Glassy eyes boring into us as we interrupted their evening program. But no, it was evident we got it right. A hetero twosome was humping against the wall. Like a red pulsing arrow on a mall map. *You are here!*

"Okay?" Andrew asked as we stepped around them.

Which was him confirming that I wanted to stay. Which I didn't. But, of course, I'd never say so. "All good," I replied. Then I grinned, and he grinned back. He'd never learned that when a woman said "All good," it almost invariably meant the opposite. I liked that about him. A layer of obliviousness. Or perhaps lack of interest. Either worked.

Andrew and I slowly wandered through the rooms. Our usual routine. Me acting nonchalant, and him evaluating all his options. Play parties were not nearly as enthralling as people thought. It wasn't like a sticky scene from a professionally shot porno. Though in fairness, each one was different. Big or small, in a private home or filling an entire club. Booze and drugs available or a strictly sober experience. Every gathering came with a set of rules. And it was honestly hit and miss. Though I immediately drop-kicked this one into the miss bucket.

The crowd was a mixed bag. What I'd expect if someone announced a "sex party in the sticks." About half the men looked like skinny college kids who spent most of their time gaming in their parents' basement. The rest of the men were older. And not in a distinguished way. The women, however, all appeared to be in their twenties, maybe thirties. Breasts still perky. Total overachievers in the hair and makeup department. Bubbly personas on full display. So, I was the oddity. On all fronts. Which was fine. I wasn't there to compete for attention.

I waited in the kitchen, the island full of supermarket snacks, while Andrew did his second round of exploration. To determine who he wanted. And who wanted him. I pondered if I could manage to eat something before he returned. I should have gone for it, as he wasn't back for easily twenty minutes. A blond on either side.

His cheeks were already pink. I waited for him to ask his question. As it was the same every time, I could have mouthed along as he said, "You want to watch?"

"Love to." I winked, and that tiny action gave me a sudden stab of . . . discomfort. Was I embarrassed? I brushed it away. Whatever. Every couple had their inane little rituals.

We managed to find an empty area on the upstairs landing. A semicircular balcony with a wrought iron railing that overlooked an expansive family room. Springy carpet and a chair made just for me. The white light bulbs had been replaced with soft violet, and the music coming from the ceiling speakers had a *chica-wah-wah* tempo. Perhaps the homeowner (or trusted house sitter) was striving for a '70s vibe?

As both blonds kneeled on either side of Andrew, I did not take my eyes off him. After the hotel incident, I couldn't risk upsetting him. With practiced expressions, I did my best to emote curiosity, pride, lust, and a dash of envy. Later, when I reclaimed him, I would tell him that he was misbehaving. That he belonged only to me. He liked it when I scratched his chest, his upper arms.

I hardly blinked, but that didn't mean my mind wasn't wandering. After my session, I'd spent several hours googling Dr. Morrison. Incognito mode, of course. Just in case Andrew decided to snoop. Even though I was ninety-nine percent sure that would never happen, I'd learned to be prepared for all possibilities.

Most of the professional mentions of him were outdated. Seemed he'd published widely in the years after my release. Not only had he won multiple awards, but he was considered an "esteemed professor." As the years progressed, those mentions grew fewer and farther between. His personal page on the college's website contained an About section with a few fun facts. He'd done an undergrad in physics. (Unexpected.) He was training to run a marathon. (Highly unlikely.) And he considered himself a foodie. (Who didn't these days?) His headshot was at least a decade old. Overall, it was lame. Or sad. I suspected those months I was dead had been the best of his life.

Details about his personal life were scant. I scanned through scores of older photos of ceremonies and gatherings, and there were none where his fingers were interlaced with a woman's. No mention of residing "with his family in blah-blah." Though I'd noticed a wedding ring during our sessions, that could be a ruse. Even the whole daughter thing could be a tactic. The artwork on the back wall of his home office there to disarm the viewer. Lull them into a false sense of security. *He's a trusted husband and dad. Go on. Spill your guts.*

Searching for relevant tidbits had mostly been an exercise in frustration. The only thing I found was a thirty-second video, posted by the marketing team at Callow College in 2014: a car wash fundraiser to build a "serenity garden" on campus. Several male professors scrubbed vehicles, with plenty of suds and laughter. Dr. Morrison and two unknowns peeled off their T-shirts, revealing torsos, still taut waists. I'd admit, the sight of foamy water trickling over his abdomen was quite arousing. The camera panned, then zoomed in. Pausing the video the moment he turned, I noted an unusual tattoo on his left shoulder blade. I enlarged the image, took a screenshot, and saved it to a locked file on my desktop. Finally, I set up an email alert for his name.

I returned my mind to the present. Andrew was kneeling now, both women on the carpet in a sixty-nine position, like a human Möbius strip. The mms and ahs were plain ridiculous. Totally performative.

I never could understand why anyone would put that much effort into pleasing a stranger. Perhaps it filled a complex emotional need that escaped me. Dr. Morrison would likely have a diagnosis, but I couldn't casually ask.

When the noises grew, a man came up the stairs and stopped to watch. He was one of the older gents with a glistening scalp. Bald, or maybe shaved.

"You don't want to join?"

"Nope," I said. "Not my thing."

"Too bad. You're the most beautiful girl here."

I rolled my eyes. "I'm hardly a girl."

"Whatever." He scowled. "It's just an expression. Why take shit so serious?"

The greaseball moved on, and I was ready to go home (grabbing a chicken wrap on my way to the exit) and initiate the second part of our dance. As I waited for Andrew's face to contort in climax, an entirely unrelated image flashed in my mind. My mother's grave marker. A garish pink-granite block with the name Janet Greene etched in bold black letters. I wondered what our relationship might be like if she were still alive. Would we be friends? Would she accept who I'd become? Then again, if she hadn't died, I'd probably be an entirely different person.

CHAPTER THIRTEEN

Mia

MIA WAS WANDERING the aisles of a grocery store, uncertain what to buy, when the music in her earphones switched to ringing. It was her mother. After tapping Answer, she said, "I'm shopping right now, can I—"

"Oh, good morning, darling." Faye sounded raspy. "I'm sorry I haven't reached out. I was nursing quite the flu but am back on my feet today."

Mia stopped beside a display of gourmet tomato products. Likely the flu was code for a massive hangover. Not only had Faye consumed an entire bottle of wine at Ian's birthday dinner, but she'd also finished the champagne and then sampled several digestifs. When they'd dropped her off, Elise had to walk her to her door and help her inside.

Ian had been livid, could not get over his gift—"that stupid fucking stone." Even though Mia had apologized again, the sourness between them lingered. Earlier that afternoon, he'd left for a two-day psychopharmacology conference. The very last thing he said was "You have to talk to Faye."

Rather than delaying, Mia needed to face things head-on. "Listen, Mom. There's something we should discuss."

"I know, I know. But before you jump down my throat, seeing you at the restaurant truly was a happy coincidence."

"I told you exac—"

"Yes, dear. But do you think I recalled? My mind's not as sharp as it used to be." She cleared her throat.

"I find that—"

"And it was kind of your husband to invite me to stay. What was I to do?"

Mia could not recall any sort of invitation. Ian had tensed, then topped up his nearly full glass.

"Sure, but sometimes we really do need family time."

"And I'm not family?"

"Of course you are, but I meant just the three of us."

A grunt then. "The three of you and that other one."

"Chloé was a last-minute addition. Elise asked us." And if parents opted to indulge their own child, whose business was that?

"Oh, it's fine. I get it. Whatever Elise wants, Elise gets."

"Seriously, Mom." She lowered her voice to a whisper. "My point is Ian and I want to get back on track." As she spoke, two women in brightly colored lounge sets brushed past her. Both were clutching scraps of paper and plucking ingredients from the shelves with clear purpose. Mia sighed. "Listen. I know you're trying to support me, but sometimes . . . it feels . . . invasive."

"Invasive?"

"Yes." She'd keep it simple. No further explanation was needed.

Several seconds of silence passed before Faye replied. "I do apologize, my darling, if you think I encroached. And if that upset you. I always want the best for you. You know that."

"It's—"

"I made a real show of myself. I drank too much. I didn't intend to. Please don't be upset with me."

As she detected no pluck in Faye's tone, Mia decided not to press any further. Perhaps the conversation might spark a shift.

"Let's put the evening behind us, okay?" She pushed her empty cart toward the produce section. There were mounds of glossy apples and lemons. Plus umpteen types of lettuce and a row of glass bottles with "artisanal" dressings. Everything picture-perfect, but nothing appealing.

"Agreed. I'm going to bring over dinner, okay? Tell me what Ian would like. We can make it up to him."

"He's away this evening, but it'd be nice if you and I cooked." She didn't mention the conference. Ian's travel already made her uneasy, and she didn't want to invite commentary. "I'm at the grocery store. What should I grab?"

"Not a worry. I'll bring everything. Some green and leafies to realign our chakras."

CHAPTER FOURTEEN

Mia

WHEN FAYE ARRIVED, she blustered into the family room and settled on the couch with Elise and Chloé. "My darlings," she chirped. "I'm so glad you're here. This old hen needs advice."

Mia was piling plates into the dishwasher. There were no grocery bags in her mother's hands. Not a single green and leafy in sight. "Weren't you bringing dinner?"

"Me? I'm sure you have plenty of things on hand."

Mia opened her mouth to speak, then closed it again.

"So what's up, Gran?" Elise said, putting down her phone.

"Well, I have exciting news." Faye clapped her hands together. "After much consideration, I've decided to dip back into the dating game."

"Wow! That's so cool!" Chloé, that time.

"But I need guidance on where to find some eligible bachelors."

"Really, Mom," Mia said as she hauled a premade lasagna from the freezer. "How would they know anything about that? They're fifteen."

"So? They're not children. Right, my darlings? Where do you think I should go?"

Chloé sat up. "Go?"

"Should I join a club? Maybe a hobby? Fencing perhaps, or woodworking?"

They both shook their heads. Confused. "Are you on any socials? You know, TikTok. Instagram. Build your following."

"Not really. I've never given it much thought. I'm a bit mature for that, aren't I?"

"You're never too old, Gran."

"There's also the apps," Chloé said. "Tons of people are on them."

"And which apps would you recommend, my dear?" Faye glanced at Mia, eyebrows lifted in a told-you-so expression.

"The usual ones. Hinge. Tinder. With Bumble, you need to connect first. So it gives you better control."

"Control over what?"

"Who you talk to," Elise said. "Losers can't just spam you."

"How do you two know all this?" Mia tried to hide her surprise over the rapid progression of their conversation.

"Mostly from listening to my mom," Chloé said. "She tries them out, then deletes, then tries them out again."

That made sense. Mia and Chloé's mother had been good friends for a while, but that ended after Sandy separated from her husband last year. Perhaps that was the reason they'd grown apart. Sandy preferred the company of her single pals over Mia.

"So," Mia gently ventured, "you haven't downloaded them yourselves, right?"

"That's crazy, Mom. Why would—"

"I did once," Chloé said, giggling. "Just for a joke. Made a fake profile. But it was super cringe. Mom says it's like fishing in a polluted lake. Usually disappointing, sometimes gross, but when there's no alternative, you got to stay hopeful."

"I see," Mia said. The discussion was making her nervous. Chloé was being honest. But was Elise? Her thoughts circled back to the laneway. Could her daughter have met someone online? Some random man who lived in one of those rundown apartments?

Faye was jabbing her phone screen with a single finger, then sighed. "I can't even find them in that store thing."

Chloé took Faye's phone and after less than a minute handed it back. "See those three new icons? Those are the apps. You need to create profiles. And then just ignore anyone who takes a gym selfie, rolls down their socks, or is in front of a car."

"Why?" Faye asked.

She shrugged. "That's just what my mom says."

"And you don't want a narcissist, Gran. They'll love-bomb you first and then crush your light."

"Oh dear. Sounds aggressive."

"Or anyone who breadcrumbs. Or pockets you."

"So much to learn. There must be a course for this!" Faye laughed and then examined her phone. "And with those profile thingies. What should I say?"

Mia shook her head. "Can't you handle that on your own, Mom? I mean—"

"Hardly!" Faye wiggled her fingers toward the girls. "I need my team."

"I'd say just be yourself," Chloé said.

"But not too much yourself," Elise chimed in. "Like, you might want to tone down the crystals and stuff. Go for mysterious but approachable."

"You two," she chirped, "are so darn smart."

"But you got to be careful. Maybe don't use your real name. If someone gives you a weird vibe, swipe left."

"Oh, I won't have any problem with that. My weirdo detector is flawless."

•

Mia was growing tired of the tittering and exclamations. Within a few sentences, her mother had transformed from late-middle-aged ethereal being to full-on sweet sixteen. Even her mannerisms changed. Jaw slack, little shakes of her rib cage, and her voice adopting an exaggerated vocal fry.

When Chloé suggested giving Faye a "glow-up" for a photoshoot, the girls dashed downstairs, returning seconds later with cosmetics bags and an armload of clothes.

"I want to look natural," Faye said. "Though I know that takes the most amount of makeup."

As they were "contouring" her mother's face, Mia went upstairs to her bedroom and closed the door behind her. Picking up her laptop from the night table, she went to the alcove at the back of her bedroom. A cozy recess with slanted ceilings and a small window. She sat cross-legged on a linen chair and logged into Other to access the latest LK video calls. There were several new files. She slid her audio controls to the lowest listenable and clicked Play.

For the most part, Lainey Kemper maintained an air of detachment, but when she spoke of her mother, Mia felt she struggled to disguise her vulnerability. Some moments, her discomfort was on display, and others she was obviously being evasive. The transitions were barely detectable, and Mia wondered if Ian caught them.

When she finished with the third file, she paused to listen. Chittering from Faye and the girls was still winding its way upstairs. Elise and Chloé were taking the task of transforming Faye seriously.

She selected the last MP4. The previous session had ended abruptly, and she was itching to know why Lainey had disconnected so suddenly.

"Sorry, Dr. Morrison. About last time. I hadn't sleep well." Her face was pale. "If I'm honest, I had an argument with my partner."

"Everything okay now?"

"Sure. I suppose. I was a bit grouchy with him. Probably because our session wiped me out."

"No need to explain. Emotional work is actual work, Lainey." Ian scratched at his beard. "If it was a breeze, I'd be out of a job."

"I did notice that. It makes you sleepy. I'm surprised I didn't remember from earlier."

"You're older now. Plus, we're digging deeper. And as you mentioned, you are striving for authenticity. Seeking help to make real change."

"Right."

"Should we revisit the topic of our last conversation?"

"I guess? What else to say? I loved my mother a great deal, but she left me alone, and that's that."

Ian flat-smiled, then tilted his head and nodded. Mia assumed he was trying to appear sympathetic, but she found the mannerism vaguely insincere.

"When you say 'left me alone,' are you referring to her death?"

"Exactly."

He skimmed the papers on his desk. "I have notes on this from Albethey. She had ovarian cancer?"

"Uh-huh."

LK shifted in her seat. She had a sheen on her forehead, and was clearly growing uneasy. Was Ian missing that as well?

"Do you have memories of your mother's illness?"

"I mean, it's mostly a blur. She must have had it for a while though.

One day everything was normal, and the next day she was a skeleton."

"Yes, it can go undetected for some time." More nodding. More beard scratching. "I'm sorry she had to go through that. And you did as well, as her daughter. How did witnessing her struggle make you feel?"

The screen seemed to freeze. Mia tapped the trackpad, but LK finally spoke. "I believe I was . . . groggy."

"Groggy?"

"Yes. Is that the wrong answer?"

"There are no wrong answers here, though I am a little perplexed by your response."

"I mean, it was sort of like I was half asleep? Seeing her melt away was only this weird dream. I couldn't imagine she was going somewhere and never coming back."

"That makes sense, Lainey. You were trying to navigate a frightening experience, essentially without tools. I assume she was hospitalized?"

"Near the end. At one point, her brother came to see us. James. He was our only living relative. My only option."

LK's uncle. The man she'd killed. Mia increased the volume by a single bar.

"Had you met him before?"

"No. Never."

"Was that a relief for her? When he arrived?"

Lainey Kemper closed her eyes for a moment and then opened them again. "No. She lost it, started ranting about how disgusting he was. Sounded like he'd dated her best friend, and it ended badly. She demanded the nurses have him removed, and then she kept clicking this button, which I believe was giving her morphine. When she fell asleep, the nurses explained that emotional outbursts could be from the cancer. Terminal delirium."

"I'd imagine that unsettled you? In a situation that was already incredibly tense."

"I-I don't know. She always was dramatic. When he appeared in that room, I was awestruck. He was this tall breath of fresh air. Dark hair and icy-blue eyes. Pure oxygen. Even the nurses changed. Using higher octaves, fluttering about. But . . ."

"Go ahead, Lainey. What were you going to say?"

Mia inched forward in her seat.

"I believed the nurses were right. That my mother was going mad. I turned my back on her. The sickness and the smell. And all I wanted was to attach myself to that perfect man's side and never let him go."

CHAPTER FIFTEEN

Lainey

AS I SWANNED around Om Bliss, teaching my lunchtime class, I was trying my hardest to stay present. My next session with Dr. Morrison was looming, and to say I was preoccupied was an understatement.

I'd already told him all I could manage of my origin story. My mother was incompetent but not cruel. Self-focused but not selfish. And she was the whole of my world until I was eight. It was time to properly introduce Uncle James. That was going to be uncomfortable. Shining a light on him also meant shining a light on myself. We were two people who belonged in the shadows.

I took a deep breath, in through the nose, out through the mouth. I had to remind myself that progress required only one step at a time. And if I was overwhelmed, adjustments to the narrative were always possible. Dr. Morrison clearly couldn't tell what was sincere and what was fiction. For a well-educated man, he seemed quite dim.

"Your choice to take a vinyasa," I told the all-woman group in a quiet tone, "if it feels right for you."

The temperature in the studio was a hundred-plus degrees. Sweat seeped from every pore in my body, trickling down my underarms, between my breasts. I hated the heat. But also enjoyed having something to hate.

"And then move into downward dog."

All of my students had purple foreheads, veins pulsing. With their shoulders hiked, they were limiting the circulation in their necks and dripping onto their mats. They no doubt believed the heat did something for them, when likely it did not.

"I'm going to come around and give adjustments. If anyone doesn't want to be touched, let me know."

I wondered if they noticed anything when I placed my palms against their bodies. Whatever festered inside me, did it transfuse through their slick skin? With their defenses down, was I imparting the slightest amount of damage? If only they had energy displays over their heads. Like in video games. A finger graze. Negative one impact. Full adjustment. Negative ten.

I had a sneaky suspicion that my thoughts were not standard for a yoga teacher. Maybe they even bordered on deviant. Not that I'd bring it up during therapy, of course. Why bother? I was already confident in the emotional label I'd selected. *Bitter amusement.*

•

Dr. Morrison's expression was unreadable. To me, at least. I wasn't sure what he wanted. The silence between us dragged. Was it normal to have a nonverbal standoff with a therapist?

Finally he spoke. "I sense we have reached a painful juncture, Lainey. Why don't we chat about something unrelated. How's your day going?"

"Today? What do you want to know?"

"Whatever you want to share."

Could these sessions possibly produce more stomach acid? Was there absolutely no guidance offered? I couldn't remember him being like that at Albethey. Back then, our time together seemed much more . . . controlled. "Well, this morning I taught yoga to a bunch of entitled women, then I drank two of those energy drinks with ginseng and thought my heart might explode. After that I had a strange craving for haloumi and ate the entire block. And later tonight I'm going to my boyfriend's DJ gig, where I'll no doubt be pushed, prodded, and propositioned by drunk men." I faked a grin. "So an engaging and fruitful day, don't you think?"

"Does your partner expect you to attend all his events?"

I sucked air through the gaps in my teeth. "He doesn't *expect* anything."

"Of course." Dr. Morrison spoke softly. "Might I ask if there's been further discord in your relationship?"

It took me a beat to realize what he meant. In a previous session, I'd used Andrew as an excuse, claiming we'd gotten into yet another argument. Which was untrue. Andrew and I never fought. But instead of smoothing over my fib, I said, "I-I can't talk about that. Or him." I knew misleading Dr. Morrison about my domestic scene was abhorrent and attention-seeking, but for reasons that escaped me, I still did it.

"Perhaps this wasn't the best way to begin. Let's try something else." His perpetual gentleness was starting to feel like a microaggression.

"I want to tell you about my uncle." There. I said it. We'd moved straight from the outer crust to the gooey center.

"Good, good." He shifted in his seat, then lifted a page, scanned some lines with an index finger. "You went to live with him in 1990?"

"Yep. Sounds right."

"And before that, you—"

"Wouldn't know him from Adam. Other than seeing him a couple of times at the hospital."

Dr. Morrison scribbled something on his notepad, then said, "The transition from your mother's care to his. Was it smooth?"

"Smooth?" The word choice made my jaw clench. A child simply accepted a situation. Assumed all the other kids were having identical experiences. The same family. The same inner world.

"I mean, you moved straight in with him?"

"Where else was I going to go? I'd already spent a few weeks in foster care, and that was plenty. After the cemetery, we drove in the back of a hired car to his place. He'd rented a small house not so far from where I lived with my mother. It all seemed so very weird."

"How so?"

"To exist without her, I suppose. Without my mother." I was like a chick suddenly smashed from its protective shell. "I had nightmares." All these years later, I could still remember them. Being alone in a cemetery, crouching by the side of her grave. Seeing glimmers of neon orange wriggling through the dirt, and my mother's painted nails emerging. Then her gray fingers. I'd grip her hand and yank. But she was stuck. I couldn't pull her out. "I would wake up in hysterics, and my uncle always rushed in to soothe me. He'd make some silly jokes, get me laughing, and then sing to me until I fell back asleep."

"Sounds very nurturing, Lainey. Similar to what you said before."

I nodded. When I was at Albethey, I'd painted my uncle as an affectionate and concerned "stand-in parent." Well, not exactly painted, as many of the examples were genuine. He was the first to take me to a doctor and dentist. He always fed me tomato soup and grilled cheese when I had a head cold. He took me to a bookstore and bought me an entire shelf of junior readers. But the thing I remembered the most?

He listened quietly whenever I spoke. He never once dismissed my childhood fears.

Those scattered memories of my uncle were still valuable to me. I decided not to tell Dr. Morrison. I wasn't ready to give them away.

"At some point, a social worker came to visit. She spoke with both of us, together and individually. I overheard her telling my uncle she was relieved I was under his care. That my mother was neglectful, at best. And while she was required to follow up, it was only protocol." I recalled the blush creeping into her cheeks as she flirted. "She came to visit once more, and then my uncle and I ditched the rental and relocated to a new town."

"How did you experience the sudden change?".

I rolled my eyes. What a stupid question. My entire life was sudden change. "I was built for instability, Dr. Morrison. But this time, I had my own room. The kitchen was full of my favorites. And there was a whole month before I needed to go to school."

He glanced at his notes again. "Your mother and uncle were siblings? Or half-siblings?"

"Full."

"But different surnames?"

"That's an interesting story. One night after we moved, Uncle James told me that he'd grown tired of being a Greene. He took down the phone book and flipped through the pages. Started tossing out random names to get my opinion. We settled on Kemper."

"I have to say, Lainey, that seems . . . unusual. Don't you think?" Dr. Morrison tapped his pen against his desk blotter. "Some issue in his past, perhaps?"

"Perhaps." Though his interest was obvious, I offered no more.

After several seconds of silence, he put up a hand. "Fair enough. We can revisit this later when you're comfortable." Then he said,

"During those early weeks and months, did you continue to feel cared for?"

"Yes. I would say I did. My mother had been . . . relaxed, while my uncle was almost ritualistic."

"Ritualistic how?"

I hesitated, searching for specifics. They weren't difficult to find. Uncle James pressing my dresses. Using the sharp handle of the comb and perfectly parting my hair. Every single morning, a Flintstones vitamin appearing next to a glass of orange juice.

Everything felt so good at the beginning. I badly wanted to place brackets around those bright spots. Shave everything else away. Though that wouldn't help me get better. I had to say things out loud. I had to release them.

". . . Lainey?"

"Huh?" My head jerked upward. My gaze returning to the computer screen.

"Sorry, I was asking if you wanted to continue. You seemed lost in thought. We can take a break, if you'd prefer?"

"Maybe." I was feeling tired again. "Though there is one more thing. We'd lived together for a couple of weeks when he reached across the table. He asked that we shake hands. Then he looked me in the eyes and with this serious tone said, 'We're a team now.'"

"How did that feel?" Dr. Morrison asked.

Heavy was the only descriptor that came to mind. But bottom line: My uncle was divinity in a man's body. Every shred of me wanted to mirror that loveliness back at him. "I just needed to make him happy, Dr. Morrison. It was all my eight-year-old brain thought about."

"And was your uncle happy?"

"Yes. I believe he was. Especially when we started to play our little game."

CHAPTER SIXTEEN

Lainey

"OF COURSE, IT wasn't actually a game. That's just how we framed it." I was back on Zoom. Dr. Morrison and I had arranged our next session for the following day. "Nothing seems out of the ordinary when you're little. Because you don't know the difference."

"That's true. Life and experience alter perspective. And perception."

"When it started, I thought the whole thing was fun. A challenge my uncle and I worked to perfect."

Dr. Morrison sat up and cleared his throat. "Would you care to elaborate?"

"You have to understand, my uncle was extremely gregarious. And charming. People trusted him. Women trusted him." I quickly blinked twice. "He had this high-wattage smile. Not unlike yours." It was the tiniest tease. I couldn't help myself. Last night, Andrew and I had made a steamy new video with the camera positioned from behind. He had week-old scruff and was naked except for the pink linen shirt I'd bought him. I cropped the frame so only the corner of his jaw was visible. Watching it back really sent me. To put it mildly. And I figured there was nothing wrong with indulging a teenaged fantasy starring a hot doctor and his prize lunatic. Especially when the material dropped in my lap.

"Oh please." Dr. Morrison waved a hand as the corners of his mouth lifted. He picked up his pen, twirled it, and said, "Continue."

"From the very start, I understood my uncle craved female companionship. He never had much of a problem sourcing it, either, but consistency seemed to be an issue."

"What do you mean by *consistency*?"

"He was a serial dater, I suppose. As far as I knew, that was how he'd earned his money. *Earned* might be a poor word choice, though relationships are hard work." I tittered and watched Dr. Morrison's face in case he revealed something about his homelife. But his expression remained neutral. "Anyway. He was single when I went to live with him, and we often discussed the best places to pick up divorced women. Or, even better, widows. He had his preferences."

Dr. Morrison scraped his fingers through his beard. "These conversations occurred when you were a teenager, I presume?"

"Hardly. We'd been together maybe a month or two?"

"So you were a child? Still eight? Nine?"

"Of course." *What was with that tone?* "I already understood the mechanics. You haven't forgotten my mother, have you?"

As I watched him taking notes, I noticed agitation flowering in my chest.

"Carry on, Lainey. Don't mind my scribbling. As you know, it's my habit."

I did know. It had always bothered me at Albethey, too. The intermittent scratching of nib on paper got under my skin. I could never decode his hand movements. Or remember what I'd accidentally given away.

"I don't know. We went over everything. Practiced, even. First we had the setup. The ruse, I guess you'd call it."

"Ruse?"

"Yeah. Basically his approach to attracting a partner. After a church service, or on the playground, or outside a convenience store, I was to stand off on my own and act distressed."

"I'm a little confused. You were distressed? Or *acting* distressing?"

"I was totally fine. I had to pretend I was lost or something. You know, look scared, sniffle, that kind of thing. Inevitably some lady would approach me with the typical line, 'Are you okay, sweetheart? Is your mommy around?' I'd squeeze out a tear or two, and Uncle James would rush forward."

When I paused, Dr. Morrison gazed at me over the rim of his glasses. "I know this isn't easy to talk about, but I do feel it's necessary to continue. You never mentioned these things at Albethey. This particular dynamic with your uncle."

"Yeah. Okay." Out loud, the entire thing sounded ridiculous. I wouldn't have bothered telling him at all if it wasn't critical to the rest of the story. "I'd feign relief, and he'd apologize that we'd somehow gotten separated. He'd chastise me—but kindly. 'You need to stay close, puppet.'"

"He called you puppet?"

"That was his nickname for me."

"Interesting."

Was it? "Then he'd stroke my hair, bend down and fix my shoelace. Or brush nothingness from the shoulders of my dress. Which I assume was meant to demonstrate care for his daughter."

"Meaning he let others believe you were his daughter?"

"Yup. He insisted I call him Dad." Probably to create the appearance of a closer bond. Though it was no hardship. Having a fake father was dreamy, to say the least.

I glanced out the north window of the den. The blinds were open today, and from that particular angle, I could peer into the backyards of the homes that lined the street behind the building. It was hard to tolerate the inequality on full display. Regular families barbecuing. Regular children splashing in miniature plastic pools.

"And after you met these women?"

"There was some . . . sorting. He preferred slightly homely, needy women. They always had a kid a little older than me. He used to say, 'You need someone too.'" That was also dreamy. Having a sibling.

"Essentially he would target someone vulnerable?"

I smothered a sigh. Such a reductionist viewpoint. Sure, the moves were calculated, to a degree, but maybe not entirely disingenuous.

"First date was always a meal. Uncle James and me, whatever woman was on the string, plus her kid. The four of us would sit in a booth at some child-friendly restaurant, and he'd explain that his beloved wife had died from cancer. He ended the story by saying he'd never trade the pain of that loss."

"Why?"

I didn't want to share that tiny detail. How my uncle always explained that he embraced the sorrow. If he'd never met his so-called wife, he'd never have had me. Pure fiction, of course, but it still warmed the stone behind my ribs. I was his. I belonged.

With bullet points, I tried to explain the cycle. Things usually progressed quickly. My uncle would be enthralling, and the woman would grow besotted. Then we'd move in with her and her daughter. For the first few weeks, it was absolute perfection. Instant mommy. Instant big sis. Family dinners. Movie nights. Sunday drives for vanilla soft serves. But inevitably the euphoria curdled. My uncle would transform into a new creature. Broody, quarrelsome, apathetic. The woman would fight to save whatever she believed they'd built together. Three months. Or six months. Once a full year.

Parting ways was always a snarl. My uncle and I would need to pack up our shit and relocate. Another nondescript small town. Another short-term rental. But with the bank account a little fatter. Or a lot fatter.

"Once we were settled in our new home, his lightness would reemerge. Seeing him happy made me feel . . ."

"Happy?"

"I don't know. Successful, maybe?" Surely that was a legitimate emotion. "And then our game would reset. Back to the start."

•

I was in a parking lot, Andrew's car idling. Slurping on a lime Icee.

Based on the dark wood paneling behind Dr. Morrison today, I'd guessed he was in his office on campus. A quick skim of his lecture schedule, posted online, and I arrived in time to watch him leave the building and head across the parking lot.

I slumped down in my seat, then took a large gulp of my drink. A punch of cold spread between my eyebrows. I kind of liked it. The predictable ache, and the inevitable recession.

Dr. Morrison's garish car growled to life, and I pulled out behind him. I promised myself it would not become a habit. Even said it out loud. "This will not become a habit, Lainey!" My therapist had a right to his privacy, his own life. He didn't need one of his clients indulging her whims. Allowing her manicured toe to drift over that line, however innocently.

This time he did not run any errands. He drove along several side streets before turning onto Main Street and then hung a left onto a wide tree-lined boulevard. After rolling through a couple of stop signs, he pulled into a driveway. The angle of his parking took up both available spaces.

I slowed to a stop a few doors down from the massive house, watched him climb out of his car and skip up the front stone steps.

Once Dr. Morrison disappeared inside, I eased the car forward. The house faced west, and the setting sun illuminated the spacious front rooms. Through the windows, I could see a lonely expanse of wall decorated with a single piece of art. Plus pale-colored furniture. A terrible choice if he had a young child, so I'd dare to say she wasn't a tadpole after all.

A wispy figure was in the front room. The ceilings were so tall, I couldn't get a solid sense of proportions, but I knew it was a woman. Or a girl. Drifting about. Too aimless to be a cleaner, and too purposeful to be a kid. Perhaps I was seeing his wife. I imagined brightly colored mules, made from impossibly soft leather. And breezy linen. Good linen too. No cheap scratchy blend for this delicate broad.

What was she doing? Was that a platter in her hands? Had she pulled a cold roast chicken from the fridge? Whatever she was holding, she placed it on a table, then turned toward a pile of what appeared to be boxes. She opened a lid, removed papers, then a large bowl. Had they recently moved in? Was she searching for the correct serving fork? Slender prongs that would glint in candlelight.

Inside that structure, Dr. Morrison had a whole life, a family. It seemed entirely imbalanced that he knew so much more about me than I knew about him. Unfair even.

I needed to fix that.

•

After parking the car, I took the side exit from the garage. Then dipped into the organic grocer that was at street level of the condo building. I grabbed two halibut steaks. Plus ingredients to make a salsa: ripe mangos, red pepper, onion, avocado, cilantro. A single-serving mousse cake to share and a bottle of Chablis.

I was relieved to find Andrew wasn't home. It had been a busy day. Video editing, yoga class, Zoom session, some light stalking, groceries. And now I needed to prep for Andrew's special evening. Our birthdays were three weeks apart, and his was up first.

My phone pinged. I opened the text from my beau. He'd just finished receiving his gift and loved the result. I emitted a tiny squeal. I couldn't wait to see it. Labeling that sensation: *antsy anticipation?*

"What's all this?" Andrew said when he finally came in the door. He was wearing a baby-blue dress shirt, slim fit.

"Oh, nothing really." I placed the plates on the island. Pulled the cork from the wine. "Just felt like making something a little fancy today."

"How'd I get so lucky?"

He inhaled his dinner like a hungry toddler. Seeing his enthusiasm for my meager domestic efforts was oddly captivating. I didn't cook often. Not that I couldn't, I was just rarely motivated. Why put so much effort into something that was going to vanish in eight to eleven minutes?

"Babe, this is delicious."

I cleared our plates and then brought the cake. A single candle in the center. "Make a wish," I said. Which he dutifully did. A sharp shot of air, and the sweet smell of smoke and melted wax filled my nostrils.

"Do you want to know?"

"Of course not."

"I wished that things'll never change. You and me. I like us like this."

He picked up the plate and, with an impish laugh, took a large chomp from the side of the cake. Held it out for me to do the same. Change might be okay, I wanted to tell him. Might make things even better. But I chose to say nothing.

When he put his open mouth on mine, pulling some cake off my tongue, the ache between my legs was instant. Within seconds, we'd stripped off our lower garments, and I wrapped my arms around his neck as he lifted me up. Carried me toward the closest vertical surface. A pant leg still attached to his foot. With the wall as stability, he pushed inside me. The rubbing was going to leave a bruise along my spine, which would undoubtedly be visible during my classes. But who cared? I was setting a good example for my students. What better way to loosen up the hips?

After the sex, we relaxed on the couch. He unbuttoned his shirt and carefully slipped out of his sleeves. Then he turned his back to me. I peeled away the tape securing the bandage on his upper shoulder. Traced my fingertips over the irritated skin. Here was the gift I'd given him. From a screenshot on my laptop, I'd created a unique design and paid for an appointment at a tattoo parlor.

"Careful," he said. "It's a bit tender."

The word *entropy* was written in bold in the center of the blade. The letters disintegrating as they went left to right.

"The woman who did it thought it was cool. Asked if she could use the pattern."

"What did you say?" My body tensed.

"I said no chance. It's made just for me. Wouldn't even let her take a photo."

I smiled. "Perfect."

"I had to look it up, you know. It means measurement of chaos."

I knew that already. As soon as I saw it in the college car wash video, I'd researched the term. A steady decline into disorder. I liked to think Dr. Morrison hadn't got it until after I was released from Albethey. He'd broken me down, then recreated me. But the rule of nature meant I was going to disintegrate once again. And I was trying to get ahead of it.

CHAPTER SEVENTEEN

Mia

MIA'S PALMS WERE damp. She was on the family room couch, her laptop balanced on a cushion. What would Ian say if he knew that multiple times a day she peered into his LK folder? Almost compulsively. When she discovered a new file, as had happened that morning, she experienced a genuine rush. Certainly it was unhealthy to be so absorbed in the details of a troubled woman's past, but Mia could not stop herself.

"These situations you describe, they continued?"

"Over the years, I lost count how many times my uncle was in a 'committed relationship.'" Lainey Kemper used air quotes. "Or how many times we moved. I knew the cycle though."

"Such extreme instability, Lainey."

"Do you think so?" While Mia immediately detected sarcasm, it seemed to fly over Ian's head. "I loved my uncle. Whenever he wasn't himself, it made me physically ill."

"Wasn't himself? Can you explain what you mean?"

"Usually, he was upbeat, positive. Learning and exploring. And wanting me to do the same."

"So being broody or quarrelsome, as you previously described, that wasn't the norm?"

"No, not at all. That was only when a relationship was ending. I was always on high alert, waiting for him to change."

"And how did you react when things came to a close? Surely it impacted you as well."

"What can I say? It stung. Every single time. I never understood why he kept blowing things up. Destroying our little families."

"Did you resent him?"

"No. I don't think so. I trusted him." She pulled in her lips and appeared to bite down.

Ian slowly nodded. "Such difficult situations to navigate, Lainey."

Mia exhaled loudly. At first, watching her husband in a professional capacity had made her proud, but her adoration had quickly transformed into frustration. Clearly the woman was uncomfortable, and his comment added absolutely nothing. Why not delve a little deeper? Delicately, of course.

"Last one was this widow. Filthy, filthy rich. But she went off the rails, totally ballistic when he told her the relationship had run its course. I remember her ranting about her bank accounts. Her credits cards. How my uncle had helped himself. She actually threw a knife at him. Full force. Just a paring knife, but still. Stuck straight into his bicep."

"You witnessed this assault?"

"I have hazy photos in my head, so I guess I did. What's clearer, though, is the two of us driving away. Car stuffed to the hilt. Me bawling my eyes out. His arm leaking blood. And when we took the on-ramp for the highway, he said, 'No more crazy bitches, puppet. From now on, it's just you and me.'"

"How old were you?"

"Twelve."

Twelve. Mia brought her hand to her mouth.

"Did anything change after he made that promise?"

"In some ways, yes. But other ways, no. The game continued, though with more honesty."

"Can you explain that? What you mean by honesty?"

The woman began picking at the lilac nail polish on her thumb. Her trepidation was palpable. For Mia at least. Ian barely blinked.

"When you know what happened, Dr. Morrison, you might wonder at what point I became fully aware."

"Aware? That your uncle was using you as a pawn to entrap wealthy women?"

"Not that. The darker part."

"I'm sorry. I'm a little confused."

Lainey Kemper stared straight into the camera, and as Mia met her steady gaze, an icy chill crept up the bones of her back.

"I understood my role," she said ever so softly. "Not at first. But eventually I knew."

•

Mia stood at Sandy's back gate, swim bag in hand.

Moments earlier a flurry of texts from Elise had interrupted her, so Mia had set down her laptop, collected her daughter's forgotten items, and dashed out the door.

"Oh thank you, thank you, thank you," Elise said, sprinting toward her. She hauled her suit from the bag and disappeared inside the house.

Mia took a moment to survey the backyard. Sandy had kept the house after the divorce, and Mia wondered how she managed the payments. Or the upkeep. Everything was pristine. The lawn, the neatly trimmed hedge. The place was a scene from a magazine. She missed spending time there and was still confused about why their friendship had ended so abruptly. Elise would have called it ghosting, which was exactly how it felt.

When Sandy first stopped responding, Mia assumed she was traveling. Or else super busy. But after several attempts, she began sifting through old conversations in her head. Skimming back through messages. Nothing seemed out of the ordinary. So why was Sandy ignoring her? Then came news of the separation and subsequent divorce. Mia once again reached out, offering support. When there was still no reply, she gave up. The silence hurt.

Squealing interrupted her thoughts. A pair of little girls, perhaps three or four years old, were seated on the bottom step of the deck. Chloé was explaining the rules to them. Water safety. The dangers of slipping on wet stone. A woman Mia didn't recognize was reclined on a lawn chair, tapping her phone.

Chloé glanced over and then hollered toward the house. "Maaaa-ohm! Mia's here!"

Mia took a step backward. She hadn't meant to linger. She'd intended to slip in and out before being noticed. But within seconds Sandy appeared at the sliding glass door.

"Oh, hi Mia," she said.

"Just dropping off Elise's things. I don't want to intrude."

"No worries." She folded her arms across her chest. "I'm taking a break anyway."

Her tone was formal. Bordering on cold. Leaving Mia feeling awkward and wondering how to leave without being rude. She turned to watch the children. Elise was already back, and the four of them were walking hand in hand toward the water. They slipped into the shallow end, the children white-knuckling the edge.

"Pool school seems to be a hit," Mia said. "Thank you so much for letting Elise work with Chloé. I hope she's not any bother."

"Of course she's not. You know I love Elise. She's such a great influence."

"That's kind of you to say."

"And yes, it's brilliant. They're busy and exhausted. Exactly how you want teens to be."

Mia smiled politely. "Well, I should—"

"Can I get you something to drink?"

She hesitated, then said, "Kombucha?"

Sandy laughed. Her shoulders relaxing. "The girls were trying to appeal to the yummy mummy crowd. But it's mostly nannies who bring the kids."

Maybe it actually had been the stress of her marriage breaking up that caused the rift between them. Maybe it had nothing to do with Mia, and it was self-centered to even consider that. Maybe the offer of a drink was an olive branch.

From the cooler, Sandy withdrew two bottles. Then gestured for Mia to sit at the teakwood table. Glass hurricanes with white pillar candles flanked a clay pot full of fragrant basil.

"And Chloé? How was her year?"

Lowering her voice, Sandy said, "Tough, if I'm honest. Splitting time between me and her father. It's not ideal."

"I'm sorry to hear that."

"And she's been fighting me tooth and nail about her meds. Same old story."

Mia cracked open the bottle and took a sip. Blueberry ginger. "Elise too. Not medication, but just her own ideas. Wanting to do what she wants to do. Like she'd prefer I disappear."

"Because we have no clue what it's like to be that age, right?"

"Exactly. Geriatric and out of touch."

A quick grin. "And what about you? I know you moved."

"We did. Still feels like a gigantic mess, but it's slowly coming together."

"Everything takes time."

Mia wanted to share what had prompted the move. To have the comfort of female understanding. But she'd already made that mistake with Faye. And with all the barbs and jabs that followed, she was paying the price for her lapse in judgment.

Instead of revealing Ian's affair, Mia said. "My mother's driving me crazy. Did Chloé tell you she showed up at Ian's birthday dinner? Pretending she just happened to be walking by the restaurant at that moment."

As Mia spoke, Sandy's demeanor changed. Spine straightening. Expression morphing from pleasant to tense. At once, she stood up. "Great catching up, Mia, but I really should get back to work."

•

On the walk home, Mia dissected the interaction. She and Sandy were having a perfectly civil conversation. Bordering on chummy even. Then it shifted. Was it her imagination, or did that happen the moment she'd mentioned Ian? As she went over it, her lower stomach cramped. That couldn't have been a coincidence.

This wasn't the first time Mia had wondered. Sandy was a beautiful successful designer, and before the divorce, her husband had constantly been away on business. It was logical to assume she was lonely, and easy to insert Ian into the equation. He'd often gone there to pick up Elise. Had she offered him a drink while he waited? Had she used him as a shoulder to lean on? Perhaps he was the reason the walls went up.

Possibly even sparked the separation. Mia had asked Ian if he'd had an affair with Sandy. And he'd recoiled at "the preposterous accusation," as he called it. Once again, he'd told Mia to stop tormenting herself. It was a woman she'd never known or met. So why keep dragging it up?

She'd apologized for thinking something so outlandish. Accepted his response. He had to be genuine. He was not that good a liar. Was he?

CHAPTER EIGHTEEN

Mia

DURING DINNER THAT evening, Mia never mentioned the odd interaction with Sandy. Though she couldn't get it out of her head, she didn't see any point in bringing it up.

"What do you think of that?"

Ian had been talking, and she hadn't been listening. "Oh, I don't know," she said. "I'm sure you know what's best."

"The hours wasted on the commute alone. I could reduce my patient load at Albethey. Or even better, take a year's leave. Settle in at the college, and just research and write."

There was an undeniable excitement in his tone. Mia suspected it was related to the case study. When LK's story gained momentum all those years ago, there'd been discussion of a book deal. Possibly even a documentary or film. Maybe Ian was pondering those options once again. Already imagining his uptick in prestige and popularity.

He wiped his mouth with a napkin and stood up. "Sorry I'm leaving you with the mess. But I'm meeting the department chair for a drink. You know, to discuss everything." A quick kiss and then he left.

As soon as the sound of his car engine faded, she piled the plates into the sink and crept upstairs to their bedroom. He'd be gone for at least an hour, and Elise was at Chloé's. Or so the blue dot indicated. She carried her laptop to the alcove and settled into her chair.

"Once the wife hunt was off the table," LK said when she appeared onscreen, "he quickly became known as the cool single dad. Well, cool single uncle, I suppose. He stopped pretending to be my father. But we always had an open-door policy. He encouraged me to be more social."

"I'd venture to say those were positives?"

Mia rolled her eyes at Ian's response. Nothing about "cool single uncle" or "open-door policy" was a positive in her opinion. More like lazy parenting.

"I thought so. I was popular. And basic as it sounds"—she glanced away—"I really, really wanted friends. But weird things started to happen."

"What sort of weird things?"

"Well . . ." LK cleared her throat.

"Lainey, you're in a safe—"

"I had a dream about him last night."

Ian frowned. Mia could barely believe it. He actually frowned. As though annoyed by a miniscule sidestep.

"Would you like to discuss it?"

"Why not? I found it super unsettling."

"Were you an adult in the dream? Or a child?"

"No clue. I was in the back of a rideshare. So maybe an adult? I was kind of ignoring the driver, like you do, but then he said my name. In this singsong way. I immediately knew."

"Knew what?"

"Seriously, Ian?" Mia hissed at her laptop. "Keep up!"

"It was Uncle James. I can't even remember the conversation after that, though I was excited to see him. But when I looked at him in the mirror, the face looking back at me was . . . distorted? Forehead larger, eyes sunken, mouth wider. I found it scary. Like hugely scary."

"Understandable. That's why so many have a clown phobia. Our brains recognize them as human, but the features are exaggerated just enough to be frightening."

"Yeah, he looked normal in his seat. But then I realized he had this creepy rubber mask stretched over the headrest. It kept nodding as he drove, like it was listening to me. I told him, 'You missed the turnoff,' and the mask nodded. Then he missed the second turnoff, and it nodded again."

"That is disturbing."

"I finally asked him, 'How am I getting home?' It grinned at me in the mirror, and in this really gentle tone, it said, 'We're going a different route tonight, puppet.'"

Mia shivered. She could easily place herself in the back of that car. The comfort first, then the confusion. And finally the visceral fear.

"I can see why you were alarmed."

"Yeah. Though once I got over the panic, I was oddly okay with it all. And then I woke up."

Ian was scribbling on a notepad. To a distracting degree. Mia wished she could somehow make him aware of his off-putting behaviors. Which were plentiful.

"That's definitely a curious dream, Lainey."

"You could probably go all Freud on it, right?"

"I'm not sure what going 'all Freud' means, but he did consider dreams to reflect repressed desires. Wish fulfillment, essentially."

"So things I want but won't admit to myself?"

"Let me be clear. It's fine and a little fun to ponder our . . . our nighttime reveries"—he twirled his hand in the air—"but Freud's theory is not scientifically based. It's a whimsy, that's all. Do you understand?"

"Sure, sure. Just a joke."

Mia snapped down the lid of her laptop. Ian had been so quick to downplay the dream. The nightmare. Why had he not asked a single meaningful question when there was so much dangling right in front of him?

Lainey Kemper loved her uncle, and clearly he had done something terribly wrong to her. Mia would have assumed sexual assault, but she'd reread the journal article, and that was specifically ruled out. There was absolutely no evidence of physical abuse either. When she was rescued at the cabin, her only injuries were severe sunburn and dehydration. Beyond that, LK was described as being a healthy teenager.

Maybe the dream simply highlighted Lainey Kemper's perception of her uncle. He was solid and steady, but also something she could not recognize. Or it indicated her emotional state. Her feeling that his actions, whatever they were, had been so hurtful or harmful, the mere imagining of him evoked fear nearly three decades later.

Mia sent a quick text to Ian. *Going well? Home soon?*

It took several minutes for him to reply. *Going great! Ill be another hour at least. This guy can talk!* Then a string of heart emojis.

She left her bedroom and went down the hallway to his home office. Clicking on the desk lamp, she dug a tiny key from her pocket. Two days ago, she'd woken extra early for a hypothetical run; but instead, she'd borrowed his keys and made a copy for the filing cabinet at the twenty-four-hour convenience store.

She tugged open the drawer. Within seconds, her crawling fingers found the mint-green LK folder. Chock full of papers and envelopes.

Mia placed the folder on Ian's desk. The first item inside was the police report from 1996, followed by Ian's summary.

Deceased male, identified as James Kemper. Additional person at the scene: fourteen-year-old female, Lainey Kemper, who was transported to Callow General Hospital for treatment of exposure. Due to ongoing mental distress, she was transferred to Albethey Psychiatric Institute. Then placed under arrest after the initial investigation. A verbal dispute had turned physical.

He also had a copy of the autopsy report. The top page was an overview, which indicated cause of death as sudden blood loss. A line drawing of a body was marked to show the position of the injuries. Bruising. Tooth loss. A single puncture wound to the neck. A note stating that a rusty nail had severed the victim's carotid artery just beneath the left jaw.

With her fingertip, Mia traced the arrows. She found it hard to imagine that a girl, even younger than Elise, could cause such damage to a full-grown man.

Beneath that was a stapled document containing reports of Lainey Kemper's diagnosis. Mia skimmed the pages. A full physical workup showed no evidence of viral or bacterial infection. The blood panel indicated no drug use. The girl was of average height, though underweight with a BMI of 17.2.

Ian had performed various psychiatric tests, but Mia couldn't understand the resulting charts and scores. An MRI revealed no evidence of traumatic brain injury or structural abnormalities. He noted that LK's delusions of death were both consistent and persistent, but she did not meet the criteria for schizophrenia or bipolar disorder. It was determined that the presentation of Cotard's syndrome was a symptom of a psychotic break brought on by major depressive disorder.

In another multipage document, he'd summarized their years of therapy. He described his patient as intially having an anxious attachment to her primary guardian after the death of her mother. During the year preceding her institutionalization, there were increasing signs of reactive attachment disorder: predominantly LK resenting the rules and structure of her uncle's home. As a young teen, she experienced recurring dark thoughts, was disinterested in her education (though showed no evidence of a learning disability), and lacked capacity to relate to her classmates. She repeatedly presented herself as a "team of one." The months prior to killing her uncle were marked by a self-imposed social isolation. Ian noted both maladaptive and antisocial behaviors.

Ian's recent notes were basically a summary of his sessions with some minor analysis and "items to explore." Much of it Mia already knew from watching and rewatching the videos, but a few lines did jump out.

Risk assessment—none identified
No notable signs of depression
No current symptoms of Cotard's syndrome
Patient has expressed desire to "correct misconceptions" that arose during former treatment. Difficult to parse which aspects of her accounts are factual or fabricated.
Described uncle (JK) as a "serial relationship scammer," yet no formal complaints or criminal charges ever brought against him.
Currently residing with a 32yo male. Some indicators of stress or discord, appears guarded when topic broached or when relating interactions. Power/income imbalance?

Range of mood—oscillating. Carefree/nonchalant to despondent in a single session. Abruptly ended one session.
Mild flirtatious behavior during sessions—attempt to manipulate?
Often displays flat affect, lack of eye contact.

Then Mia noticed a line that made her pause: *No apparent female friendships. No close emotional bonds with peers.*

How strange to consider she and Lainey Kemper had something in common.

CHAPTER NINETEEN

Lainey

"SHALL WE PICK up where we left off? You were describing things happening in your home."

Over the past two days, disturbing scenes had played on a loop inside my skull. And I'd accepted that the only way to cut myself free from the iron manacle was to admit everything.

"I remember. I was telling you about my friends."

I enjoyed having Dr. Morrison's eyes on me again. Knowing he wanted more. That morning I'd clipped several sound bites from session recordings, then slowed them and deepened the pitch of his voice. *Do you have anything to ask me? You have full control. Are you comfortable?* I also isolated his breathing and then meshed the audio files with my newest video—a leisurely shag with the camera focused on a sweaty back and a healing tattoo on a shoulder blade. In my mind, he clearly wanted more then too.

"Were you finding the social dynamics challenging?"

"Honestly? Not so much. I mean, I was close with the girls. We did mostly silly stuff, really. Playing with makeup and drooling over movie stars. Hanging out at the school playground until it got dark." I smiled slightly.

"You were establishing a strong network, Lainey. I'm not sure I understand the oddness you mentioned?"

"It's a strange age, you know? We were all eleven and twelve. And the entire world starts to transform into this peculiar, heated place."

"True, it is a time of significant change. Being on the cusp of puberty."

"Right? During the summer, when my uncle walked around without his shirt on, my friends would totally roll over themselves."

"Yes, I can see how that might be disconcerting. Or perhaps embarrassing."

"I didn't blame them, really. We were only kids. And as I said, he was an attractive man." I took a deep breath. "But let's just say I was sharply attuned to it. Sharply attuned to him."

A slight nod, then some annoying note-taking. "We call that hypervigilance. It's often a survival response to past trauma. An attempt to reduce the risk of harm."

Perhaps. Even now, I monitored my environment and the people in it. Kept tabs on Andrew. Watched my yoga students. Studied Dr. Morrison, while he studied me.

"One time, one of the girls flipped out when my uncle walked into the bathroom when she was using the toilet."

"An understandable reaction, no?" Dr. Morrison wrote something else down. "Did you ever feel your privacy wasn't respected?"

I knew immediately where his dirty probe was aimed. "No, never."

"Any other instances you might label as *weird*? I believe I'm using your own term here."

This next tidbit was bound to raise an eyebrow. "One time I was having a sleepover. Three or four of the girls from my class. And my uncle accidentally left his porno movies out. VHS tapes. Remember those?"

"Well, that's incredibly irresponsible."

"I mean, yeah." I sniffed. "But we watched them. Of course we did. Kept the volume on low, but the grunts and moans, well, were pretty recognizable. Our eyes were glued to the screen. My stomach was sick and fluttery at the same time."

Dr. Morrison cleared his throat. "Was your uncle aware you'd discovered his . . . collection?"

"He was. At some point, I noticed him crouching on the top step, looking down at us. I honestly thought he wasn't sure what to do. Whether to come down and stop the film, or retreat and act like nothing was happening. It was so awkward and awful. But for a few minutes . . ." In my mind, I could still see him with crystal clarity. His perfect face pressed to a gap between two painted spindles. I opened my mouth to say something, but he slowly brought his finger to his lips. *Shhhh.*

"Are you okay, Lainey?"

"I'm always okay, Dr. Morrison."

"You paused mid-sentence. You were about to say . . ."

I was supposed to cough up the missing detail. Fill in his blank. But I was incredibly tired. I glanced at my wrist, even though I wasn't wearing a watch. "It's gotten late. I have things to do." Then, with the subtlest hint of faux dread, I whispered, "Before my partner gets home."

"Of course, of course, let's wrap up. We're doing important work here, and that can be taxing."

"I don't know. It's just . . . I'm beginning to realize the closeness between me and my uncle eclipsed the bigger picture."

"Oh? How so?"

"I made too many excuses, Dr. Morrison. I should've paid closer attention."

I clicked Leave Meeting.

•

Always leave 'em hungry. My mother had told me that repeatedly, from the time I was old enough to wobble across the room.

I knew I was breaking my promise to myself to take my therapy with the utmost of seriousness. But what was the harm in engaging in a little play here or there?

And it totally worked. Not sixty minutes later, Dr. Morrison emailed to "check in." Asking if we could schedule our next appointment at the soonest opportunity.

I didn't make him wait long. After I finished teaching my next morning's classes, I sent a reply, and we soon had a session set for that afternoon.

"She kept telling everyone he was a creep."

I was employing more of my mother's advice. *Throw 'em a scattered bone.*

"A particular friend?"

"No, she wasn't a friend. Just someone who'd tagged along. You see, there were a lot of freedoms at my uncle's place. Lots of kids wanted to hang out."

"And this girl's assessment of your uncle? How did you feel about that?"

"I thought she demonstrated poor manners. Given his hospitality."

"That's a logical response, Lainey. I'm more interested in your emotional reaction."

"If I'm honest? I wanted to hurt her." In my defense, I thought she was going to ruin everything. I thought I might lose my friends.

He nodded passively. "And did you act on that feeling?"

"I suppose I did, Dr. Morrison."

After he made a note, he said, "Let's walk through that together, shall we?"

This man could win an award for his clunky suggestions. He obviously wanted to evaluate my early communication skills. What could I say? They were effective and concise.

But still, as he stared at me with expectation, my shoulders tensed. I knew I was balancing on the tip of a fulcrum. If I shared all the details of that day, there would be no turning back.

"Right," I said, without meeting his eyes. "I spoke to her at the beach. A group of us went to swim. Some moms came, and Uncle James did too."

"Was your uncle close with the mothers?"

"Hardly. But they still fluttered around him. That never changed."

More nodding. More note-taking. "Please carry on. I'm listening."

"One of the women gave me a bottle of root beer." I paused for a second, then said, "That's important."

"Because she demonstrated generosity?"

"No, because the bottle was glass."

As I waded into the water, the girl was gaping at me. I sipped my drink, and by the time I'd finished, an idea had arrived. I never really thought it through; I just dunked beneath the surface. When I reemerged, I called her over.

"She stomped toward me. With this childish indignation. Water frothing around her legs. And then she stopped. I can still see the shock on her face. Her mouth opened and out came this piercing scream. It was so shrill. She fell sideways and kicked one of her legs out of the water. Blood was pouring out of the bottom of her foot."

Dr. Morrison shifted in his seat. "Can I assume the injury arose from . . . from broken glass?"

Ding. Ding. "Yes, you assume correctly." When the sun passed behind the clouds, I could see the shards of my root beer bottle, barely a glimmer on the bottom. "It was my uncle who rushed into the water and scooped her up. He bandaged her foot with his T-shirt, and we all took her to the hospital for stitches."

"That sounds quite serious, Lainey. Quite—quite significant."

It was all a tangled blur. I remember being startled by the brightness of her blood. And the severity of the injury. I couldn't recall what I'd expected to happen, but not that. Yet mixed with my surprise had been an undeniable splinter of . . . satisfaction? Whether right or wrong, the sight of her pain relaxed the spring inside me. Alleviated my tension.

"That night, after everything calmed down, my uncle told me something I'll never forget."

"Could you share it with me?"

"Basically, he saw what I did. Smashing the bottle. But instead of punishing me, he said, 'We all do unsavory things, puppet. But we won't tell on each other.'"

I exhaled. Repeating those words out loud made my stomach churn.

"You believed that absolved you?"

"No, it wasn't about absolving me. Though I probably thought that at the time." How could I explain things? "It was like he was telling me that on some disturbing level . . . we'd become . . . equals."

Dr. Morrison chewed the end of his pen, then said, "I apologize, Lainey. I'm not quite following."

I had to lay it all out. So there was no confusion. "I was a troubled girl, capable of emotional detachment with a propensity for calculated violence. And my beloved uncle? He actually was a creep."

Another annoying blank stare.

"Don't you get it? All those relationships he had? He was never interested in the rich mothers. It was always their daughters. The young girls."

CHAPTER TWENTY

Lainey

I'D BEEN LYING in bed for ages but could not drift off. The bedroom blinds were wide open, as was usual, and the city lights illuminated the room. I flipped the feather pillow, punched it twice, then lay back down.

Even though hours had passed since that uncomfortable exchange with Dr. Morrison, I couldn't stop ruminating. A noisy gridlock inside my skull. Every single thought: negative. Was I supposed to feel better? Was all our chitchat a waste of time? Was I participating in *real* therapy?

I was still awake when Andrew returned home. It was well past two in the morning. He flopped down on the clean duvet beside me.

"Man, that was a crazy good gig."

I leaned over to kiss him. His skin smelled almost electrical. Like overheated wires.

"Awesome," I replied, using the required intonation.

"You should've come."

"Next time."

He got up from the bed and went into the adjoining bathroom, rummaging through the medicine cabinet. "I'm so wired." He held up an orange prescription bottle, rattled the sleeping pills. "Hey? You want one?"

"No." I'd taken enough drugs at Albethey to last a lifetime.

After stripping down, he climbed under the covers. Snuffled toward me, then rubbed himself against my thigh. Usually I was insta-ready to roll, but I lay still. The penile prodding was doing zilch. Totally nada. I wished that I could feel him. Well, some other part of him. Besides *that*.

•

"Shall we pick up where we left off?" Dr. Morrison was in his home office. The child's artwork once again on full display.

"With my uncle. And his . . . predilections?"

"Exactly."

"Well, I mean, after that day he seemed lighter. Really upbeat all the time. Maybe he felt there were no more secrets? He was freer to be himself?"

"I don't want to extrapolate, Lainey, but I assume you're referencing his apparent interest in young girls?"

I hesitated. "I want to be clear, Dr. Morrison. Nothing obvious was happening. I just knew something was . . . off. But maybe I also rationalized it."

"Rationalized how?"

"I don't know. I knew he liked my friends. He always teased them. Complimented them. But I figured they liked him too. He pretended not to notice if we stole his cigarettes. Or his gin. They all wanted to be there. None of his attention seemed *that* bad."

Dr. Morrison gently shook his head. "Makes sense you would find those dynamics confusing, Lainey. That you didn't recognize the inappropriateness of it. You and your friends were very, very young. And from my vantage point, quite unprotected."

"Maybe." A drop trickled down my underarm. Why was I sweating? I wasn't even warm. "I see it now, but back then, not so much."

"Yes, but you're reflecting as an adult."

"I suppose. But then something happened that was a little harder to ignore."

"Which was?"

"I found a bunch of shopping bags on my bed. He'd bought me lingerie and makeup."

"Did he explain those purchases?"

"I mean, he told me I was getting older and might need those things." I gazed out the window for a moment. An east view of the park, the clock tower. People milling about. What I wouldn't give to trade places with any one of them. "My friends and I would dress up. Act totally ridiculous. Stuff tissues into empty bra cups. Smear on lipstick. That sort of thing."

"Ignoring the source of the items, I would stay that's quite typical exploration."

"Yeah, at first, it seemed like a joke."

"Did your uncle know what you were doing?"

"I don't see how, but maybe? A Polaroid camera appeared next." The box resting on my pillow. "I started snapping pictures of the girls. You know, they'd pretend to be models. It was a little provocative maybe, though we just thought it was funny."

"What did you do with the photographs?"

"I hid them." Beneath the gym clothes in my closet. "But then they disappeared."

"As in, someone took them?"

"Yeah. Obviously my uncle."

Dr. Morrison brought his fingertips to his chin. "After you realized, I assume you stopped taking photos?"

"Of course I did. I was embarrassed."

In the weeks after, my bedroom was always in disarray. Books tipped from the shelves, drawers hanging open, clothing piled in mounds. My uncle's mood was intensely sour. That was my punishment. I no longer had access to his good side. When he was content, something inside me soared.

"That makes sense, Lainey. Certainly there's some sort of attachment—" Dr. Morrison's head jerked toward the right. "Hey! What are you doing?"

For a nanosecond, I was stunned by his tone but immediately realized he wasn't talking to me.

"Yeah, but I need printer paper. Like, now."

A figure shuffled in behind him. Her back to the camera.

"Elise. I'm working. I've told you already, you can't barge in here."

Elise. The uncommon E of his artwork. His daughter was a teenager.

"Jeez, Dad. You're so extra." She tugged open the top drawer of a credenza. "My stuff's important, too, you know."

I leaned forward. How badly I wanted to see what she looked like.

When the girl turned, I clamped my teeth together. Felt a sting in the soft flesh of my cheek. Her heart-shaped face. Wide set eyes. Perfect scowl. The taste of iron filled my mouth. She looked nothing like him. Nothing at all.

"I'm sorry, Lai—"

The host has ended the meeting.

CHAPTER TWENTY-ONE

Mia

FAYE BROUGHT THE stylus to her lips and audibly sucked in air.

"You look like you want a cigarette."

"Hardly, darling. But in a previous existence, absolutely."

The past two days had been hot and humid, and they were seated in the afternoon shade on Mia's back deck. Faye had arrived earlier with iced teas and a paper bag of triple-berry scones.

"If you must smoke in this life," Mia teased, "a stylus is a healthy choice."

Faye laughed, then said, "Now, I said I'd stop being a nosey parker, but you're practically radiating tension."

Mia leaned back and put her feet up on the wicker coffee table. She was desperate to talk about Lainey Kemper. The disturbing childhood details and the dysfunctional interactions with her uncle. Even Mia's own fear over her family's safety. But she knew any sort of discussion about Ian's work would be a mistake on multiple levels.

"No tension, Mom. Usual worries, I suppose."

"Well then, I have an interesting tidbit to share. I've been a busy, busy bee."

"With?"

"My palmistry course." She took a big bite of a scone. "It's a fascinating science, but quite intense. For our final project, we had to submit scans of our handprints to our prof. Along with an analysis. Needless to say, my results were illuminating."

"Is that a good idea? Giving someone your fingerprints?"

Faye snorted and brushed away a spray of crumbs. "What do you think, Mia? He's going to use my assignment to cover up a crime ring? It's a reputable institute, you know."

"It was a legit question. I wasn't making fun."

"Yes, you were, but I'm not the least bothered by ignorance." She took another drag off the end of her stylus. "My professor says I have the palm of a mystic. All kinds of rare lines and mounds. I even have Odin's eye." She spread her hand out, palm up, and pointed to the inner joint on her thumb. "Impressive, no?"

"Neat," Mia managed, though she could see nothing that resembled an eye.

"Give me your hand. So I can see who you are."

"Mom, seriously. I think you know who I am."

"Yes, but let's pretend I don't. It's good for me to get practice before the final."

Faye shuffled her chair closer, and Mia had no option but to play along.

Several ums and ahs as she delicately examined Mia's hand, front and back. Finally, she gave her head a sad shake. "Look at those knuckles. Hardly a wrinkle in sight."

"Moisturizer?"

"No, no, dear. It has to do with raw intelligence." She smiled gently, a fragment of strawberry stuck to her front tooth. "But don't fret. Learning is a lifelong process. Nothing is stopping us."

"That's a relief."

"And look here." Fingernail digging into Mia's palm. "Your head line is fractured. Repeatedly. Which indicates a suspicious nature, you know. And all those shallow intersecting lines? You're naturally prone to troublesome thoughts."

"Somewhat accurate, as you well know. Though I'm working on it."

"That's good. We can't control destiny, but we can always improve our lot." She leaned closer. "Your line of life splits. A complete fork."

"Is that bad?" Mia asked, trying to sound serious.

"Not necessarily. Means you'll be moving to another country. Fairly soon, I think. Or else some other huge life change."

Mia pulled her hand back and picked up her iced tea. Last thing she needed was another major change. "I sound like a mess."

"It's not ideal, but as I said, nothing is written in stone. I have a triangle where my fate and heart line meet, and that didn't amount to much."

"Was it supposed to?"

"I was meant to have a wealthy partner. And clearly I don't. Which, as you might imagine, is deeply upsetting."

"Well, you never know what the future holds, right?" Though with an eye on her thumb, Mia mused, perhaps her mother already did.

Faye's phone buzzed, and she held the screen at a distance. "Speaking of the future, I've just made another new friend on the apps. Keith is texting. Says I'm a total betty."

Mia frowned. "I don't even know what that is."

"It's old slang, darling. He's being retro to catch my attention. Means he finds me attractive."

"Gotcha." There was never a dull moment with her mother. Faye was constantly discovering. While her focal point might be outlandish, at least her days were never stagnant. Unlike Mia's. In recent months, there was very little she found engaging or exciting. Besides the ridiculous obsessing over LK. Perhaps Ian was right and her near-constant low mood and behaviors were signs of depression. She needed to find a purpose, a new interest.

"Maybe Keith is going to make that triangle thing true?"

"Could be!" Faye stood and pocketed her stylus-cigarette. "It's been a lovely visit, sweetheart, but I can't while away my entire afternoon." She bent and loudly air-kissed Mia. "I'm off to chat with my new prospect. See what he's got to offer."

•

Mia watched out the kitchen window as the sky darkened at an alarming speed. Black clouds scuttling to eclipse the late afternoon sunshine.

She checked her phone notifications. No texts from Ian or Elise. Nothing from her mother either, which was not surprising, given her excitement to chat with an online stranger. Mia just hoped she was being careful and not leaving her personal security up to "fate."

A weather alert appeared: flash shower warning with potential lightning. Swim school would be canceled, and surely Elise would hunker down at Chloé's until the summer storm passed. She opened the Branches app. The blue dot appeared, then the background map loaded. Mia inhaled sharply. Elise was not at Chloé's after all. The dot showed she was back in that grungy laneway. Standing still.

Rain splatted against the windowpane. Single fat drops that quickly transformed into a hose-like spray. Bouncing off the sill, blurring the glass. The dot began to move. Out of the laneway, speeding up Main Street, and then turning into their neighborhood.

Mia went to the window and monitored the road. Monitored the app. Within minutes, Elise appeared, bounding along the sidewalk.

Hoodie plastered to her thin body. Puddles of water splashing as her flip-flops slapped the concrete.

Front door closing, items dropping, then an exasperated cry: "Oh my god—I'm soaked!"

"That's a real downpour," Mia said, trying to keep her voice steady. She stepped away from the window.

Elise skipped down the hallway and into the kitchen without responding. Each step leaving drips on the hardwood floor. Following behind, Mia found her standing in front of an open fridge, chomping bites of watermelon from a plastic container.

"Elise?"

She did not turn around.

"Elise!"

Elise's hands jumped, a chunk of watermelon splatting against the milk carton. She scraped an AirPod from her ear. "What the hell, Mom."

"You couldn't hear me."

"So you need to yell? I'm listening to music. What's your problem?"

"You tell me."

"Tell you what?" Elise chewed her bottom lip. "Is this a test or something?"

This close, Mia caught the odor of chlorine and saw the chemical dryness in her daughter's hair.

"Where were you?"

"Where do you think? We started a business, you know."

"And after that?"

"We rescheduled the kids, and I hung out at Chloé's."

"You hung out at Chloé's."

"Yeah. That's what I said."

"Then why'd you come home?"

"Because I, um, live here?"

"I mean, when it was pouring."

Elise's eyes narrowed. "Like, seriously, Mom. What is wrong with you?"

Mia blinked and took a step backward. Elise was lying to her. Looking straight into Mia's eyes and outright lying. To make matters worse, there was no way for Mia to tell Elise why she was pressing her. Not without revealing the tracking app.

So she was stuck. Her mind pulsing with alarm and simultaneously trying to calm itself. Maybe there was a logical explanation. Maybe secrets were inevitable with teenagers. Wasn't that what Ian had said? Elise was guarding aspects of her life in an effort to break away and stand on her own. *Your concern is bordering on toxic, Mia. What's most important is that she's safe.*

•

As Mia was wiping up the trail of rainwater, she heard the mailbox lid clang, then the front door open and close. She froze. She wasn't expecting anyone. Had Elise left the door unlocked? Had someone followed her home?

Then came Ian's voice, calling "Hello."

Mia exhaled and met him in the hallway. "You're early."

"No one showed for office hours, so I cut out."

"Maybe the weather." She gestured toward the pile of mail in his hand. "Anything good?"

"Nah. All junk."

She held out her hands. "Here, I'll toss it."

He brought the papers to his chest and smiled. "No worries, Mia. I'll sort through it in my office."

Then he slipped past her, walking up the stairs without even removing his wet shoes.

CHAPTER TWENTY-TWO

Mia

MIA WAS ALONE in the kitchen. She opened the refrigerator, the freezer. Then the cupboards, one by one. There were groceries galore, but she could not think of a single thing to prepare. After flicking through several online recipes, she ordered cheeseburgers and fries. A strawberry milkshake for Elise.

"Oh wow," Elise said after the food arrived. "You totally read my mind."

"Well, I am my mother's daughter," she replied. When Elise giggled, she felt a flicker of joy.

"Can I eat in my bedroom? Please? I'm watching *Love Is Blind*, and it's, like, totally messed up."

Usually Mia was firm—dinnertime was family time—but she nodded. And in a blink, Elise grabbed one of the greasy bags and vanished downstairs.

Moments later, Ian appeared. "This is perfect," he said. "Good for you to take a break from cooking." Mia was surprised when he went to the wine fridge and grabbed a bottle. "Why not?" he shrugged, as he popped the cork on a red. After pouring two generous glasses, he slid onto a stool at the island and pulled a paper-wrapped burger from the second bag. She sat beside him and did the same.

"Good day?" he asked, after taking a huge bite.

"Mostly. I tried out some color samples in the dining room. And have been researching wallpapers for the powder room. There's so much choice. But it's fun." Well, it wasn't fun exactly. But at least it was something. She nibbled the bun. "You? How was your day?"

"Busy, Mia. Just super busy." He took another bite and, with his mouth full, mumbled, "Oh, there's something I forgot to mention."

She gulped nervously. "To me?"

"Just an email that might interest you. The department is looking for a volunteer to head this year's fundraising gala. Can I offer you up? Everyone at the college loved you last year, and you really enjoyed the role."

She sipped her wine as she pretended to consider his proposal. By no stretch had she "really enjoyed the role." The initiative was organized by a group of women, and much of the work involved managing those difficult personalities. If she voiced that, Ian would accuse her of being judgmental or socially inept. "I don't know, Ian. If I have the time."

"Really, Mia? Elise is crazy busy with her summer job, we're mostly settled here, and you hardly leave the house. You've isolated yourself. Wouldn't it be good to diversify your day?"

"Diversify?" What was she? Some sort of portfolio?

"I just mean mix things up. Put yourself out there."

"I-I've been busy." Which was somewhat true. The move had been a huge task. Not just unpacking; she'd been slowly painting each room from the original builder beige. She'd also constructed shelves in the garage and planted a flower bed in the front garden. Pile on cooking, cleaning, plus nonstop visits from her mother, and a day could easily dissolve.

"I see that, but why not give it a go? You might even make some new friends."

"I'll think about it."

"That's all I ever ask. Model a full, healthy life. Elise pays attention, you know, whether you realize it or not."

Mia closed her eyes for a second. How easily he piled on another layer of guilt.

As they ate, he talked once again of his plan to increase his research work and reduce his patient load. "Taking a risk. But if not now, then when?" The more he spoke, the more she drank. By the end of the meal, her burger was barely touched, and the bottle of wine was empty. Perhaps she actually was her mother's daughter. The thought made her chuckle to herself.

Ian cleared and tossed the greasy garbage, then poured two digestifs and carried both tumblers and his laptop to the sofa in the living room. "Come," he said. "Join me. No reason I can't finish things up while spending time together."

"Okey doke," she said with a slur. "Let me grab my laptop too."

They were seated on opposites ends of the couch, facing each other. Perhaps Ian was right, and Mia should try to model a fuller, healthier life. Instead of sticking so close to home, with Faye being the bulk of her social life. The college offered a ton of continuing education courses, and it was easy enough to gather some information. Even if it amounted to nothing, at least it would give her discussion points for her next conversation with Ian.

She was tipsy from the wine. Growing tipsier with each sip of amaro. Not what she'd intended for a Tuesday night, but why not, as Ian had said. Over the top of her screen, she watched him. Short bursts of typing, then periods of intense focus. Was he reading or just gaping? Captivated or distraught? It was impossible to tell, but she sensed his expressions were connected to LK.

"H-how are things going with your, with that girl. That woman?"

He looked up and brightened immediately. "It's been a roller coaster, to be honest. Her history and psychological profile are complex. Riveting actually . . . Though things are taking quite a turn from Albethey."

"Her diagnosis has changed?"

"No, not that. I'm confident in my assessment. I'm talking about her familial history."

"But I thought she had no family. Other than the man she killed."

"That's right. When I first treated her, she presented herself as an instigator, I suppose. She was the source of friction in her relationships."

"And now? How is she now?"

"I can't share much more," Ian replied. "Though at times I'm struggling to decipher what's reality and what's construction."

She nodded. He'd mentioned the same in his notes. "You think she's lying?"

"*Lying* is a strong word. It's not my job to condemn her. Perhaps better to say that she can't acknowledge her own darkness." Then he bent his head and refocused on his laptop.

Mia was surprised by Ian's openness. He never spoke about his patients, but maybe the alcohol had loosened his tongue. Or else he was deeply excited about some aspect of his interactions with LK. Mia shouldn't look, she really shouldn't, but the desire to know what he was doing on his laptop was intense.

Nothing wrong with a quick peek.

She turned her volume to silent. Another glance at Ian, and she selected Other. Within seconds, her husband's desktop appeared as her own. Instead of work documents, as she'd assumed, he was on Goodreads, having searched for famous case studies. The list had a variety of subjects from hoarding to multiple personality. He had two tabs open on writing the perfect query letter. Plus a page detailing a nonfiction editor's manuscript wish list and a publisher's website. Ian was indeed planning to write a book.

He suddenly threw his right hand out to the side, then sighed loudly. "The hell is going on?"

"What is it?"

"My computer keeps acting strange."

The booze-induced serenity skittered out of Mia's body. "Um, how so?"

"Like tabs shifting. My font size increasing. Several times, folders opened after I closed them. One was even moved to a different spot."

She'd been stupid. Unbelievably stupid. Not realizing something so very basic: While she could see what he was doing on his desktop, he could also see what she was doing on the mirrored version.

"Is it your mouse? Maybe it's your mouse."

"I'm not even using a mouse. I think I might have a virus."

She tried for a light laugh, though it sounded strangled. "Let's hope not."

Her finger fumbled over her trackpad, and acting as casually as possible, she logged out of his desktop.

"Look, there it goes again." He pointed at the screen. "My search history just popped up."

"How, um, bizarre." She coughed. "Are you certain you didn't do it?"

"Positive. You know, I should take it to the IT desk over at the college. Get them to run a scan."

"I'm sure that's unnecessary, Ian. You probably just need to update your software."

"How do I do that?"

"Easy," she said. As she explained, the knot tightened in her stomach.

"You totally called it, Mia. The system is out of date." He reached over and squeezed her foot. "Phew!"

"Yeah, phew."

•

The next morning, as soon as Ian left for Albethey, Mia scooped up her laptop and went upstairs to his office. Though it might be paranoia, there was something about the way he'd gripped the mail yesterday that indicated it wasn't just junk.

The room was immaculate, as it always was. A small pile of books and papers on the console table, but nothing else. She pulled out his chair and reached beneath his desk to withdraw the tiny blue recycling container. Elise had given it to him as a birthday gift, insisting he needed to help save the environment. "Greta can only do so much, Dad." Inside, Mia found the colorful flyers and a mound of shredded paper. She poked the thin strips; they appeared to be handwritten pages. Likely patient notes he'd already transcribed.

She shook her head and sat down. Then mumbled, "Clearly no Odin's eye on my thumb."

Placing her palm on her laptop, she wondered if she should dare. Last night had been a very close call. She could not imagine the repercussions if her actions were discovered. But Ian had been gone no more than fifteen minutes. His drive would easily take an hour at this time of day. She had time to check the folder for new recordings.

There were two.

She opened the earlier of them. When Lainey Kemper appeared, Mia felt the usual anxious exhilaration. Her mouth was even dry.

The corrosive relationship between uncle and niece was coming into tighter focus in LK's telling. Mia found the grotesque details overwhelming. Especially when Lainey Kemper described hiding inappropriate photographs and her uncle taking them. And the emotional manipulation when he realized it was a one-time occurrence.

A voice filled Ian's office then. Familiar but completely out of place. Mia rapidly glanced at the open doorway, found it empty, and then turned back to her computer screen.

Elise?

"Jeez, Dad. You're so extra. My stuff's important, too, you know."

"I'm sorry, Lainey. I'm sorry. I need to end the session."

Mia's mouth fell open, and she brought her hand to her forehead. How could Ian have allowed their daughter to be seen? Why didn't he lock his office door? His patient now knew not only what Elise looked like but also her name. And the thrill of that newfound knowledge was slathered all over Lainey Kemper's face.

Picking up her phone, she wanted to call Ian. To give him an earful. But she put it down again, took a deep breath, and forced herself to relax. She checked the date on the video. It was recorded two days ago. Nothing had happened. No doubt, she was misreading LK's expression. Besides, that woman could be anywhere in the world. Hours away on a plane. It was not a catastrophe. It was not a threat. It simply wasn't.

She closed her laptop, and as she was about to leave, she noticed a corner of paper jutting out of his day calendar. Was it the letter Ian had been gripping so tightly yesterday? Noting the date where it was inserted, she removed the envelope and opened it. A financial document with a red and white logo in the upper right corner: *Dear Dr. Morrison, Please find enclosed a copy of your recent transactions for your records.*

Mia blinked, assuming the numbers would adjust themselves. The zeros would blend. Ian had opened an account at a new bank and taken out a line of credit. Only to immediately withdraw a hefty sum. He'd made no mention of these funds, or their purpose, to her. His wife, his partner.

The moment he arrived home that evening, she'd demand an explanation. Face-to-face. But as soon as that thought formed, she reconsidered. That would not necessarily yield an honest response. When backed into a corner, Ian was lightning fast with his lies. She needed to figure this out on her own. To understand why thirty-eight thousand dollars had been borrowed without her knowledge or consent. And why Ian appeared to be hiding it.

CHAPTER TWENTY-THREE

Lainey

"I SINCERELY APOLOGIZE for what happened during our previous session, Lainey. We were talking about something quite delicate and—"

"No biggie, Dr. Morrison. Don't worry about it."

"Well, it was regrettable. And I thought it important to acknowledge that."

"That was your daughter, right? Elise?" He squirmed in the leather chair of his campus office and did not respond. I offered him some comfort by saying, "I heard her come in but didn't see her."

Which, of course, was untrue. I saw her quite clearly and desperately wanted to track her down. But locating Miss Morrison was more challenging than expected.

Even with her full name, an online search with all conceivable keywords offered no related results. I perused the usual socials. Nada. Perhaps she had some serious privacy settings. I then wasted an entire afternoon sifting through snooze-worthy posts from nearby schools, both private and public. I went back a couple of years before finally finding the most miniscule of rewards. A blurry snapshot from her middle school volleyball team. The name Elise M. included in the caption. She was standing at the end of a middle row. To her left, a basic blond named Chloé G.

"Can we put the unfortunate incident behind us then?"

"All good, Dr. Morrison. The perils of working from home, I suppose."

I wasn't the least bothered that my privacy had been breached. In fact, I would say it was a fresh development. Or *diversion* might be a better word. In the past, I'd perched Dr. Morrison on a pedestal and fantasized about him relentlessly. But lately he seemed less godlike and more dishwater-dull. I wondered if he might actually be a subpar clinician. Was it reasonable to say, without arrogance, that the high point of his career had been me? Would he be where he was—the fancy house, expensive car—if our paths hadn't crossed? I'd admit, some degree of ennui had been creeping into my attitude, but when I saw his daughter's face, my perspective did a somersault. His sheen was fading, but his family was starting to glisten.

This led to several days of speculation. Even a hotel romp Andrew had arranged offered minimal distraction. I maintained my voyeuristic pose, but my mind drifted endlessly. I envisioned Dr. Morrison's wife. The perfect little life she'd built around her husband and her strikingly gorgeous child. I imagined exotic vacations and laughter-filled dinners with chichi friends. Toe-curling sex even after years of marriage.

I had none of those things (well, except the toe-curling sex). My reality involved pacing around a high-rise condo with a boytoy, while choking through childhood memories with a lame shrink. Who delusionally assumed he was helping me achieve that sense of mental freedom others took for granted. I was beginning to realize I could not rewind my life and correct mistakes. I could, however, start anew. Setting my own rules this time.

"Perhaps we can return to where we were?" Dr. Morrison said. "Delving into the complex relationship between you and your uncle. You mentioned Polaroids? Lingerie?"

"Thanks for the reminder." Which I needed as much as a hammer to the head.

"Did things escalate from there?"

"Yeah. I did something. Something that helped him." Saying those words made my neck hurt. Like I'd swallowed a jawbreaker, and it was stuck in my esophagus. "At night, if I had a friend sleep over, my uncle made us hot chocolate."

I explained the performance of it. How he acted as though he was a professional chocolatier. Calling us into the kitchen with the words "I'm going to whip up a spectacular treat." White apron on, he'd be standing at the counter, blocks of semisweet and dark on a butcher board. As he chopped, he'd ask us questions about school, mocking the teachers that we hated. Or teasing us about trends and teenager fashion. Everything lighthearted and laughter-filled as he added chocolate chunks to scalding milk. A few drops of vanilla, and then he'd dance the metal whisk across the bottom of the pot. When he handed us the steaming mugs, he was gravely serious as he said, "Liquid gold, my darlings. Don't waste a drop!"

"Pink one's for you, puppet." The sunflower one was always meant for my friend. That was the rule, and I did what was expected and pushed the correct mug in the correct direction.

We'd retreat to my bedroom. He'd given me a television for my last birthday, and it was perched on top of my dresser. Mugs in hand, we'd snuggle under the blankets and watch something banal like *Blossom* or *Home Improvement*. Drowsiness would strike my bedmate about twenty minutes later. She'd invariably fall into a deep slumber before the first episode had even ended. Chocolate crescents at the corners of her mouth, and her breath milky sweet like a kitten's. I'd wiggle the mug from her loose grip and place it on the night table. Then click out the light.

Eventually I'd doze, too, curled on my side. But when nightmares jolted me upright, which they usually did, I'd sit up. The moon creating a spooky glow inside my bedroom. I'd notice the bedspread had been peeled back. Mattress beside me, empty.

"My friend was gone."

A sting in my right palm. I unclenched my fist, revealing the sweaty skin. Four deep indentations from my fingernails.

"Gone? I'm afraid to ask . . ."

As I lay awake, I knew something was very wrong. But my mind fabricated a myriad of reasonable explanations. She'd simply woken. Gotten up to use the toilet. Gone to the kitchen for a glass of water. I would repeat those possibilities over and over and over again, until they were real. There was no worry. There was no danger. And then I was able to doze off again.

"She was always back in bed before morning."

He was nodding slowly, his expression grim. "And the next day?"

"My friend would be sleepy, slow to wake up. And my uncle would be pleasant as can be. Jovial even. He'd blame the grogginess on too many sweets. Or on staying up late watching nonsense. Usually he'd threaten to remove the television from my room, and then he'd feed us breakfast. 'Something hearty to start your day,' was what he always said."

"Do you recall how you felt during those moments?"

While I certainly felt something, it was an indecipherable snarl. "I don't recall."

"No?" He scribbled on his notepad. "Then what about your thought pattern?"

Now *that* was crystal clear. "Do you really need to know?"

"It's not about me knowing, Lainey. It's about you working through these difficult memories in a way that feels supported."

I hesitated. My spine grew rigid. Did I feel supported? Had I ever felt supported? Then I said it. "I told myself that whatever happened, those girls were none the wiser. I told myself it wasn't causing any harm."

He touched a finger to his lip, then lowered his hand. "Do you still think along those lines? That there was no harm in what your uncle was doing?"

"Of course I don't." What a vulgar question.

"What are you feeling now?"

Not much, besides a crusty loathing toward Dr. Morrison. He'd scratched the scab off a wound and offered nothing to soothe the pain.

"Don't you get it?"

"Can you articulate what you'd like me to understand?"

The inanity of our exchange made me want to explode. "My uncle was my entire family." As depraved as he was, he also took care of me. I believed he loved me. "There was nobody else."

Dr. Morrison's face remained passive, but behind the veneer, he was judging me. Judging what I'd done. It didn't matter that I was essentially a child. I had known right from wrong. I needed to betray my uncle. To tell someone. But day after day, I had been unable to find the courage to take that step. I lied to myself constantly. Made up reasons, excuses. Minimized, rationalized. And in doing so, became complicit in his criminality. My uncle had shaped me into a predator. His prey was my prey. We were aligned.

Still to this day, the only sound that made me shiver was a door in the darkness. Creaking on its hinge.

CHAPTER TWENTY-FOUR

Lainey

FOR SEVERAL DAYS, I waited up the street from Dr. Morrison's house. Far enough away to have a good view but remain undetected. I tried various times, early morning to late afternoon, but my surveillance never overlapped with the girl's arrival or departure. My aggravation was growing. So much effort with no result. On the fourth day, the heat inside Andrew's car was making me feel vomity, so I climbed out, used the side of my sneaker to slam the door. Then trudged a few streets over to grab a cold energy drink.

I knew I was taking a chance wandering around that neighborhood. If he saw me, he'd assume I was exhibiting stalker tendencies. Or that I was obsessed with him, or some other annoying label to add to my pile of psychological maladies. When nothing could be further from the truth. Dr. Morrison was of minimal interest. Even the doppelgänger videos I'd made with Andrew now seemed cringeworthy.

The break came when I returned to my car. As I approached, icy beverage in fist, I noticed a bright blue sheet of paper pinned under the windshield wiper. *Elise and Chloé's Swim School.*

I chuckled. The timing was uncanny. If I believed in all that new-age crap they spouted at the yoga studio, I'd say it was by ethereal design. The universe had finally decided to stop fucking with me.

Sliding back behind the wheel, I gulped a few mouthfuls of liquid caffeine. I could sense it skidding through my bloodstream. Chemical fists pumping. *Woot!* I took a grounding breath, then dug my cell phone from the bottom of my bag. Punched in the number on the flyer. A youthful voice of pure effervescence answered on the third ring.

"Hi, there," I said, using my best entitled-mommy purr. "Elise?"

"Nope, it's Chloé."

Shit. Wrong one. "But you are running a swim school, right? I just got a flyer."

"On your car? My mom must have put it there. She helps out with the marketing."

"Wow. Nice mom. You two girls teach together?"

"Yeah. We only do private lessons, and both of us are in the pool at all times. We both completed the water safety instructor course, as well as being Red Cross certified. And we also did . . ." She droned on. The adolescent lilt was comical.

"Well, I have an adorable five-year-old boy who won't go near the water. He'll barely take a bath."

"Lots of kids are nervous, but our lessons are in my backyard. We're, like, super friendly, and we want the moms to wait and watch. Or the nannies."

"That sounds, like, ideal. It just might work."

"Well, we have a slot opening Tuesday morning, if you're interested."

"Where are you exactly? I'm on—" I peered through the windshield and read out the name on the street sign. "Just wondering if it's walkable."

"Totally. We're, like, literally around the block from you." Then she offered up her address. Like candy from a baby.

"Could I pop over and take a peek at the setup? Won't be long."

"One sec, okay?" Some mumbling in the background, and then she said, "Sorry, but we're actually done for the day. Is tomorrow good?"

"Sure, no prob," I chirped. "See you then."

I hung up and immediately looped the car around. Two minutes later, I turned onto her street and saw the girls standing at the bottom of a stone driveway. Dr. Morrison's daughter was instantly recognizable. They both checked their phones, and then side by side, gaits matching, began striding along the sidewalk. Wet hair sharply parted in the middle, wearing identical cutoff jean shorts and matching white tanks. Muscular tanned limbs.

I felt a pang of . . . I wasn't sure. Perhaps it was envy. Maybe pity. Possibly plain old animosity at the sight of their casual beauty. Young people were oblivious of their power. Or their vulnerability.

I parked the car and stepped out. Nothing wrong with an unplanned stroll on a summery day. I took a left, followed by a right. When the girls dipped into an alley behind some buildings, I dipped in too. They stopped beside a pair of spray-painted dumpsters. As they lingered there, they kicked tiny pebbles across the pavement with their Converse sneakers.

Before the guy even slinked out of the shadows, I knew exactly what they were doing. And the revelation gave me a heady feeling. Only label that made sense: *fundemental delight.*

Once the transaction was complete and their customer retreated, I sidled closer. "Hey," I said.

They both jumped slightly, then recaptured their cool. "Hey," they replied at the same time.

With a conspiratorial tone, feigning a nervous vibe, I whispered, "You guys, uh, selling?"

Rapid glance at each other, and the other one said, "You a cop?"

"Do I look like a cop?"

"If we ask, you got to identify yourself. That's the law."

"I'm not a cop. And for the record, that's only true on TV." I spoke with confidence, though I had no clue one way or the other. "Every adult knows that."

Elise jammed her friend with her elbow, then lifted her chin an inch. "What do you want then?"

"Any jellies?" I figured one of them had pinched their mothers' stash. So many of my yoga clients were that type of women. Uppity lives, organic this and that, self-care up the wazoo, but needing sedatives to get through each day.

"Jellies? Huh?"

"Or some k-pins?"

Another dart of confusion between them. "No?"

"Well, what do you got?"

"Just Addies."

Adderall. One of them had pocketed their own ADHD meds.

"Seriously? That's exactly what I need. My boyfriend's a DJ and he's got this new gig, and I absolutely have to go. Probably an all-nighter."

Quick glance between them. "Really?"

I knew what they were thinking. I looked too old for any of that. Boyfriend. Gig. All-nighter. "I usually don't go hunting in random alleyways for help, you know. But I'm kind of desperate."

"If it's, you know, your boyfriend's thing," Elise said with a small smile, "you shouldn't have to go if you don't want to."

Was that a sliver of kindness?

"Nah, it's going to be a blast. If I can stay awake." I laughed, hoping I was convincing. Though I had no intention of ever using Adderall. "And hey, you guys are totally welcome to come. I can get you in if you're interested."

"Oh wow!" Elise's eyebrows shot up. "That'd be, like, seriously cool."

"Yeah," the friend said. "I'd be down for it. How much stuff do you want? They're instant release, so thirty for a twenty."

"Actually, we can do twenty-five, okay?"

Was this chick giving me a deal? Was my talky-talky approach endearing?

"Can I Venmo?"

The friend shook her head. "Nope. Sorry. Just cash."

Ugh. I wasn't a fan of Number Two. But then my psychiatrist's daughter came to my rescue. "You can Venmo me. Here"—handing me her phone—"add yourself as a contact."

"Super-duper," I replied. Once I'd typed in my digits, I quickly skimmed through her apps. The usual teen time-wasters, but then I noticed an unexpected icon. A green leaf. Was Dr. Morrison spying on his own daughter? Was he that sort of creep?

I clenched my jaw, then said, "Did you know someone's tracking you?"

"What?"

"Yeah, your phone is being monitored. I recognize the logo. I used to work at a software company." My short-lived dip into the corporate world. "That was our competition." I pointed at her screen.

"No, that's just a step counter." She took back her phone, then opened the Branches app. Turning the screen toward me, she said, "See? I've done over six thousand so far today. That doesn't even count the swimming."

"Yes, but if you minimize that. It's a standard overlay." I reached and tapped a nearly invisible X in the upper right corner. A detailed map appeared.

She gaped at her phone. Blinked several times. Then whispered, "What the actual fuck?"

"You're the blue dot."

Even with the tan, her face paled. I estimated she was genuinely upset.

The other girl pressed closer, peering over her shoulder. "Wow. That's, like, so crazy. Guess who, right?"

Elise gnawed a fingernail. A bubblegum-pink home manicure.

"Your dad, I presume?" Offering my suggestion.

She rolled her eyes. "Hardly. He couldn't care less. Totally my mother."

"Oh dear," I chirped, attempting to appear sympathetic. "Well, I'm transferring enough for three twenties, okay? Plus a tip!"

•

On the drive home, I evaluated the interaction. I was honestly perplexed. It was the opposite of what I'd anticipated or intended. Every time I watched the screen-capture snippet from my session with Dr. Morrison, my acrimony had grown. The girl's carefree attitude. Her entitlement. Her obvious self-possession. But in person, she hadn't been the snarky snippy teen from the video. She was actually kind of sweet. We clicked. Practically got on like gangbusters.

With all my energy-from-a-can, I decided to take the stairs up to the condo. Hopping them two at a time was an easy alternative to leg day. As I reached the upper landing to our floor, my phone buzzed.

A search engine alert. About an Ian R. Morrison. No mention of the doctor title, but more than likely, it was him. I scanned the brief piece of information. Not a particularly interesting post, but I thought I might use it. See how far I could go.

That was what friends and family did, I figured. Horsed around with each other.

CHAPTER TWENTY-FIVE

Mia

"MAAAAHM!"

Even over the spray of water, Mia could hear the sharpness in her daughter's tone. She hurried to finish her shower, rinsing away the sweat and salt from an afternoon run. After watching the most recent therapy session, she had been too angry to sit still.

Instead of acknowledging the depravity LK described, or assuaging the woman's misplaced guilt, Ian had glossed right over it. He'd offered no warmth or compassion and simply questioned her about the next day. Was he oblivious to the distress his patient was experiencing?

All Mia could fathom was that Ian was so ravenous for Lainey Kemper's story, he'd lost his ability to evaluate his client's needs. Perhaps even his ability to treat her.

More yelling.

"Mom? Where are you? I need to talk to you! Like, now!"

"Be right there."

Mia threw on a linen robe and belted the waist as she trotted down the stairs. Rounding the corner to the living room, she could see Elise pacing back and forth. Her hood was up, face hidden, and hands locked like hammers.

"What's going on?" Mia said as she moved closer. "Are you okay? Did something happen?"

"Don't come near me," she growled, yanking down her hood.

"Elise, you're scaring me."

Then she turned toward Mia, and with narrowed eyes, said, "What the fuck, Mom."

Mia recoiled. Her daughter had never sworn at her. "Don't talk to me like—"

"Like what? Like I'm so mad I-I'm going to lose it?" Yanking her phone from the back pocket of her shorts, she slammed her finger into the screen. Then a snap of the wrist and she shoved the device at Mia. "What's this? What did you do?"

The floor tilted. Mia pressed her fingertips into the nearest wall to balance herself. There it was. A line-drawn map of their street. A blue blinking dot. Now nestled inside the rectangle of their home.

"I-I don't know."

"You installed that on my phone. Admit it! No, don't bother. I know it was you. Dad would never. Wouldn't even know how."

"I wasn't—"

"How long? Huh?"

"Elise—"

"I said how long!"

Mia swallowed. "A few months. Not long. I promise. And I forgot it was even there."

"You're such a liar."

"I mean, I just had this feeling something wasn't right. I can't explain it."

"Then why didn't you talk to me? Why didn't you ask?"

"I didn't know what to say."

"You're supposed to be a parent. You're supposed to be my mom."

Sadness washed over Elise's face, but it was quickly recoated in fury.

"You kept going to that laneway. I thought you might be in trouble. Or making a terrible mistake."

"Yeah, right. You were so upset and couldn't bother to say a word?"

"I . . ." Mia didn't know how to respond. The question was justified. Why hadn't she addressed it? Instead of doing nothing and worrying incessantly.

"You really want to know what we were up to?"

Mia stared at her, afraid to speak.

"Well, I'll tell you, Mom. I went with Chloé. She was selling her fucking pills to these two losers who live there. She wanted me to come along so they wouldn't scam her."

"What? Why?"

"What do you think? For money."

"But you're both working. The swim school. Isn't that enough?"

She huffed. "Consider it a side gig."

"My god, Elise. You can't do that. What if—"

"I couldn't care less what you say. Why can't you leave me alone? Why can't you let me grow up?"

As Elise raced away, Mia stood frozen in place, water dripping from the ends of her hair and soaking into the collar of her robe. What had she done? She'd convinced herself the surveillance was harmless. It was necessary. When it was neither of those things.

From the lower level came the whoosh of a closet door, drawers banging. Not sixty seconds later, Elise flew up the basement stairs with a small duffle gripped in her fist.

"Can we talk about this? I'm—"

"Talk?" A wry laugh before the thousand-daggered stare. "Why would I talk to somebody I hate?"

•

Tingling, weak, nauseous, cold. Mia imagined being tased was not much different. She moved toward the couch, sinking into a triangle of sunlight. As she waited for the shock to pass, she listened to normalcy through the open window. Birds chirping and cars driving past. A pair of chatty neighbors walking their dogs along the sidewalk.

Eventually she got up and retrieved her phone. She tried texting and calling, but Elise had blocked Mia's number. She even clicked the Branches app multiple times, willing the blue dot to blink. But of course, it had vanished. Just a pop-up reminding her that her single offshoot had disconnected. Her branch was severed from the trunk.

When Ian arrived home later that evening, Mia was forced to explain what had happened. Confess the reason behind the massive argument with their daughter. When he began to nod knowingly, she stopped. "You've talked to her?"

"Certainly. She called me at work. She was distressed."

His words were a slap. Elise had never looked to Ian for emotional support before. Or anything else, for that matter. "And?"

"She's okay, Mia. Well, not okay, but she's fine."

"At Chloé's?"

Expressionless, he gazed at her for one, two seconds. Then said, "I do want to hear your side, you know."

She had no choice but to continue. In part explaining, and in part defending herself. Even though she knew the app could not keep Elise safe, she still paid a monthly subscription fee to maintain that self-deception. She also understood that spying was not a solution, and all it did was show Elise that her mother didn't trust her. But that was not the main issue. The larger part was that Mia did not trust herself. Her ability to be a decent parent. To communicate. She feared she hadn't planted the proper seeds. Hadn't done enough to nurture confidence and independence.

As she spoke, she could see his demeanor shifting. First the tensed eyebrows, then the inevitable beard scratch, and finally a string of probing questions. Did Mia recognize her maladaptive tendencies? Was she struggling to accept a diminished role with their daughter? Did she want a carbon copy of the relationship she had with her own mother?

Mia stammered, and before she could cobble together a response, he offered further observations. She should examine her expectations of their daughter. She needed to strike a balance between providing comfort and room to grow. "Roots and wings," he said. And a final gem: Mia should consider getting help. "Maybe," he suggested, "there's some unresolved trauma."

"What are you saying?"

"Let's be honest, Faye wasn't the best example. I'm sure her . . . her ineptitude has had an impact. Probably to a significant degree."

"I don't know, Ian. That seems like an overreach?"

"Perhaps it is. But on the other hand, perhaps it's time to explore your own teen years."

CHAPTER TWENTY-SIX

Mia

MIA HADN'T HEARD from Elise in over twenty-four hours, and the not knowing was almost unbearable. For her, at least. Ian's reaction was the polar opposite. He'd gone to work as usual and was now downstairs "planning a surprise." He'd asked her to stay in their room and "try to relax."

As he bustled about, she could hear him chatting to himself. "Looking good," then, "Yes!" His exuberance grated on her nerves. Once again, she was reminded how differently they experienced the world. She carried all the family's concerns, which allowed him to skate on by, embracing the belief that everything would be fine. "You're aging yourself prematurely," he'd said to her years ago. A casual insult she'd never forgotten.

"Nearly set," he called out.

"Can't wait," she called back, then took a slow, steady breath.

Perched on the chair in the alcove, she scrolled through her emails. She'd used the same address forever, and these days it was filled with more mindless junk than actual correspondence.

Perfect gifts for the home chef!

Get tax debt assistance!

Ugly and horny? These moms will reply!

No, she did not want to attend an evening for local fashionistas. Or save five percent on fresh pasta delivery.

Delete, delete, delete. Her spam filter was clearly worth nothing.

The only email that appeared to be legit was about the grand opening of Callow's newest hotel and spa. She skimmed the message. Luxury suites and five-star amenities. Introductory discounts on salt scrubs, seaweed wraps. Even a gold facial. They were offering a chance at a free night.

Wouldn't Elise love a luxurious day of pampering? Then a squishy bed with a thick duvet and a trolley with room service. Even though a mother-daughter outing seemed like an impossibility right now, she felt oddly hopeful as she clicked the bright blue Enter to Win button.

"Mia? Could you come down?"

Something in the watery smoothness of his tone made her insides flip-flop. She stood up, straightened her cotton dress with damp hands, and went to see what he'd done.

The main floor was pitch-dark. "Ian," she said. "I can barely see." With her fingertips, she lightly felt along the wall for the switch.

"Don't." His whisper hovered around her. "It's like this on purpose."

As she shuffled toward the kitchen, a lighter clicked. Ian's grinning face now illuminated by a pair of taper candles. The table had been set for two. A romantic dinner.

"O-oh my," she stammered. "I wasn't expecting this."

"Sit," he said, tugging out her chair.

"You've gone to so much trouble." And he had. Proper plates and cutlery, plus thick fabric napkins and a vase of yellow wildflowers. He'd transferred take-out Thai into proper bowls. Ian didn't cook, but he'd chosen all her favorites.

"I thought it'd be nice to have a quiet meal." He popped the cork from a bottle of prosecco and poured two glasses. "And really focus on you and me."

"You're right, we should talk. We have things to discuss."

"Yes, we certainly do." Another wide smile as he handed her a full flute.

They clinked glasses, and after she took a gulp, she said, "Ian, I really do need to know where Elise is. Have you spoken to her today?"

He stroked her hand. "I have indeed. And she's just fine. Not to worry."

"But just fine where?"

"Can we leave this for now?"

"Absolutely. Just tell me what's going on."

His mouth tightened slightly. "Look, I promised her. And I think it's important that Elise feels she can count on one of us."

"Are you serious? I have a right to know. She's my daughter."

"*Our* daughter. Who is very sore at you. And rightfully so." He exhaled loudly. "Tracking her without her knowledge was unconscionable. That kind of betrayal is about your needs; it has nothing to do with her."

Each sentence was a sharp punch, expertly delivered, and she pushed back her chair. "Need I remind you she was selling drugs?"

"Her friend was selling her own prescription medication. Elise tagged along to make sure things didn't go sideways."

"So? Cushion it all you want, they still put themselves in danger."

Mia could not look directly at him. The candlelight was highlighting all the wrong hollows and crests, making him appear as a photographic negative.

"Listen, I know the consequences could have been catastrophic. But teenagers are going to do stupid things. This was just a bad one. But they're both okay."

As always, he was rational, serene, and balanced, and his placid expression gave her a hot pulse of rage. She envisioned the tines of her fork stabbing the fleshy part of his hand. Closing her eyes, she waited for the frightening sensation to pass. It was the fatigue, she told herself. The helplessness over Elise. She lifted her glass and took another mouthful, then said, "Why would they even do that?"

"I won't break Elise's confidence, but she hinted that Chloé wanted to buy new clothes. Some designer stuff. There's a lot of pressure on these kids to fit in."

"That doesn't make sense."

"To me and you, it doesn't. But to a teenager who was used to certain things and whose divorced parents have tightened their belts? It might. And I discussed things at length with Chloé's mother."

"You spoke with Sandy?" *Thud, thud, thud.* Her heart was suddenly pounding.

"Absolutely I did. We're all on the same team here. Communication is critical."

"A-and what did she say?"

"That Chloé will no longer be managing her own medication. Sandy's confiscated the tablets. And she's grounded her for the remainder of July. But the girls can continue their swim school."

"That's it?"

"I think it's a fair result. Elise will face the same when she comes home. She understands her error. The risk of it. But right now, she's requested a cooldown period."

"A what?"

"A time-out, Mia. And I agreed that made sense."

"I see." Mia straightened the knife and fork beside her plate. This entire discussion was feeling like an attack. She'd essentially raised Elise on her own since birth. Every need or want, she'd handled it.

Detangling her hair, reading her books, sewing her torn blanket. Doctor's appointments, bandages on scrapes, comfort after a nightmare. All of it. Yet here was Ian. Posturing as a dedicated family man. As though he'd been there every step of the way.

"Now can we relax a little? I've been pondering something and wanted to run it by you."

"Something serious?"

"Yes, very serious."

She finished her glass and reached for the bottle. What possibly could be next? Surely he wasn't aware that she was following his case study. Acting, yet again, in an intrusive and immoral way. If he'd caught her, then why the dinner and bottle of bubbly? Maybe he'd done something. Maybe he was feeling guilty.

"Is this about your line of credit?" She hadn't planned on bringing it up, but she was out of ideas. After snooping through all the documents in his filing cabinet and his laptop, she'd found nothing else.

"What?"

"From your office. There was a letter from a new bank."

"How did you come across that? You know my workspace is off-limits." He cleared his throat. Hard. "I have client notes. Forms, and what not."

"I was dusting and knocked some papers off your desk." When had lying become so easy? "And really, Ian. A banking document isn't related to your work."

"No, it's not. I appreciate, um . . . It's . . ."

"It's a hefty sum."

"Yes."

"And no mention of it to me."

Placing both palms on the table, he sighed. "This really wasn't how I planned our evening. I-I do apologize for not bringing it up."

"No time like the present."

"Well, this is a little embarrassing." He adjusted his glasses. "You're going to think it's outrageous, but I purchased cryptocurrency."

"What? Really? You mean that fake money with the dog on it?"

A feathery laugh. "No, not Dogecoin. Other ones like Ripple and Stellar. That's where the value is. I just went ahead on my own, as it was a tight window of opportunity. And if I'm honest, Mia, it's really quite a learning curve."

She brushed off his not-so-subtle insult. "I know enough that it's high risk. We just bought this house and your new car."

"Fair point, but rumor is I'm getting a substantial bonus this year from Albethey. Plus who knows what opportunities will arise once that journal article is published. It's going to make for a fascinating addendum, and I'm seriously mulling over a book again. It could be huge."

She took a slow breath to steady herself. Ian's smug expression was both deeply unattractive and nonsensical. If he reported accurately, wouldn't it show he'd initially been duped by the subject of his famous case study? That during not months but *years* of treatment, his patient had misled him? Would anyone still care about his diagnosis? Or would his capabilities as a psychiatrist be called into question? Not that she could broach those concerns, of course. Instead she said, "What if she doesn't want you to? What if she wants to remain private?"

"Not to worry. She's already given me permission."

"How?"

"With signed documents. All covered in the fine print, my darling. Plus, we've developed a good rapport."

There was something in his tone. A distasteful slickness. Had he always been that way? Why hadn't she noticed it?

"Now if we can regroup, I'm bursting to tell you my idea."

"Okay?"

"I've been looking at this from all angles, Mia. You might think it's out of left field, and admittedly it is, but I can't shake the excitement. What do you say . . . to another baby?"

She began to sputter. Grabbing the napkin, she pressed it to her mouth, hacking until she recovered. "I'm sorry?" she croaked.

"Hear me out. Lots of women are giving birth well into their forties, right? Can you imagine having another little one around? Elise would be an amazing big sister. You and I would go through all those firsts again, without the same fears. It would bring us that much closer. And just picture it, so much love to fill up your days?"

No was what she would say. Was he delirious? Did he think a baby would solve their problems? Plaster up the cracks in their marriage?

He reached across the table and gripped both her hands. "What do you say, my love? Will you give it some thought?" Then a sly and deliberate wink. "We could even start trying tonight."

CHAPTER TWENTY-SEVEN

Lainey

AS I WAS settling in for my next therapy session, I opted to engage in a mini experiment. My hypothesis: Dr. Morrison had white knight syndrome. I assumed most practitioners in his particular field did. I wanted to test how far I could go.

"Things have been super stressful." I gave him my best dejected expression. "Not great."

"How so?"

I threw a quick glance over my shoulder. The door to the den was right behind me. "Um. I . . ."

"Is there something specific that concerns you, Lainey?"

"I don't know." A second glimpse. As though I was concerned a raging bull might barrel into the room at any moment. Which was unfair to Andrew, and also dumb because he was at work. "I don't think anyone can help. I made this mess m-myself." An expert hitch in my voice on that last word.

"Lainey, I understand." He moved closer to his screen, searching my face for obvious signs. Remnants of a black eye. Tiny bruises from the squeeze of fingertips on my cheeks. "You've alluded to friction at home. There are plenty of resources if . . ."

He was waiting for me to fill in the blank. That was a technique I'd noticed repeatedly. Allowing silence to dangle between us. That tiny trick made most people uncomfortable, and they'd rush in to fill the empty space. But not me.

"No, no. It's all good. I don't need resources. I just thought I heard, um . . . It's totally fine." Dabbing my eye, I smiled resolutely. "Forget I said anything, okay?"

"Know I'm here if you need anything. You can reach me anytime. Night or day."

I wrapped my hands around my coffee mug and shifted into high gear with an expression of pure vulnerability. I'd even practiced the face in the mirror. "Can I though?" I whimpered. "Can I reach you?"

And boom. Step one complete. I had his personal cell number.

"Now, shall we pick up where we left off?"

I straightened my spine and gave myself the slightest of shakes. "Okay," I said. While I would've preferred to carry on with my miniscule diversion, I also wanted to continue therapy. As depleting as it was, I'd discovered this desire—this need—to say everything out loud. To have another person hear the truth. Even if it was a dud like Dr. Morrison.

"I told you about the special hot chocolate, right?" Eyebrows up, he gave a quick nod. "I mean, that sort of thing went on for a while. Somehow I managed to pretend that everything was fine. That I lived an average life in an average house. But then it happened." I ran my damp hands over my thighs. "One of the girls. I think she woke up."

"Would you like to tell me about it?"

Yes. And also absolutely no.

"In the morning, she wanted to leave. Didn't even want to stay for breakfast. Wanted to call her mom immediately." Her eyes were glassy, pupils wide. She was standing on the porch, her back pressed against the front door. I kept asking her what was wrong, but she wouldn't look at me. Her hand was gripping the fabric near the neck of her pajama top. When she released it, I saw the tag. Sticking out the front. Her shirt was inside out.

Dr. Morrison was writing furiously. Each session, the blur of his pen was bothering me more.

"That sounds quite startling," he finally said. "Do you recall how it made you feel?"

How did thirteen-year-old me feel? Confused? Panicked? Like it was somehow all my fault? That everything in my life was about to blow up? "I would guess I felt unsafe."

"I see."

He sees? Why was he tapping his pen against his paper?

"Once again, I needed to find a solution."

"And did you?"

"Not in so many words."

"Can you clarify what that means, Lainey?"

"Well, let's say a solution found me instead."

He nodded. "I'm here to listen."

And that he was, but I decided to withhold the details this time. Bone thrown, but without much meat.

I didn't mention how I tried to talk to her repeatedly. Following her in the school hallways. Knocking on the door of her house. I was desperate to tell her that nothing had happened. That she'd put her top on wrong and just hadn't noticed. That we'd snuck rum into our hot chocolate, and it had unsettled her. I wanted to use the same trick I used on myself—saying the same lie enough times so the worry resolved and we could still be friends. But she rushed away from me at school. At her home, no one ever answered. Sometimes she'd peek out from behind a curtain like she was afraid of me.

We weren't face-to-face until my uncle and I attended a neighborhood party two weeks later. A group of parents and children. And a long thin pool of aqua-colored water. The backyard was buzzing with chatter and laughter, all the tones blending together into continuous white noise. The adults were sipping vodka punch from plastic goblets, and a few of the kids were stealing whatever they could. Not me though. I had this awareness, a premonition almost, that I needed to stay sharp.

My uncle was stationed at an enormous barbecue, grilling hotdogs. He carried the piled-high plate to a nearby table covered with a checkered tablecloth. There were paper plates and condiments. Opened bags of chips and cheese puffs. Juice boxes. Music blared from speakers tucked up in the leafy branches of the trees, and the kids were dipping their toes into the pool, then squealing about the cold.

My friend was there, but this was a different experience than I'd had at the beach. She wasn't prancing about like some snotty poodle. She just continued to avoid me. In some ways, that made it worse. Losing her made my chest ache.

The afternoon wore into evening. Most of the parents were some degree of soused, and the kids sleepy from the sunshine and the sugar crash. I caught sight of her then, standing on the opposite side of the pool. We stared at each other, and I wished she'd tell me her decision. If the offense was a) the liquor or b) my uncle. And if it was my uncle, did she plan to announce it? I needed to know, but I couldn't ask. The tension of it was unbearable. The spring in my gut tightening.

But instead of giving me some signal, she lifted her arms above her head, hands perfectly overlapping. Then, bending slightly at the waist, she dove in. I stayed where I was, watching her body slip through the clear water. Her long black hair was like fabric covering much of her back, a mermaid ripple each time she kicked.

Using hips and legs, she was gliding along the tiled bottom of the pool. When she eased past a slotted white square, everything changed in an instant. Tendrils of hair sucked up and vanishing. Neck cricking sideways. She must have blocked the pool's filter, as the sound from the jets morphed from smooth flow to desperate gulching.

As I stood there, I could not move. My body fixed and my eyelids refusing to lower. But my brain . . . my brain was revving at a high rpm. *I had to help her. But what was her plan? I had to help her. But what was her plan?* My friend, with a few choice words, could destroy our lives.

She tore at her hair, thrashing about wildly. Though her efforts were silent. A large bubble appeared near her face. In slow motion, it wobbled upward. When it burped the surface, something in me woke up. I opened my mouth, and I screamed.

"Lainey? Where were you just now?"

I looked up. Where was I? Fused to the stone edge of a pool in a damp bathing suit. Trying to process what I'd done. Or failed to do. Until it was too late.

"Sorry," I said. "I'm suddenly tired." Or perhaps I wasn't tired at all. I was just more aware of my weakness.

"Not to worry. Are you comfortable sharing what happened?"

I took a sip of my coffee and pushed the memory down. Distancing myself from that moment. "It was sad, really. There was an unfortunate accident . . ."

Shortly after that, my uncle and I were on the move again. This time he didn't mention a fresh start, his usual line. He said he was convinced I'd been deeply affected by what I'd witnessed. That it was better to be far away from the town where it had happened.

And he was right. I was affected. I'd finally realized that something inside me was broken.

•

After the session ended, I paced around Andrew's condo. Why did it seem so much smaller than it had yesterday? Every single possession felt like clutter. The fruit bowl, the empty glass near the sink, the black leather couch. Even the fridge and cupboards and countertops. I wanted to be in a clean room. A blank room. Engulfed by a brilliant whiteness, where nothing solid existed.

But I couldn't go there. I couldn't go back to that dead place, after I'd fought so hard to climb out of it.

I snatched my phone from the charger. Skimmed my brief, but pleasant, exchange with Elise Morrison. She'd followed up on my earlier invitation.

I sent a new message. Like a barbed hook. The club link, and then:

Here are the details for the jam

Welcome to join

Within seconds, the three dots were undulating.

cool well be ther

CHAPTER TWENTY-EIGHT

Lainey

FROM MY PERCH at the bar, I monitored the bouncer. I'd already handed him a C-note and described the guests I was expecting, but I didn't trust that concussed baboon to get it right.

Andrew's gig was at a club in downtown Callow. Basement level. Purple and orange lights whizzing over the walls, the ceiling. Young women with white-blond hair carrying trays of shots. Already there was a solid crowd, but it wasn't packed yet. Would be soon, though, as Andrew's reputation as a DJ had exploded. Sometimes he pondered giving up his career, but I cautioned against it. Every night in a bar would take a toll on his health, I said. But in truth, his job in security systems was a nine-to-five affair. Which worked for me. I couldn't handle attending nonstop late-night events.

He was standing behind his equipment, headphones covering his ears. More than once he'd tried to explain the process—mixing, crossfading, twisting knobs, scratching up something or another. Deathly dull, and if I was honest, the product mostly sounded the same to me. Random tunes mashed with a generic beat. Though it was highly possible I wasn't the target demographic. A woman tiptoeing into her mid-forties.

I was beginning to wonder if they'd gotten caught sneaking out. But then I saw them. Dr. Morrison's progeny and her sprightly sidekick. Tweedle Dee and Tweedle Dum in their matching short shorts, crop tops, and white platform sneakers. Looking entirely underage and pathetically nervous. The bouncer performed his job and unclipped the velvet rope to let them pass.

Instead of immediately rushing to reintroduce myself, I took time to study my subject. To see how she'd operate in this unfamiliar environment.

The girls hovered around the edges. Clinging to each other. So I stopped one of the willowy servers and, with another C-note, sent her in their direction. She kindly encouraged them to sample her wares. The shooters were called Wolf Bites. Spooky bright green absinthe, and a few drops of grenadine skulking near the bottom. They downed them, shuddered, and reached for seconds.

Not more than fifteen minutes later, they'd taken to the dance floor. Putting the legal-aged occupants to shame with their moves. Effortlessly shuffling their feet, like in the reels I'd seen on Instagram. I recognized the running man. And something that looked like the Charleston on steroids. They were so carefree, as though nothing had ever happened to weigh them down.

How different I'd been as a teenager. After the girl drowned at that party, something in me disintegrated. I gave up trying to blend in or pretend I was normal. I didn't deserve friends. I didn't deserve much of anything. In a way, I tumbled inside myself. I began to fail at school. I refused to bark like a seal to get a pointless grade. At one point, I dyed my hair black, let it hang lank and greasy over my eyes. Plenty of pale foundation. Tried to pierce my lip, too, but I botched it (and still had the tiniest scar as proof).

Andrew moved through his set, and the crowd grew, though I had no issue keeping track of the girls. Their skin had developed a greasy sheen, but they did not slow down. In time to Andrew's music, their torsos shook. As though something other than primitive hearts pulsed inside their chests.

When an older man infiltrated their space, I immediately slid off my stool. Spray-tanned with a basketball belly, he was wearing shorts that looked like patchwork denim. His garish floral shirt had an oversized collar, and to polish off his look, he'd unbuttoned it to mid-chest.

Knees loose and arms bent at right angles, he shimmied in between them. His dancing akin to muscular spasms. The dude was an optical assault.

His focus was exclusively on Elise. Grinding his hips on her. He kept touching her too. First her cheek. Then her shoulder. He even plucked up a lock of her hair and trailed it beneath his nostrils.

As I watched, I brought my hand to my neck. I sensed a discomfort in my trachea, and wondered if I was having a mild allergic reaction to my beverage.

When he looped his hand around her waist, my breath quickened. He octopus-armed her into an embrace, whispering in her ear. He was nodding, but she was shaking her head. Another whisper, and he clutched her wrist. Grinning playfully, but I knew there was nothing playful about it.

Without thinking, I flew toward them, toward the man. Feigning drunkenness, I punted his body with my own. He was knocked backward.

"Watch it," he snarled.

"Sorry, crowded in here." I smacked him again.

"Hey, back off, lady. I'm busy."

"Yeah?" I yelled into his face. While he wasn't quite geriatric, he was easily older than me. "You like pretty girls, huh?"

"Not your concern."

"Is my concern, asshole."

I waved at the bouncer. Gesturing for him to hurry over. Told him that the guy was harassing my guests. Thirty seconds, and the offender was escorted off the premises. Amazing what sort of favors a few dollars can produce. Well worth the humble investment.

"What'd he say?" the other one asked Elise after we'd stepped off to the side.

"He asked me to be his ice cream."

"Seriously? What does that even mean?"

"So he could lick me," she said. But instead of being affronted, she emitted a burst of disgusted laughter.

"Ewwwwww. That's totally gross."

I was getting tired of the music and the people and the sticky floor.

"You girls hungry?"

They turned to face each other, nodding in agreement.

"Totally starving!"

•

Like puppies, they trailed me half a block to a Chinese restaurant that stayed open until 3 a.m. We piled into a booth, and I ordered the late-night basics: egg rolls, dumplings, honey garlic spareribs. A plate of bok choy to be healthy. The lazy Susan in the center of the table was soon full of platters.

"That was, like, awesome," the friend said, as she gnawed a rib.

"Yeah, thanks for inviting us."

Elise Morrison had good manners.

"A pleasure. You guys saved me in a tight spot, remember?"

"Oh yeah. The Addies. I hope you don't need anymore. My mom took them all."

"I'm totally good." Then I casually asked, "So how'd you two get so cool? Guessing cool parents?"

Two loud groans. And then they started. Firing gripe after gripe against their mothers and fathers. As though their families had no part in their evolution, and they were products of spontaneous generation. Frogs burbling up from the mud.

While I ignored the other one's yammering, I gave Elise my undivided attention.

"Dad does absolutely nothing."

"Your father? How do you mean?"

"Never ever wanted to hang out. Or take me anywhere. All he does is work and talk about where he should be. Published here or invited there. I'm like, 'Well just do it. Get on with shit.'"

"You say that to him?"

"No, but I think it though. And his car is a totally cringe color."

"Well, that's the tru—" I caught myself. "I mean, that's too bad. That your father's not more involved. He's missing out." The artwork on his office wall was just for show. "And what about your mother? She still in the picture?"

"Oh, yeah. She totally sucks."

"Geez. Bad luck on both fronts, it seems."

"And she was the one who put that app on Elise's phone. Remember you found it? It's practically stalking, right? Like, is that even legal?"

"Maybe?" I said, but when they both frowned, I added, "It's totally shady, though, no matter what. Who does that sort of thing?"

"Exactly, and she won't leave me alone. Wants to know every single detail of my existence."

"I'm sorry to hear that. She sounds like a trash mother."

"Yeah. I guess." Elise twisted one of her earrings. "But she's not, like, total trash or anything. She just doesn't really have any friends. And she never leaves the house." A slow sigh. "All she seems to do is worry about me. I just wish she didn't treat me like some stupid kid."

"I totally get it," I said, but my mind was yelling, *You are some stupid kid. Didn't a strange man just try to drag you out of a club? And you thought it was amusing?*

I was finding the plethora of complaints difficult to evaluate. While I wasn't shocked by Dr. Morrison's behavior, Elise's description of her mother was a genuine surprise. I couldn't have said exactly what I'd expected, but it certainly was not that. I'd had experience with an undercarer, but I wasn't sure how to make sense of an overcarer. The first was ignorant and thoughtless (even if unintentionally), but the other approach seemed like a painful preoccupation. More self-abuse than anything else.

"Do you have anyone to talk to about it? Like a relative, maybe?" My performance of concern was award-worthy. Gold star for me.

"Not really. Just my grandmother, but she's, like, ancient. Nearly sixty."

"Right, right," I agreed, resisting the urge to roll my eyes. "That's a different generation."

"But"—a toothy grin—"me and Chlo gave her a glow-up and put her on Tinder."

"Really?"

"Not going to lie," the friend added. "Girl looked hot. And she's getting tons of matches, right, Elise?"

"Younger guys too."

"Well, good for her," I said. Nothing wrong with a younger guy. "Your family sounds like a total riot."

CHAPTER TWENTY-NINE

Mia

"ELISE. I'D LIKE you to come home. This evening. After your last lesson."

Mia had walked over to Sandy's house, slipping through the back gate about ten minutes before the start of swimming lessons. The girls were sprawled on lawn chairs in navy suits. When Mia approached, Elise did not look up.

Face angled toward Chloé, she said, "Can you hear something? Like an annoying rumbly sound?"

"That's not funny," Mia replied. "We can discuss this, okay? Sort things out."

"Chlo, can you tell that stranger there's nothing to sort out?"

"Elise says there's nothing to sort out, Mia."

"And that I don't want her messing with my life."

"Um, she doesn't want you messing with her life."

"And that she's trespassing."

"Well. You kind of are, Mia. But it's okay." A sharp finger jab from Elise, and Chloé added, "Mostly."

Mia sighed. "Okay then. I'm not going to push." Though she really wanted to do just that. "I'm here, Elise, whenever you're ready to talk."

"Tell her not to hold her breath."

Sandy appeared on the back deck. "Hey Mia. Everything okay?" She looked at her watch.

"I'm sure you know it's not."

She looked at her watch. "Listen, we're all upset here, but perhaps you should give your daughter some space? Isn't their class starting soon?"

Mia took a step back. "You're giving me advice? Chloé was the one selling medication!"

"Could you be a little more sensitive?" Sandy tilted her head sideways. A young mother with a toddler in her arms was coming through the open gate. She walked quickly past them with a tight smile and down the stone pathway toward the pool. "I'm up to my neck in work today, and I don't need this. I've already spoken to Ian at length."

"He told me." He'd taken full control of the situation with an unsettling degree of ease. Discussing things with Elise. Working through a resolution with Sandy. Making an outlandish suggestion to Mia, as though a baby would be a cure for her issues.

"Then I'm sure he told you what Chloé's father and I decided. What you do with your own kid is your business."

Elise and Chloé had climbed into the shallow end. The child was arm-flapping excitedly on the side, and with a life jacket on, splashed into Elise's arms.

"I do hope you let her carry on with her work." Sandy's voice had softened a little, and she pointed toward the pool. "Look at them, Mia. Things are not all bad, you know."

Without saying anything further, Mia left Sandy's backyard and stood on the sidewalk in front of the house. She was lightheaded, and it wasn't just the heat. Between her former friend and her husband, her role as a parent had not just been diminished. It was obliterated. Mia had no clue what she was supposed to do.

She did not want to go back to an empty house, so she hauled out her phone and texted, *You free?* In seconds, she received the response. *for u? Always.*

Mia met her mother on Main Street. A quaint little café about the size of a walk-in closet, that served drinks in mismatched mugs and had colorful woven wall hangings. It was her mother's suggestion. She claimed it "jelled" with her "boho vibe."

When Mia arrived, Faye was already at the counter. "Two iced hibiscus. With stevia."

The barista cleared her throat, then flat-toned, "Name?"

"Faye. With an E. Like Dunaway."

"Like who?"

"Faye," she repeated. "Just put Faye." Then to Mia, "The education system these days is pitiful."

Mia smiled. Today she welcomed her mother's antics. Even though Faye could often be self-absorbed and overinvolved, she was always available when Mia needed her most.

As soon as they sat down, Faye twitched her hands through the air. "Your aura, sweetheart. It's clinging to your body."

Mia laughed lightly, then said, "I'm not surprised. My sleep has been absolutely awful."

"I promised not to pry, but Ian, I'm guessing?"

"It's okay, Mom. You're not prying." A sigh. "Yes, it's Ian, I suppose, and Elise too. Where to even begin?" She took a deep breath and explained what had happened. "Then she exploded at me."

Tut-tutting, Faye said, "Justifiably so, Mia. What do you expect? Such sly behavior on your part."

"But what she did was incredibly risky. I wanted to protect her."

"The best way to do that is to teach her how to protect herself."

Such a simple approach that made solid sense. It was odd advice coming from her mother, as she'd never had that mentality when Mia was young. For the most part, Mia was left to manage things on her own.

"She's never looked at me that way before," she said. "Like she despises me."

"Obviously. She's a teenager." Faye slurped her bright red drink. "Frankly, these are normal trials and tribulations. I should know. I went through it all with you."

"With me?" She could not recall ever fighting with her mother. In fact, she remembered herself as shy and obedient.

"Yes with you. And it was all so tedious."

"I never hated you."

"No, not hate, but our relationship was often difficult, wasn't it? You weren't happy unless the focus was on you."

"Mom! That's certainly not true." Mia found the characterization outlandish. A total fabrication. Wasn't it?

"If you say so, dear. Perception is a funny animal, isn't it?" Faye shrugged. "Anyway. Why don't you just take these couple of days and relax a little. Read a good book."

She rubbed the side of her neck. It had been stiff since she'd woken up. "I don't know, Mom. I can't manage to relax. Everything seems to be coming at me all at once. Thinking about my life. What I want to do. What I don't want to do."

"It's the stars. I did check your sun and moon signs just this morning, and based on your chart, you're entering a time of transition, you know. A period of chaos." Eyebrows flicking upward. "Coming out of the shell can be painful, darling."

Usually her mother's predictions were easily ignored, but this dart struck its target. "Yeah. I actually feel that."

"Of course you do. Now you also mentioned Ian. What has he done this time?"

Mia hesitated. She wasn't going to bring it up, but as her mother gazed at her intently, she opened her mouth, and out it spilled. "He wants us to have another baby."

Faye's hand stopped midair. "A what?"

"He thinks it would, I don't know, enrich my days. And we could enjoy the experience more this time around."

"So he wants to tether you for twenty more years. Corral you." Her cheeks flushed. "It's almost maniacal."

"I agree it's a crazy idea." Mia's initial view had been similar. Even though he may have been sincere, the idea of it still felt like a bear trap. The jaws stretched open, and if she made a misstep, its teeth would snap, sink into her ankle. "But I don't think he's that way."

"Why? Because you know him so well?"

"Really, Mom. That's unnecessary."

"I'm not trying to be mean, Mia. Just sometimes when a person is too close to something, they can't see it properly."

"I'm his wife, so I'm supposed to be close, aren't I? And I think I see him properly."

"Listen, I'm not going to interfere, but I urge you to exercise caution."

Mia nodded. "To be clear," she said, "it's not something I'm considering."

"What *are* you considering then?"

"Nothing for sure. But it did cross my mind to take a class at the college. Maybe something in fine arts? Or entrepreneurialism? That might be interesting."

Faye straightened her back. "Not to dampen your enthusiasm, but if anyone's got an entrepreneurial energy, it's me, Mia. You really should explore other avenues. Based on your life number, you might consider a career as an organizer."

"Organizer?"

"Yes, one of those women who goes into other people's messy spaces and helps them learn to fold properly. You know, donate things or recycle. There was a whole television series about it. People tuned in to watch that lady."

"I-I don't think I'd enjoy that." Mia felt deflated by her mother's suggestion. In that moment, she desperately wished it was a friend sitting across from her. Someone her own age who could relate to her situation, her struggles. She couldn't grasp why that seemed so far out of reach. What was wrong with her?

"Come now. Why so glum, chum? You shouldn't close yourself off to new experiences. Take me, for an example." She brought her fingertips to her chest. "Putting myself out there. Searching for my life partner. In the filthiest corners of the 'net, I might add. Those apps can be a daunting place."

Mia gripped her glass, slick with condensation. She had to resist slipping into despair. Things would eventually improve. They had to. "Sorry," she said. "I forgot to ask." Maybe hearing about her mother's online escapades might offer some comic relief. Cut through the gray mood. "Have you met anyone?"

"Oh, no one meets just like that, dear." Finger snap. "These things take time, effort, and careful consideration." Faye pulled her phone from an oversized bag and slid on a pair of reading glasses. "But I have participated in multiple chats."

"And?"

"Let's just say I've got a few viable options." She tapped her phone, swiped upward with exaggerated motions. "There's Barry. Fifty-eight. Investment adviser. Or so he claims." Quick glance over the top of her reading glasses. "Likes travel and golden doodles." Screen turned, she showed Mia a photo of a portly middle-aged man "I can feel the upbeat energy, can't you?"

"Sure? He looks promising?"

"And oh, there's Roger. Accountant. Says he's addicted to golf."

"Well, that rules you out. You hate golf."

"Do I? I don't believe I've ever taken a hard stance. Perhaps it's something I might enjoy. Though using the word *addiction* at all seems questionable."

"Maybe he's being silly."

"You can't be too careful, Mia. And just yesterday I matched with Mateo. Doesn't say what he does, but he hums to himself and can't tell his left from his right."

"Bit off the wall."

"Yes, a couple of beige flags, but the hair makes up for it."

Mia had no clue what a beige flag was but decided not to ask. "You're being cautious, though, right?"

"Yes, there have been a few slicksters. You know, the too-good-to-be-true kind, but as soon as they ask for a gift card, I unmatch in a flash." Faye smoothed her hair. "I even had a college boy wanting 'sugar,' I think they call it."

"I hope you didn't entertain that?"

"In the end, no," she said calmly. "We discussed the possibility, but it's really not my jam. Especially with my budget. Can you imagine?"

"No, Mom. I can't." Mia had never seen the inside of a dating app. She could not fathom trying to appraise another person from a few contrived photos and a sentence or two. Then again, was meeting someone at a bar or a gym or a lecture hall that much better? Everyone presented a polished version at the beginning. Or perhaps forever? She and Ian had been together for years, but as Faye had just said, did she really know him? Or only the side of him he'd chosen to display?

"It's like a junk food store. Lots of stuff you'd never eat, but fun to peruse."

"Fun is okay." Mia glanced at Mateo's image, cupped in her mother's palm. Tanned, dimpled, streak of gray. Handsome, but he could be anyone. "As long as you don't take it too seriously."

"Of course I'm taking it seriously. The entire experience is arduous, Mia, and I'd prefer if you didn't dismiss my efforts. Elise and that annoying girl, they did such a stellar job with my profile, I can barely keep up. I'm worn out."

"Speaking of being worn out." Mia recalled the surprise email she'd received that morning. "I have something to give you. To unwind."

"Really? I do like surprises."

"I won a hotel stay, if you can believe it. A single night. First time winning anything in my life."

"And how did that happen?"

"Totally random. I filled in this promo thing on a whim."

"Oh my, Mia." Faye was shaking her head. "Even I know those things are scams. I hope you didn't give anyone your credit card."

"No, I think it's just marketing. I called the location, and sure enough there's a reservation in my name. For me and a plus-one."

"Oh. So you're going with Ian?"

"No, Mom. That's why I'm telling you. I don't want to go."

Nodding, she said, "I can understand why."

"Okay, I'm trying to do a nice thing here. They've got a spa attached to the hotel. The prize comes with a treatment of your choice. I thought you might want to use it."

"Well, thank you then. I could definitely use it. Me and *my* plus-one."

"I thought you hadn't actually met anyone?"

"Not yet, dear. But who knows what tomorrow brings. There are plenty of Rogers and Barrys in the world, and I am going to leave it all up to my spirit guides. What's meant for me won't pass me by."

CHAPTER THIRTY

Mia

AS IAN WAS getting ready to leave for work, Mia once again asked about Elise.

"I have nothing to add," he said, as he placed his canvas backpack on the dining table. "It's for your own good. You need this break just as much as she does."

"That's not fair." Mia did not need or want a break from being a mother.

"Listen. It'll fix itself. And in the meantime, I'm keeping a close eye on things."

Which could mean anything.

"Is that new?" She gestured at a leather satchel. Ian was transferring his laptop and folders into the tawny-colored bag with a sleek silver buckle and crossbody strap.

"Figured it was time to grow up," he said, backpack now emptied. "Apparently it's all the rage in Europe. You like it?"

"Sure," she said. "Looks dapper."

"That's all that matters. I'll send you the link; you can get one too." He pecked her cheek, then breezed out the door.

She went to the front window and watched him stroll toward his car. His outfit was not the usual either. Instead of a dress shirt, he was wearing a linen sweater over a white tee. He backed onto the street, and just before driving away, checked his reflection in the rearview. Picking away a smudge of breakfast from his mouth and then ruffling his own hair.

After discovering Ian's infidelity, she'd read a vast number of articles detailing "surefire ways" to know if your partner is cheating. The basic premise was that men settled into a comfortable routine, and change might signal an outside influence. Perhaps he'd begun reading a different genre of book. Or recently developed a taste for spicy food. Or even had brand-new opinions on foreign politics. A man rarely divulged an affair but often could not resist newfound enthusiasms that arose because of it. Even when talking with his wife, the very person he was betraying.

Was Ian's sudden reservation about his tattered backpack a sign? What about the subtle shift in his attire? All meaningless scraps, but they gave her a bad feeling.

•

Upstairs in her bedroom alcove, she settled into her chair with her laptop and a glass of sweetened iced tea. Something else to focus on, that was what she needed. Despite her mother's career advice, she perused classes in the college's creative arts department. Pottery. Glass blowing. Photography. They even offered a course on turning a passion into a viable business.

All the images on the department website were the same. Every single person was young and brimming with energy. Big toothy smiles. Doubt immediately percolated through her. Was she capable of doing any of those things? Was she too old? Then her mind drifted to Ian. Did he spend his days surrounded by such vibrant twenty-somethings? Were those the sorts of students who took his classes? Might one of them recommend a fancy new bag to their professor?

Clearly her attempt to shift gears was not working. She peeked at the computer's clock. Ian's morning lecture had started, and after that, he had office hours. He would be away from his computer until noonish.

A few clicks and she had accessed his desktop folder. She felt a ripple of nervous excitement when she noticed an unviewed file. As though there was a flashing headline. Next chapter: now available.

"I was getting fed up with it."

"With what?"

"Relocating. Constantly."

With Ian and his patient now onscreen, Mia sat up. She took a long sip of her drink.

"And what did 'getting fed up' look like?"

Ian's fawn eyes flicked to his open notebook, then back to Lainey Kemper. Mia could easily decipher his expression. *Desire* was too strong a word, but it was painfully obvious he wanted her to elaborate. Probably to describe an instance of violence or aggression. Believing, no doubt, he could pinpoint the moment when a fuzzy little seed of reprisal began to sprout. Mia was almost relieved when his patient didn't take the bait.

"Mostly I started to resist bringing anyone over."

"That's it?"

"Yeah."

"Did your uncle react to th-this new boundary?"

"I mean, for the first while, he never mentioned anything. But then, I guess, he'd press me. 'Any new friends?' That sort of thing."

She paused for a moment, then said, "You might not think so, but his concern was legitimate. He had his . . . his disorder, but he also wanted the best for me. It was all . . . I don't know. Intermingled?"

Ian was nodding in the most unconvincing way. Was he that unaware of himself? Mia was finding it increasingly difficult to watch him.

"And were you meeting any young people?"

"No. I decided I was done with that. I never wanted another friend. It was better that way."

"That must have been difficult, Lainey. Teenagers are naturally social. Wanting to be accepted by their peers."

She smiled. "You'd have direct awareness, right? With your daughter. She's about what? Fifteen? Sixteen?"

Mia shifted in her seat. If the woman hadn't seen Elise, how could she estimate an age?

"I'm simply saying it seems like a lonely life."

"Well, company is overrated." She folded her arms across her chest. "But I'd be lying if I said I was alone for long. I did meet someone . . . eventually."

"Oh?"

"It was unexpected, and as I said, I was dead set against friendship. But it's time to talk about her. That girl." An unmistakable scowl. "She became like a little sister to me. Or so I thought at the time."

"She sounds important to you. Please go on."

Mia tapped a fingernail against her front tooth. Ian's response made no sense. She'd read his private notes from Albethey, and there was never any mention of a little sister type friend. Which suggested, to Mia at least, that the person was not important at all.

"It was a few weeks into fall term at a new school. I let down my guard. Which I realize was a mistake. But hindsight, and all."

As Lainey Kemper spoke, her expression flattened. Mia listened intently as she described with caliper precision the details of that first interaction.

"I was skipping class, hiding in the bathroom, marking up the walls of a stall." With a quick tap on the keyboard, Mia increased the volume by a single bar. "I was about to leave, but I heard noises coming from the next stall over. Like someone smacking themselves. Then this whimpering. I don't know why I spoke up, but I asked if she was okay, and this tiny voice whispered, 'I'm bleeding.'"

"An injury?" Ian said, making a note on his yellow legal pad.

Mia rolled her eyes, and Lainey Kemper gave him a withering look. "Her period."

Apparently, the girl was not distraught about ruining her clothes but over the reaction she anticipated from her mother. A fury that "female things" had started.

"I told her that was beyond dumb. Not like she had control over it. And if her mother's that screwed up, why even tell her? She should go with her friends and get her own stuff. But she didn't answer me. I just heard more smacking sounds. Even worse. So I did something entirely out of character."

Pen poised, Ian said, "Which was?"

Mia shook her head. Could he get any worse? Lainey Kemper was sharing a simple moment of adolescent kindness, one girl supporting another. The only reaction required was gentle attentiveness. Not a bent head, hand and pen a blur. Gathering up the details, as though fleshing out a chapter of his future book.

"I offered to meet her after school. Then I unzipped the front pouch of my bag, plucked out a pad, and held it close to the bottom of the stall. This chubby hand appeared and snatched it. When she emerged a minute later, she was a . . . surprise."

"How do you mean?"

"I don't know exactly, but she was small and round and wore these clunky glasses. Her eyes were freakishly huge." LK smiled then, her gaze momentarily distant. "Like she was in this permanent state of alarm. Though maybe she was?"

"Would you say you felt, perhaps, some tenderness toward her?"

"Tenderness? I don't think I felt much of anything. But she, on the other hand, she looked . . . hopeful. For what, I had no clue."

"Did she show up after school?"

"She did. We went to the mall, and on the way, she held my hand. As though it was the most natural thing in the world. I recall thinking it was pleasant and unpleasant at the same time. I fought the urge to snap it back."

"An innocent expression of affection, no doubt."

Lainey Kemper did not respond for several seconds. Finally she said, "I was drawn to her, Dr. Morrison. In a way I can't explain. Being next to her made me feel unwell."

"Unwell?" He wrote that down too. "Emotionally?"

"I don't know. Almost queasy."

"That does make sense, Lainey. Any form of attachment involves risk."

"Yeah. Sure. So . . . so I decided to do her that one favor. Steal a shitload of sanitary products and then never speak to her again."

When Mia's cell phone rang, she jumped. Her finger darted to press the pause button on her laptop. Glancing down, she saw the caller ID. Her mother. Mia let it ring out, but within seconds, it rang again.

"Sorry," she said when she swiped to answer. "I was in the washroom."

"I needed to call you, darling. We must talk."

"About?"

"The hotel stay. I wanted to thank you."

"I'm glad you enjoyed the room."

"The room was ho-hum, but the massage knocked me off my feet. It was positively life-affirming. I'm reinvigorated." A shuddering moan. "My masseuse was a genius with his fingertips. A very muscular man, I might add, and he made short work of my knots."

"That all sounds, um, positive?" Mia adjusted her laptop so the sun was not obscuring the corner of her screen.

"At first I felt a little sheepish, taking your prize, but I quickly let that go. I've given so much, you know. And I've come to some realizations."

"About?"

"Basically it's time to dig a little deeper. To discover who I really am. Not allow old vibrations to drag me down."

"Do vibrations have an age?"

"You don't understand. I mean days gone by. I'm not going to be afraid anymore."

There was something odd about the image frozen on her desktop.

"Afraid of what, Mom? Maybe don't, um—"

"You know how hard I've tried to get my footing. I know you've had a bump here or there, so I'm . . . one to begrudge . . . but I will call a spade a . . . and I refuse to keep . . ."

Faye's voice began to fade away. Mia brought her face closer to the screen. Usually Lainey Kemper's blinds were closed, or perhaps Mia had never noticed before. But in this session, they were raised. Through the window, Mia could see a wide expanse of weeping willows and oaks. And a distinctive brick structure rising right in the middle. Could that be a clock tower?

"Mom?" Mia whispered. "I have to go."

Ian had never given a single hint: Lainey Kemper still lived in Callow.

CHAPTER THIRTY-ONE

Lainey

I LICKED MAYO from the side of my thumb. With only ten minutes before my next session, I'd thrown together a sandwich. Thick slice of salted tomato on farmhouse toast.

As I hacked off bites, I paced around Andrew's condo. Hoping to quell the vibration in my shoulders, my neck. Almost a low-level fizziness. Like my damp skin was pressed against a nine-volt.

Had the sensation been there when I left Om Bliss? Or did it arrive when I stopped at the convenience store to buy tampons? At some point, I'd become aware of my body's movements. My slow stride, the way my hand reached to grip a box. Almost as though I could see myself. And I had the tingly awareness that someone else saw me too. For a split second, I was certain Elise Morrison had drifted around the end of the aisle, but when I checked, she wasn't there.

Likely it was all in my head. *Calm the mind, calm the body* was one of the lines I whispered at the start of cooldown during yoga. Mostly I thought it was drivel, but perhaps there was something to it. Since I'd mentioned the bathroom girl to Dr. Morrison, she kept crawling into my head. *Bug.* That was the nickname I'd given her all those years ago. She was bug-eyed. Bug-sized. If I wanted to, I could've squished her bug skull with one stomp of my Doc Martens.

After my kindness at the mall, we went our separate ways. It was a large school, and I didn't expect to see her again. But the following day, she appeared on the sidewalk behind me. Her feet skittering over the concrete, skipping to catch up.

"Hey," she said. "Where you going?"

"Nowhere. You wouldn't like it."

"I might. Can I come?"

I didn't answer, but she scampered along beside me. Tried to hold my hand again, but I yanked it away. We were not toddlers. We were not freaks.

Without a blink, she trailed me through a slit in a chain-link fence and then into an abandoned low-rise office building set to be demolished. I remembered wondering if the structure understood its fate. That something taller, sleeker would take its place. Which, I'd already determined, was the way the world worked.

I had a tiny Maglite in my back pocket, and as I entered the stairwell, I clicked it on. With every step I took, I could hear her footsteps. Mirroring my own. It gave me an odd comfort, which in turn made me uncomfortable.

We climbed the stairs until we reached a door that had already been kicked open. All I needed to do was push, and we emerged onto a flat roof. Based on the mess, it was popular spot. Smashed bottles, empty cans. Exterior walls tagged with symbols. Boring hearts and various initials. *Auggie was here.* When a fluffy cloud skuttled across the sun, we were both cast in shadow. Wind moved around her. Wind moved through me.

She leaned against the wall and slid downward. Her palms pressing on the ground. "I don't like heights," she murmured.

More lameness, I thought, as I drifted closer to the edge. "I love them."

"Why?"

"Gives me vertigo." I hopped onto the concrete lip that bordered the roof and let my arms jut outward. To my right, a modest eight-story plummet. A paved wasteland of faded yellow lines and spindly weeds rising up through the cracks.

"You're afraid you might fall?"

"No, it's being afraid of wanting to fall." I wobbled my limbs like an inflatable tube man outside a car dealership. "It's l'appel du vide. The call of emptiness. I read that somewhere."

"You must have weird books. Doesn't that scare you? The . . . the call?"

"Who cares? I like to tease myself with the potential. Play with it."

For several moments, I wavered on the edge, gusts nudging me toward oblivion. In the distance, I could see the city's crappy downtown. When I turned toward her, her face was sheet white. Her chin quivered, and she hiccupped several times. Then she started to cry. "Don't," she said. "Don't play with it."

The sight of her weeping made my muscles seize. I had a feeling, but I could not identify it. In my gut, I knew she wasn't faking. And I really wanted her to stop.

I leapt down from the edge, stormed past her and through the door. Down the stairs into the safety of the top floor. Beige light poured through the windows, revealing a series of empty cubicles. Stubby white divisions that had once contained entire lives. Everything was covered in dust and debris. Mold flourished in the stained industrial carpet.

I sat down on the dirty floor. Wiped my sweating hands on my school kilt. In a moment, she was nestled in beside me. Her freckled face was wet from tears, but she grinned and said, "What do you want to do now?"

Opening my book bag, I pulled out paper and pencil. "Here. Write down your biggest wish. I'll do the same. Then crumple it up."

I'd never admitted the words I wrote. A syrupy sentiment that I attributed to being a hormonal teenager. Though even in my forties, I was still an absolute loser and desired the same thing: a genuine friendship that lasted forever.

I brought a flame to the tiny scrap that lay on her palm and then to mine. She didn't flinch as her secret caught and curled. Fragments of black lifted by an invisible draft. Ash stuck to her hair, her cheek.

I reached over and swiped the fragment that clung to her forehead. Creating a gray smear just above her eyebrows. A new beginning.

"Now they'll come true?"

"Who knows."

"Cool," she whispered.

"Cool," I whispered back.

Even now, I still struggled to identify the emotion that flooded me in those moments. It was akin to a visceral sense of want. Almost vulturous. All I knew was that my loneliness, which had pulsed and hollowed for as long as I could remember, was suddenly gone.

•

"So you took a chance?"

"I did, Dr. Morrison."

After that day, Bug and I were inseparable. Walking to school together every morning, swapping lunches, meeting after class to explore. Nowhere was off-limits. We climbed trees, traipsed through cemeteries, and sat under old bridges during heavy rainfalls. We smoked stolen cigarettes, listened to cassette tapes backward, and sliced open our fingertips, smashing our blood together. Once she had me pretend I was blind and then led me along the streets for hours. I never so much as stubbed a toe.

She experienced life with a fullness that was foreign to me. Nothing in half measures. I marveled at how her happiness was the happiest of happy. Her sorrow, a deep and debilitating suffering. Her anger, a passionate punch to the proverbial gut. It wasn't long before I loved her. I wanted to keep her for myself and took steps so our connection would stay hidden. But at the same time, I believed I was breaking my uncle's rules. I was concealing something.

"Did he find out?"

"At first, he didn't."

But everything changed that afternoon she knocked on the front door of my house. And my uncle, with a warm and wide smile, welcomed her in.

CHAPTER THIRTY-TWO

Lainey

ANDREW HAD TAKEN a sleeping pill, and I had restless legs. Restless arms too. And possibly even a restless skull, which had to be a legitimate medical phenomenon. I could not close my eyes without seeing Bug.

When I was at Albethey, she never came to visit. No one did. At the beginning, I was so disconnected from myself, I was oblivious. But when the ghost of me receded, I discovered not a single soul was waiting on the other side. There wasn't even a letter. I didn't resent her for that. However, I did expect us to pick up where we'd left off when I reentered the world. She'd acknowledge what I had done, and our crazy-glue attachment would be even crazier. Friendship resumed.

After I left the institution, I tried to locate her. First thing I did was go to her home. But instead of Bug answering the door, it was an irritable man with two chihuahuas. I went to all our old hangout spots. Scanned every unfamiliar face. I even went to our high school, but she'd ceased to exist beyond a sullen photo in a yearbook. After that, I conjured up reasons for her disappearing act. She was traveling the globe. Or had joined a commune. Maybe we were having identical experiences. Each struggling to find the other. I had reverted to my original name, after all. Not that Lainey Greene would be complicated for her to figure out. Bug knew all about my mother. She was the only person I'd ever told.

Eventually I accepted that she'd consciously chosen obscurity. She no longer wanted a friendship. From that rejection, a kernel of hatred slowly germinated. More recently, though, it had begun to flourish.

When Andrew rolled onto his back, his chainsaw-loud snoring forced me from the bed. I tugged on a pair of yoga pants and a thin black hoodie. Then went to the kitchen, where I perched on a stool at the island and opened my laptop.

During a recent session, Dr. Morrison and I had discussed my "difficult" relationship with my partner, and he spoke of the importance of building out my life. Recognizing that I was an individual with independent interests. With that in mind, I'd decided to start a fresh project. It was research-based. The results of which were entirely unexpected. Empowerment: *check!*

In the glow of my screen, I pondered the next steps of my personal endeavor. How best to present my findings in a creative and engaging way? And who might I present them to? Perhaps a write-up was unnecessary, and a photo compilation would be the most arresting. I got down to business.

Crop and drag. Crop and drag. Enhance. Adjust brightness. Crop and drag. The exercise was repetitive but it settled my mind, and I was finding the task to be immensely fulfilling.

Once the project was completed, I wasn't sure what to do with myself. My energy still hadn't dissipated. Sex was out of the question, as Andrew was down for the count, and I wasn't in the mood to self-serve. I stuffed my feet into my runners and slipped out the front door of the condo.

I had no plan. I even whispered that to myself as I rode the elevator to the lobby. "Lainey. You do not have a plan." A quick nod to the smiling concierge, and I strode out through the gold and glass doors.

A recent rainfall made the light from the lampposts splinter. Other than a folded figure dozing on a bench, the sidewalks were empty. I wandered, inhaling the humid night air until I nearly smacked into a glass enclosure. At that moment, Callow's night bus was pulling up to the stop. When the door opened, I barely gave it a thought and climbed the grimy steps.

I rode west across the city. Then took an alternate bus north, and I exited by a quaint strip of stores and restaurants. Behind those, a quiet pocket of family homes. Almost everything was closed at that hour, but I followed a reedy thread of jazz music and discovered a cocktail joint above a French bistro. Luck was on my side that evening; I'd just made last call. I ordered a gin and tonic, double lime.

It took the man at the end of the bar all of thirty seconds to sidle over. A local, no doubt. I imagined that he had a wife and baby at home. That his interest in his marriage had waned, but he was dedicated to keeping up appearances. The white shorts and white polo screamed tennis enthusiast.

"Are you with someone?"

Was I? At this specific moment, I was not. "It's complicated," I replied.

He unhinged his oversized maw and out shot a boisterous laugh. "You're one of those."

"Perhaps I am." I had no reason to be snarky to the gentleman.

He was nursing a deep brown martini. Balanced on top, a thin metal skewer with a spiraling tongue of lemon peel. "I see you enjoy a decent cocktail"—he gestured toward my drink—"but what else are you into?"

Another ambiguous question. And of course, my mind went *there*. Down on all fours. Double mounted. Gimp suit. I could say any of those things to tantalize him, but what I really wanted was small and simple. Someone to call late at night. Someone who'd laugh at my moronic jokes. Someone who knew the grittiness and perversion of my origin story and continued to care.

"I'm looking for a friend."

"I've been told I'm very good at that. Being a friend."

"I might've guessed." When I offered my best coquettish tee-hee, his meaty hand settled on my upper thigh. A question mark for me to ponder.

I suspected he viewed himself as subtle and suave. Assumed the effect of his touch had caused a hot rush of blood, parts of me blooming. Totally unaware that my muscles had locked in a painful clench.

Next move was mine.

As I leaned my cheek onto my palm, my left hand searched the contents of my purse. Then I shifted forward in my seat, allowing his knuckles to reach their destination: the warmth between my legs. Edging even closer, I plucked up the skewer from his drink, and the rind toppled off. As I stirred seductively, I also opened my palm. Three tiny Adderall tablets disappearing in the dark liquid.

"So," I said to spark conversation, "I'm Sylvie, and you are . . ." I could have left immediately, but I'd spent seventy-five bucks on those drugs, so I deserved a visual.

"Tim."

I nearly snorted. Another Tim. Was there a rulebook or an *Idiot's Guide* for these sorts of encounters? When in doubt, be inoffensive Tim.

"Well, Tim. While we finish up our drinks, why don't you tell me about yourself."

Few of the male species can resist the invitation to brag. After fifteen minutes of droning on about his investment career, his boat and lakeside cottage, the size of the carp he'd caught last weekend, he unbuttoned his shirt. His right knee began to jerk up and down.

"Doing okay, Tim?"

"Yeah, just my heart's racing." A shaky grin. "Must be your effect on me."

"Or the espresso?" Gesturing toward his near-empty glass.

He nodded vigorously, and after another few minutes elapsed, he began tapping the bar with his fingertips. Trying to get the server's attention. "Was that a double shot?"

"You really should watch the caffeine," I offered, trying to be helpful. "We get more sensitive to it as we age."

I stayed with my bar buddy for a short while longer, but when he gripped his chest, used profanity, I took my leave. Our bartender could offer support. A sixty-milligram dose wasn't going to kill him, but he'd be awake for a while. Maybe even productive?

After my miniscule diversion, I roamed the leafy side streets. The first shock arrived when I caught sight of a pricey little sports car. The second when Dr. Morrison's palatial home appeared before me. I stood on the sidewalk, staring at it. "Ah, Lainey," I whispered. "You had a plan. Don't be coy with yourself."

Every window was dark. Even the lamppost bulb needed replacing. I waffled, I honestly did, before I strode across the driveway, past the garage, and slipped around the shrubs at the corner.

I assumed they had a security system. But I was banking on the fact they were the same as most people. Never bothering to arm it. They paid the monthly charge and relied on the window stickers to keep them safe.

I crept along the side of their house. Peering through a casement window at ground level, I was surprised to discover Elise Morrison's bedroom. Whose else could it be? A night-light, in the shape of a rabbit's head, softly illuminated the space. She had a queen-sized bed, neatly made with a puffy comforter, umpteen pillows and stuffed animals. Her clothing was folded at the foot. Floral decals adorned the walls. The room was oddly spotless for a girl that age, but perhaps they had help.

Not only was her window unlocked, it was also slightly ajar. Just enough to wriggle my arm through. With a swift shove, I managed to pop out the screen. Then cranked the lever. Several twists, and the gap was wide enough to slide my body through. Other than a scrape on my hip bones, entry was pathetically easy.

I exited the bedroom, nothing more than a shadow among shadows. As I drifted up the stairs, I took a moment to check in with myself. My legs were limber, jaw loose, shoulders completely relaxed. No physical identifiers of tension or fear, which I'd have expected during a burglary. Not that I intended to take anything. (The opposite in fact.) Unfortunately, I'd be unable to get Dr. Morrison's perspective on my current emotional landscape. Which I labeled *chill exhilaration*.

The area at the back of the house was open concept, and compared to Andrew's condo, the scale was cavernous. There were two built-ins on either side of a grand fireplace, full of books and decorative white pottery. Matching glass hurricanes flanked an ornate mirror. A set of three succulents sat on the windowsill behind the kitchen sink, and a KitchenAid mixer was tucked into the corner on the countertop. The house was magazine-perfect, but something was off. The combination of their belongings did not spell h-o-m-e.

I wandered down the hallway, past a dining room and a living room. Then another flight of stairs to the upper level. The landing was enormous, but all the doors were closed. A wall sconce, dimmed to its lowest level, barely illuminated the mostly empty space.

In a corner, there were several paint tins, plus a roller and tray. Beside that, a couple of carboard boxes. I stepped closer. Balanced on top was a wicker basket full of what appeared to be dirty laundry. I plucked up one of Dr. Morrison's dress shirts from the pile and brought it to my nose. I expected citrus and tobacco, but it mostly smelled of sweat. Turning in a circle, I knew one of the doors led to the primary bedroom. No one used the phrase *master suite* anymore, unfortunately. But I decided further investigation would be ill-advised. I tossed the shirt back into the basket and retraced my steps.

When I reached the kitchen again, I heard a door opening above me. Then somebody tiptoeing down the stairs. Instead of scrambling, I quickly backed into a darkened corner by the oversized windows. Moments later, Dr. Morrison's wife appeared in the kitchen. Standing stock-still, I held my breath. The woman was fifteen feet away from me, if that. I did not budge as she poured a glass of water and then opened the fridge. For what felt like forever, she stared at her groceries but did not select anything. Instead, she closed the door and leaned her forehead against the stainless steel. I thought she'd dozed off, but then I heard a shuddery sigh. Finally she retreated. Her slippered feet slishing over the hardwood. Up the stairs. Click of her door closing.

The noninteraction was unsettling. Not once did she turn toward me. She did not sense my presence or notice my energy. Didn't even detect a whiff of unfamiliar perfume. How was that possible?

As I waited in the corner, ensuring the coast was clear, I thought about the night nurse at Albethey. Each shift, she was responsible for bringing me pills in a tiny white paper cup. Same as they showed on television. But in reality, there was no hiding medicine under the tongue or tucked into the cheek. Blue glove snapped on, she'd check every crevice with exploratory fingers. I did bite her once, and though the crunch was satisfying, it did not serve me. For weeks after, they restrained me, and the medication was administered through a needle. So I acquiesced. No matter how hard I fought, those chemicals were going inside me.

At the end of every visit, after I'd raged like some sort of injured animal, she said the same thing. Which, at that time, I thought was a pacifying statement of fact. And if I was honest with myself, there were moments when I still feared it was true.

"Okay, okay, Lainey. I can't even see you. You're not even there."

CHAPTER THIRTY-THREE

Mia

MIA KNEW HER behavior the previous afternoon had been incredibly impulsive. She felt jittery when she thought about it.

The online sleuthing had seemed innocent enough. She had two facts to go on: Ian's patient resided in Callow, and she worked as a yoga instructor. Mia was systematic in her approach. Creating a Word doc with a complete list of all the studios in town and then moving through the city geographically, radiating out from locations by the clock tower. Most had colorful websites. And nearly all had an About section with photographs of their staff.

Finally, Lainey Kemper appeared on the site of an upscale natural health center called Om Bliss. A flawless headshot with an earnest expression. Underneath the image, the name Lainey G.

When a "Would you like a free class?" pop-up appeared on her screen, she checked the schedule. "Lainey G" was teaching at that moment, and her session would end in exactly thirty-five minutes.

Then Mia did a terrible thing. She'd driven across the city, at high speed. Rolling through stop signs and running yellow lights.

She'd found a parking spot close to Om Bliss and lingered until the woman emerged. Without thought, Mia had trailed her for two blocks and then waited as she entered a convenience store.

Through the glass, she watched Lainey Kemper gliding up and down the aisles. Selecting items, evaluating labels. Every action was mundane. No one would ever guess her past was riddled with darkness. She was simply a striking woman, skin still dewy from exercise, buying hygiene products and barbecue chips.

It was disorienting. Being so close to Ian's patient. She could never have predicted she would engage in such brazen behavior, or feel the adrenaline rush that resulted from it.

•

Taking a deep breath, Mia accessed Ian's computer. She'd already accepted that her actions were ethically wrong. And probably evidence of OCD or some other psychiatric disorder Ian could identify. But when her mind was filled with thoughts of Lainey Kemper, she did not think about his affair. She also did not think about her estrangement from Elise. Or the penetrating worry that the years ahead held nothing for her except dullness and decay.

Her cursor hovered over the file folder. She double-clicked.

"He had his pattern, Dr. Morrison. The hot chocolate never came right away."

"That must have been incredibly stressful."

"Yeah. I was on edge all the time. He kept inviting her back, and she kept showing up. I could tell my uncle was getting irritated with the way I was acting."

"Can you be more specific?"

"I don't know. I threw away all the lingerie, and I never offered her so much as a sip of alcohol. His porno movies were out, but I just feigned embarrassment and threw a blanket over them."

"And the Polaroids? Did you keep the camera?"

"I told you already. I didn't take any more."

"Understood."

"Though that's not the total truth. I did hold the camera out and take a photo of the two of us. She had this huge grin. Her face was mostly teeth." As Lainey Kemper spoke, her shoulders drooped. "I still have it, you know."

Watching her expression, Mia experienced an unexpected wave of compassion.

"So you were on a tightrope, would you say? Trying not to upset your uncle and still holding on to your new relationship. Shielding your friend."

"As much as possible given the circumstances. But I was always waiting."

"Waiting?"

"Yeah. And it finally happened. She was sitting on the carpet near the coffee table. I remember she had a needle and thread in her hand. Maybe there was a dish of beads? Anyway. I was on the couch, reading or something. It was almost a relief when he called out. Asking us to join him in the kitchen. He was the one who suggested that Bug sleep over, and after she called her mother for permission, he started with his elaborate show. When he slid that yellow mug toward her, he gave this friendly wink."

"And then?"

"As soon as he turned his back, I whispered, 'Don't drink the hot chocolate. Don't even taste it.'"

"I'm assuming she questioned you later?"

"Of course she did. It was weird, and she was confused, Dr. Morrison. I couldn't explain. But he'd made his intent clear for that night, and I knew I had to ward him off." She paused, and scratched at her neck. "We squished into my bed, and I pulled a length of kitchen twine from my nightstand. I bound our wrists together."

"No doubt that led to more questions?" Ian's head was angled, reminding Mia of a dog asking for a treat.

"Not so much. I said I was the worst sleepwalker. I can recall her exact response. 'I'll be your security.' And then I said, 'I'll be your security too.' We locked pinkies. Swore to protect each other forever. Even though we were essentially kids, that promise had weight."

"She trusted you."

"She did. I trusted her too. Though I knew there were limits."

"Did the trick work?"

"Yeah. When we woke up, the twine was still intact. After she'd gone home the next morning, I told him I wanted her to be mine. 'Just this one, Uncle James.' I literally begged him. 'Please. Just her.'"

"What was his response?"

She shook her head. "I could see it in his eyes. They were dark and shiny. And he said to me, 'That's not how this works, puppet.'"

The hair on Mia's arms stood up.

"And how did that make you feel?"

"I don't know. I must have been scared. Or upset? Maybe both? I knew our game would not end. I knew he would never let me keep her for myself."

•

Mia shoved laundry into the front-loading machine. She needed to reorient herself before Ian came home for dinner. That last video was deeply draining. She could not imagine the emotional complexity for a child. What were the options? If Lainey Kemper told an adult, her guardian would go to jail, and she'd become a ward of the state. But keeping her uncle's revolting secret put other children at risk. How could a young teen possibly handle that situation? Day in and day out, it must have created such a snarl of fear and guilt and self-loathing.

When Mia tossed in one of Ian's shirts, she heard a metallic clink. Something had fallen from the pocket. Digging through the mound of items in the drum, she expected to find a coin or a button, not a thumb drive. It was such a brilliant red, it was practically glowing.

Her fingers closed around it. For no reason she could articulate, her palm suddenly started to tingle. She immediately abandoned her chore and returned to her laptop.

As soon as she opened the USB drive, images began appearing on her screen. *Pop. Pop. Pop.* One opening after the other. Five. Ten. A hundred. Then two hundred. So quickly, she could barely register them. Innumerable stills from a video. A bare backside. An erect penis. Familiar hands gripping slender hips. An entropy tattoo across a shoulder blade. And then: the ugly contortion of Ian's face.

Mia's body turned icy cold, while her brain scrambled for a soothing explanation. *These are old. He'd forgotten about the drive and brought it home to destroy it. He was ashamed to admit he'd made a recording of his one-time-only tryst.*

Drip disclosure. That was the term she'd read online. The truth revealed in dribs and drabs. A slick approach that made it easier for the liar, while each new piece of information created fresh devastation for the one betrayed.

But then she saw it. Leaning against an unfamiliar bed frame. Ian's brand-new leather satchel.

CHAPTER THIRTY-FOUR

Lainey

"MY UNCLE INVITED her to join us on our summer vacation. At that cabin."

"I'm sorry, Lainey, I'm not trying to contradict you, but all past accounts indicate you and your uncle were alone that entire week. The property owners, the police, your own—"

"And as I explained, Dr. Morrison, I'm telling the truth *now*. Unless you'd prefer I lie?"

"No. No, of course not." A faux smile replaced the consternation. "I apologize for my interruption. I'm eager to hear what you have to share."

Eager. That was obvious. At the beginning, having a rapt audience had been ego-boosting, but I'd since concluded two things. First, the man who'd once enthralled me was patently dull. And second, talk therapy was a total time waster. Even so, I'd decided to trudge onward. I was always one to finish what I started.

"This cabin," he continued. "I have my notes, of course, but why don't you tell me about it. As you remember it today."

"I doubt my description would be much different. Rustic. Nothing fancy. Two bedrooms on either side of the upper floor. An attic full of board games and moth-bitten blankets. There was a huge lake." When my uncle and I arrived, I had thought the setting was almost magical. "The only flaw was a pile of gray boards."

"From?"

"Oh, come on, Dr. Morrison. You know the answer to that."

"Yes, of course. The construction debris."

"Exactly." The owners had built a new dock but hadn't removed the junk. "We were told to use it as firewood."

He gazed at me over his glasses. "Any neighbors?"

"And you know that already too. There were no neighbors for miles." The cabin was completely isolated.

"Just gentle questions to aide your recollections."

I needed no gentle questions. That place was seared in my mind.

"My uncle had offered to drive Bug, but her mother said she needed to accompany her daughter. And they'd make their way on their own."

"Did your uncle hesitate? Having another adult around?"

"No, he came alive, actually. Like when I was younger and he had th-those relationships."

We'd been there a couple of days before they arrived. My uncle and I were on the front veranda when we saw their car, puttering through the thick brush. The passenger door kicked open, and my friend scampered out into the yard. My uncle's hand tightened around the flaking banister.

Bug shook herself like a puppy released from its cage, then squealed, "We're here!" She raced toward me, sweaty feet squeaking in her cheap flip-flops. A tight hug for me, and then a hug for my uncle. "I seriously thought I'd ralph in the car."

"When Bug's mother emerged, the sight was a ground-tilter."

"That's an interesting turn of phrase. Could you define that for me, Lainey?"

"She'd driven there wearing only a skimpy bikini, cherry colored, and a mesh beach wrap knotted around her waist. Let's just say the fabric was thin and overfilled." Soft mounds of her spilled out the sides.

Under his breath, my uncle whispered, "Oh."

I was confused. Remembering what Bug had said ages ago in the bathroom. How her mother hated all that girl stuff. But here she was, sashaying her hips, her ass as she moved around the car. The body of a Venus on full display. I whispered to Bug, "Your mom's, like, va-va-voom."

She grimaced. "You think?"

"Total sexpot."

"Maybe James will like her, and they'll get married, and we'll be real sisters."

"Yeah, maybe." I resisted the glimmer of hope. I already knew how such a scenario would inevitably play out, and I certainly didn't want that.

"Allow me," my uncle said as Bug's mother started to hoist a full-sized suitcase from the trunk.

"Oh thank you, James. I've overpacked a titch." She flicked her hair. "Like women do."

"Not to worry. I'm at your service."

When they shook hands, I caught sight of a ruby-colored fingernail poking the veins of his wrist.

Within minutes, Bug had changed into a tiny blue swimsuit. Her limbs were pasty white, stomach distended like a toddler's. Hair its usual bird's nest.

"Who's coming in?" she hollered. Then she announced her own intentions with "I am, I am!"

She ran to the end of the dock and cannonballed into the lake. When she came back up, she sputtered and cried out, "Rotten eggs! All of you!"

A quick glance at my uncle. He was transfixed.

Minutes later, she clambered back onto the dock, water dripping, teeth chattering. My uncle rushed toward her with a plush towel. A snap of fabric in the air, and then he wrapped it tightly around her shoulders. His hands rubbed up and down her arms. "Give it a sec," he said. "You'll warm right up."

"He was so gentle with her, Dr. Morrison, I remember thinking to myself that maybe . . . maybe it would be okay."

"That's a common response during periods of high stress. Ignoring past experiences and establishing a false narrative so you feel safer."

I inwardly groaned.

"In the days after that, everything was about my friend. Did she need sunscreen? Did she want to borrow his ball cap? Did she like sweet sauce on her ribs? Was the coleslaw too vinegary for her? Did she prefer egg or dill in her potato salad? Was this stick suitable for her marshmallows?"

"And the mother?" Dr. Morrison asked. "Did she notice any of this?"

I honestly couldn't recall. That woman was fused to my uncle's flank. Exhibiting the usual female fluttering around him, but as that was de rigueur, I barely noticed.

Each day Bug and I swam in the lake and traipsed through the cool woods. Filled ourselves with junk food and diet soda. Lying side by side on the dock, we compared tan lines and pored over her teen magazines. Usually, I deemed that sort of reading beneath me, but Bug insisted there was vital knowledge to be acquired, such as "True Love or True Crush?" We laughed at an article on "dating terrors" and examined the umpteen images of "cool guys on the scene." We did personality tests—"Sly or Shy?" and "What's Your Style Era?"—and with a little cheating on my part, we always came out the same.

One afternoon, she tried to teach me how to make a daisy chain. We sat across from each other in a small patch of flowers near the lake. Long thin stems, pinched and knotted, one bloom added to the next. While mine fell apart in my hands, hers was perfectly woven, and once she'd joined the ends, she leaned forward and balanced it on top of my head. After a slow admiring whistle, she removed a tiny compact from her beach bag and opened it. Used her thumb to wipe the beige powder from the mirror. Then held it up to my face.

I had a difficult time staring at my reflection. Looking myself in the eye.

Then she said, "You're the prettiest person I know."

I wasn't sure what her words made me feel, but it wasn't good. Like a heavy blanket had been dropped over my face, my neck, and I couldn't breathe. I couldn't move. I desperately wanted to be whatever it was that she saw. My ugliness invisible. No, not invisible. I wanted my ugliness gone.

•

After an evening campfire, Bug's mother and Uncle James were on the couch watching an old movie. The musical score was eerie. Mostly cellos. Bass drumroll. "Oh, I can barely look," she said, wriggling closer. She threaded her limbs through his, so tightly she was practically sewn onto his side. "She's such a stupid girl. Why are the lead actresses always so ditzy?"

"To move the plot along?"

"Oh James"—she lightly slapped his upper arm—"you're just so clever."

Bug and I were barely paying attention, but her mom suddenly said in a sickly sweet tone, "This film isn't for you two scamps. Go on. Get!"

Bug whispered, "I think they want some privacy?"

"Whatever. C'mon." I swiped my uncle's cigarettes, and with Bug close behind, we went out the back door, screen door banging.

We crawled into the mildewy tent we'd set up in the yard. I tied a flashlight to the frame with an old shoelace I'd found in a drawer.

"They like each other. James put on a horror movie to get my mom closer."

"You think?"

"Why else would he?"

To move the plot along?

I reached up and knocked the light, so the beam flowed around us, over us. We were both wearing oversized T-shirts we'd found in an upstairs drawer. Mine had colorful dancing bears, and hers a white dog with an alien's head.

"You're grumpy."

"Am not." I flumped backward onto the mound of blankets and cheap foam-filled pillows. "I'm just . . . I don't know. Maybe I'm angry."

"With me?"

"No, you idiot. Of course not." Then I managed, "With myself."

"Oh, that's not good. Not good at all."

I thought of the daisy chain she'd given me. I'd left it on the kitchen counter. Only hours later, the stems were wilting, the petals already curling inward. It wouldn't last. Nothing was going to last. Everything that connected Bug to me, me to Bug, was going to be destroyed. How could it not?

"Probably just cramps," I said and lolled out my tongue.

"Ugh. That rots."

I lit a cigarette and inhaled deeply. After a minute of quiet, I said, "Totally weirdo question."

"What?"

"If-if your soul had a smell, what would it be?"

"That *is* a totally weirdo question."

"I think mine would smell like smoke." As though I had this inkling there was chemical destruction in my very core. "Not like this though." I waved the cigarette, then passed it to her. "More like an incinerator. At a dump."

She didn't laugh at my ridiculous pronouncement. Instead she scratched her scalp and said, "Mine probably just smells like wet feet. Or maybe grass. Or, or maybe apple juice."

We both startled when a hulking shadow rose over the wall of our tent. Someone tugging at the zipper.

Then my uncle appeared, crouching before the open flap. His happy handsome face. "Night got chillier, hey girls? That darn lake air."

"We don't mind," Bug said as she stubbed out the cigarette and tried to frantically wave away the fumes.

"Oh, don't fuss." A reassuring murmur. "I'm not going to tell your mom."

"Thanks, James," she whispered. Shy (not sly) eyes lowered.

"Well, here's a sweet surprise to warm you both up," he said, reaching for something on the grass. Then he pushed the mugs through the opening. One pink, one yellow. As we accepted them, his gaze met mine. Lids slowly blinking over his brown eyes. I caught his unspoken message loud and clear. I was not to interfere.

"Uh. Th-thanks," I whispered. My throat in a vise.

"Drink up, little cuties. Lots more where that came from."

He was abruptly reabsorbed into the night, zipper teeth biting back together. Before I could strategize, I heard an ahhh. Bug had already downed the contents of her mug. "I know it's fattening, but it's just so delicious." She wiped her mouth with the hem of her T-shirt. "And I changed my answer. My soul smells like your uncle's ho-cho. I kid you not."

"No, it doesn't. Wet feet's way better."

"Hardly! Do you want yours? Can I have it?"

"No." I gulped mine, believing it was simply milk, sugar, chocolate, and vanilla. As it always was before.

I'd hardly finished when rain started pelting the roof of our tent, seeping in as though the fabric had pores. When rivulets formed along the floor, we hurried out and dashed into the cabin. Up the stairs to our attic bedroom.

The slanted ceiling was covered in webs and spiders. We tucked inside musty sleeping bags. Our skin tight from sunburn. I curled my body around hers. Best friends. Sisters. Underneath the desperation and the dread, I was drunk on joy. I was also being pulled strongly toward sleep.

"And I forgot, Dr. Morrison. I forgot to tie our wrists together."

CHAPTER THIRTY-FIVE

Mia

"MIA, WHAT'S GOING on? My assistant actually interrupted a critical meeting. Said it was a family emerge—?"

"Ian." She could barely get his name out. The sobs wracking her chest. "H-how could you?"

"I'm sorry?" She heard him shuffling. The sound of his office door closing. "How could I what?"

"You know exactly what I mean."

"Christ," he hissed. "You disrupt my day over ancient history? Haven't we been through this a hundred times? This might sound harsh, but you need to get over it."

"This week is not history."

"This week?" A comfortable laugh. "You're confused. It was last year. You know this, Mia." Then in a lower voice, "Are you okay? You don't sound stable. Do you want me to come home?"

"I saw the photographs."

"The what?"

"You were at her house. In her bedroom."

"The only bedroom I've been in this week is ours."

"That's not—"

"Do you want me to account for every hour, Mia? Because I can, you know."

Her mind looped around. Could she possibly be mistaken? But then she remembered his leather bag. His tattoo. His entire face on full display.

"Stop the bullshit, Ian."

Silence for a moment, before he said, "Listen, let's talk when I get home. I've got no clue about photos, but we'll figure this out."

"No, we won't. This time, I'm done talking." She hung up.

All those months of trying to forgive him. She'd been so naive. Anxious to believe the story of a single time. A curiosity-fueled lapse. Or whatever idiotic way he'd framed it.

And he'd apologized repeatedly, promised it would never happen again. Hadn't he spent the past months trying to convince her to put it in the past? That their relationship would only get stronger? He'd even suggested another child.

Now she knew all of that was fake. Ian was doing whatever he wanted and then manipulating her. Sowing seeds of paranoia or delusion so she doubted herself. When he was the one who stood to lose the most. His wife, his home. The respect of his colleagues who valued family and stability.

"Yoo-hoo! It's me!" The front door closing. "It's a scorcher today." Bare feet padding down the hallway.

"Mom," she sobbed. "Everything's a mess."

Faye rushed toward her. "Sweetheart. What's happened?" Then her jaw clenched. "Or should I guess?"

They sat side by side at the kitchen island, and Mia told her everything. Even showed Faye the photos. At that moment, she needed her mother's support. She felt so isolated, and there was no one else to turn to.

With her reading glasses perched on the end of her nose, Faye examined the screen. "That skin does look quite supple. Don't you think?"

Mia nodded. It did look supple.

The bedroom could be in a house or an apartment. Maybe even a college dorm? Both the furnishings and bedding were basic. The only distinctive item was a white throw blanket with a blue octagonal pattern, but that could likely be purchased at any home store or online. Dropped on the doorstep the following day inside a cardboard box.

"Well, what I've brought seems even more timely now." Faye lifted the flap on her crocheted bag and pulled out an orange file folder. She slapped it down on the marble. "I've continued looking into things."

Mia wiped her nose with the back of her hand. "Sorry, what things?"

"For my courses. I've been delving into astrology. Horoscopes and tarot reading and such. It's an applied science, Mia. Evidence-based."

"I know you're keen to tell me, but can we put a pin in it? I need to think about what I'm—"

Faye put up her hand. "I'll be concise. You're fire and water."

"I am?"

"No, you and that husband of yours. He's fire, and you're water. His moon is in Aries, too, which is a terrible red flag." She patted Mia's shoulder. "If only I'd been more educated when you two met. I could have guided you with much better clarity."

Closing her eyes for a second, Mia tried to control herself. All those years ago, her mother had made no attempt to guide her, with clarity or otherwise. The coldness was sudden, total, and inexplicable.

"And of course," she continued, "I'm stating the obvious that you're both very self-centered. Naturally so."

"You're joking, right?"

"Not at all. This is not coming from me. These are not my opinions, dear."

"Mom. I can't believe you."

"What? Do you think I'm making this stuff up? I've gone over the data with my professors." She licked her fingertip and flipped through several pages. "And they're all doctorates, you know. Leaders in their field."

"I don't care if they're leaders. I don't care if they can levitate."

Head jerking backward. "Now you're just being ignorant. And saucy."

Mia shoved back her stool and stood up abruptly. "How do I already regret telling you?"

"Excuse me?"

"I do, Mom. I wish I hadn't opened my mouth."

"Yes, well, there's nothing wrong with your voice chakra." Faye jammed the folder back into her bag.

"I'm leaving."

"Where are you going?"

"Away from this house." Perhaps she could spend a few days at a hotel. Or, even better, their rental property. It was currently vacant, had all the basics, and that would give her a chance to clear her head.

"Come on, Mia. Running off like a petulant child."

"You can let yourself out."

She grabbed her purse, her mother's sudden yelling propelling her forward. "It's the definition of a toxic partnership! I'm surprised it's lasted this long."

CHAPTER THIRTY-SIX

Lainey

I KNEW SHE was coming. Well, not quite *knew*, but I had an inkling it would happen at some point. Especially after I took a few mischievous steps to set things in motion.

Getting Dr. Morrison to give me access to his condo was much easier than I would've guessed. When I'd initially told a few fibs about mild abuse, I hadn't considered the faux strife might come in handy. But after receiving the Google alert for his rental property, I leaned into the narrative of misdeeds. I wanted to see where it might go.

I began by mentioning random arguments. Then layer by layer, I piled on other problems. The verbal sparring. A heated shoving incident. His control over my finances and food intake. During one appointment, I wore an ivory linen sweater. The pale color and boat neckline highlighting a substantial bruise over my left clavicle. I'd spent over twenty minutes using a blend of eyeshadows and a tickly brush to create it. Purples, yellows, even a slender streak of green. And not to toot my own horn, but the result was impressively convincing.

During the most recent session, I feigned severe jitteriness (taking my inspo from my bar buddy Tim) and then confided that I felt in imminent danger. I told him my partner was furious about a lipstick I'd purchased. A flutter of damp eyelashes, and I whimpered that I had nowhere to go. Couldn't use a credit card. Andrew was in security and could trace my every move. "With all this stress," I mumbled, balancing the cherry on the sundae, "I don't know if I've got the strength to continue treatment."

What followed was entirely predictable. As I'd guessed, Dr. Morrison's savior complex kicked in, and bingo, the dear man coughed up the goods. He gave me the condo address, a building in midtown, and said he'd drop a set of keys at the concierge. He offered to meet me, show me around the unit, but I insisted I could manage. I promised that I'd only stay a night or two. If he was comfortable with that.

"Absolutely," he'd said. "You'll be in a secure place, until we can get you sorted."

I squeezed out a few grateful tears. "Thank you. I mean it." I didn't mean it.

"There are resources. I can help you with everything."

"Thank you," I repeated. He was clearly a man who welcomed a bootlick.

"You're not alone, Lainey. Don't forget that."

Of course I'm alone. We're all alone.

During my free time, I hung out at his place. Wasting the hours. Reading magazines, playing *Fishdom* on my iPhone. I allowed myself the guilty pleasure of a cigarette. I liked being inside something he owned. Enveloped, so to speak, in Dr. Morrison's world. Though the finishes were builder grade and the furniture kind of crappy.

Finally the loitering was paying off.

Sixty-seven minutes ago, I received a text from him. *I think a colleague might need to use the place for a few nights.*

u think?

not confirmed yet. She's in a bit of a spot.

She. As I reclined on his sofa, I quickly replied. *No worries. The place is available.* I told him I'd never actually stayed there. Things between my partner and I had settled, though his offer had been kind and oh so very generous. (Another bootlick.)

I said I'd leave the keys with the concierge, and he was welcome to retrieve them at any time.

Thx. I'll do it shortly. I have a spare.

I also had a spare.

The three dots on my screen were bouncing. He was typing another message. Then stopped. I counted to thirty, but he never started again.

Placing my phone face down on the coffee table, I stood up. The waiting was interminable. I tossed out the old magazines, wiped down a spill from my mochaccino. Took a quick assessment of my body (back muscles tight, jaw clenched). I identified the emotion as *stage fright.*

Then a key, jamming into the lock. Furious twist, and the person arrived. The *she* he'd mentioned. Gingery hair disheveled, eyes rabbit-red from crying. An adult, sure, but remarkably similar-looking to the girl who had emerged from the bathroom stall all those years ago.

"Hello, Bug."

CHAPTER THIRTY-SEVEN

Mia

KNEES TO JELLY. Mia fell back against the condo door. She was standing only a few feet in front of Ian's patient. Dark hair and dark eyes with an expression on her heart-shaped face that was impossible to read. After nearly thirty years, Mia and Lainey Kemper were complete strangers. But their shared past was fixed in amber.

"You've grown," Lainey finally said.

Mia swallowed. "H-how are you here?"

"Is that the first thing you want to say to me?"

"I'm . . . I'm just surprised."

Lainey shrugged. "It was your husband. My psychiatrist. We've reunited, as I'm sure you're acutely aware. And he gave me the key. Quite readily, I might add."

"Okay." Mia nodded quickly. "I understand." She could guess the reason. Based on what she'd seen, Lainey's partner was abusive. It must have worsened—she hadn't yet viewed the most recent sessions—and Ian had offered up a temporary solution.

"If you think we're fucking, you shouldn't worry."

She winced. "I don't. I don't think that at all." Which was true.

She'd never imagined him breaching that particular boundary. Or this patient having interest. Lainey may have been attached to him at Albethey, but in their current sessions, she exuded only disdain.

"Good." Lainey chewed her bottom lip. "And you? Why are you here?"

"I-I'm not sure," she stammered. "I should go. I can go."

Lainey took a step closer. "Let me take a stab. Mr. Perfect did something to upset you."

"No, nothing like that." Her hands fumbled behind her back, and she grasped at the doorknob.

"Are you sure?" she continued. "My guess is your dear hubby is screwing around. And you need some space?"

Mia lowered her head. Her skull ached from all the mental chatter. Ian's pompous denial. Her mother's callous reaction. Now this woman's words, hitting the nail on the head. Much to Mia's dismay, tears dripped on the laminate flooring.

"Oh, poor chicken. Do you need a tissue?"

When she looked up, she discovered Lainey was even closer. Within arm's reach. But the expression on her face was one of controlled rage, not empathy.

"It's okay," she whispered. She wiped her nose in her sleeve. "I-I've barged in on you. I'm going to go."

"Why so soon? Are you frightened of me?"

"No," she replied. Too quickly.

Lainey eyed her up and down. "I always knew when you were lying." Then she scowled and added, "I'm not frightened of you either."

Mia gave her head a tight shake. What possible reason could anyone have to be scared of her?

Turning on her heel, Lainey took several long strides across the room. Tugging open the sliding door, she said, "Well? Are you going to stay glued to that door, Bug? Or are we going to settle some things?" Then she held up a crumpled brown and white package. "This is our brand, if I remember correctly." She stepped outside and disappeared from view.

Mia did not move. She could easily leave the condo. Nothing was stopping her. No one was blocking the door or making a threat. But as she weighed her options, she discovered that the intensity of her anger had tempered her fear. She was curious. And in that moment did not care if it was reckless. So she peeled herself away from the safety of the front entrance and followed.

The balcony was a strip of concrete barely six feet deep and ten feet wide. Over the glass and metal barrier, there was a death drop of nineteen floors. Her legs felt wobbly, and she quickly slid onto the edge of a rattan chair. She picked up the package of cigarettes and plucked one out. Lainey offered a flame.

Mia hadn't smoked since she was a teenager. Stealing them from Faye, while Lainey had stolen them from her uncle. After taking several deep drags, the nicotine brought a near-instant calm.

They smoked in silence for a few moments, and eventually Mia worked up the courage to ask, "Did you know I married Ian? That I was his wife?" Based on Lainey's nonreaction when Mia had entered the condo, she suspected the answer was yes.

Lainey flicked ash over the edge of the railing. "I wasn't totally sure at first. When your daughter appeared on Zoom, I actually thought I was having a delusion."

"But you sa– I mean, Ian told me you never saw her face."

A snort. "Of course I saw her face."

Mia blew out a stream of air. "We look that much alike, huh?"

"Yeah. The resemblance is insane. You two are carbon copies."

"I guess so." At least, she used to feel that way.

"Needless to say, it was a jump scare. But once I got over the shock, I tried to trace a path between you two. I assumed he didn't seek you out, right?"

"No. No, he didn't."

"So. Let me see if I get the sequence of events right. His trashy case study was published, and somehow, you happened upon it. I mean, it was all over. Talk television, news radio. I even saw the write-up in *People* magazine. Why they considered it worthy of a two-page human interest spread, I've no clue. But"—she put her finger up—"no doubt you realized who the subject was. And you clearly wanted to know more, so you hunted down my dear doctor. Were you his patient? Or was he your prof?" She raised her eyebrows at Mia. "Either way, it's kind of juicy, right? But clearly that wasn't enough, and beyond all comprehension, you went full steam."

"Yeah. Um. That's about it." A wave of embarrassment settled on top of her overwhelming mound of feelings. "I met him on campus."

"Well, A-plus for me." Lainey leaned farther over the barrier to toss her cigarette into the parking lot below.

"Can you come away from there?"

"Why? You still don't like heights?"

"No—not really."

Lainey laughed but didn't change position. "I just have one question for you. Why did you fuck, and even worse, marry the man who medicated me. Electrocuted me. Kept me locked in a box?"

Mia's thoughts began to race. "I didn't know any of those things. My relationship with him . . . it was—it was unexpected."

"Unexpected." She sneered. "Whatever."

"Like you said, the only reason I approached him in the first place was for information about you. I wanted to know if you were okay."

"You expect me to believe that?"

"I'm just trying to explain. I couldn't talk to you, obviously. My mother and I moved. I changed schools. I knew you were in a hospital somewhere, and I assumed you were sick and getting help. We were kids, weren't we? But I never stopped wondering about you."

"Right. And you wondered so hard, not once did you try to find me."

"How could I?" That wasn't Mia's fault. "It was part of . . . you know, a condition of you going to Albethey. We weren't allowed to see each other."

"But when I got out?"

"No, I mean, not see each other ever again."

"Said who?"

"My mother told me. I wasn't allowed to reach out. Couldn't try to visit you. Or even write a letter without, you know, consequences. You could've ended up in jail."

"What the hell?"

Mia was taken aback. Lainey's reaction made no sense. How could she not know the details of her own situation?

"I really did ask my mother to fix things. To get the police to remove the condition, but she said it wasn't possible. What was done was done. I was devastated." The more Mia had moped and complained, the more irritated Faye became. At some point, Mia was no longer allowed to even say Lainey's name. Her mother insisting that the friendship was a figment of an overactive imagination. The remainder of Mia's teenage years were a chasm of loneliness. "Which, of course, I shouldn't even be saying. I'm sure whatever you went through was infinitely worse."

"Huh," Lainey said, her fleeting reaction gone. "That's something."

She slid into the chair beside Mia's. Their bodies very close together. "I've thought about this a ton," she said. Too softly. "Like, really, really thought about this. Part of me wanted to damage you. I wanted you to feel some of the pain that I've felt all these years."

Mia gazed at the cigarette pinched between her fingers. Tendrils of smoke curling upward. "I'm sorry," she whispered. She didn't know what else to say. Everything was so complicated. And because of her spying, she knew much more than she should.

"I don't need your shitty apologies. And I get why you did that to my uncle. I mean, I know what happened. You just reacted."

Reacted?

"What are you talking about?" Even though Mia now knew about James Kemper's revolting behavior, he had only treated her with warmth. Nothing questionable. That she could recall, at least.

"You destroyed my life, but I was still your friend. I did it all to protect you. I never said a word at Albethey."

What was Lainey suggesting? That not only had her uncle done something to Mia . . . but Mia had also done something to him?

"I don't understand what you mean about—about any of that. I can't even imagine how traumatizing it was for you. But . . . but nothing happened to *me*."

She sucked air through her teeth. "Do I look like an imbecile?"

"Of course you don't. I-I never said that."

"So what then? My uncle did it to himself?" She tilted her head and, with a fingernail, jabbed just beneath her jawline. "He stabbed his own neck?"

What? Sweat trickled down Mia's underarm, and the cigarette dropped from her fingers. "You don't actually think *I* did something, do you? That *I* hurt him?"

"I don't think," she growled. "I know."

Mia's mind raced. She should have left when she'd had the chance. But instead she'd put herself in danger. Believing that on some level she still knew who Lainey Kemper was at her core. Now she was trapped with a woman who was clearly unhinged. Making irrational statements. Mia knew enough about psychology to know that trying to contradict those delusions might intensify the situation. Lead to a confrontation. And they were on a thin balcony way up high. But she could think of no other way to respond. Other than with the truth.

"I didn't even see him that morning. I wasn't anywhere near him."

Lainey slowly examined every inch of Mia's face. "Are you lying?"

"No. I'm not. I—I promise."

As Mia sat there, barely breathing, Lainey stared out at the city. Identical buildings, evenly spaced trees, every street in shadow.

"So, if it wasn't you," she said, "and I know for certain it wasn't me . . . then who are we left with?"

Mia's mouth was suddenly bone-dry. She did not want to answer that question.

CHAPTER THIRTY-EIGHT

Lainey

I HAVE RARELY ever been surprised. Throughout my life, I invariably found people and situations mind-numbingly predictable. I could identify ulterior motives from a mile away. When a scammer approached, he was practically luminescent. But I had to admit, in that instance, I was stunned.

When I arrived back at Andrew's, I unrolled my yoga mat next to the desk in his office. I lay down, limbs relaxed, and waited for clarity to arrive. As I reviewed the death scene in my head, it seemed shockingly obvious now.

I'd left Mia sleeping on the attic floor and gone for a walk in the woods. I needed to calm down. At some point, I heard noises. Yelling maybe. The echoes brushing over the cabin, weaving through the trees. When I got there, I saw a body curled on the dock. A pool of thick blood. It was my uncle. His mouth was smashed, red hands limp by his sides. Faye was standing right there, a length of graying wood from the old dock gripped in her fist. Wet shiny nail protruding from the end. I screamed, ran toward my uncle. "What happened? What happened?"

And in a wavering voice that was deeply infused with adult concern, adult authority, she'd said, "I don't know. Mia just . . . lost it."

On the mat, I squeezed my eyes closed, trying to center myself in my new awareness. No escaping how naive I'd been. During the most critical moment of my existence, I'd allowed a ruthless liar to light my way. Without question or consideration.

The longer I lay there, the more agitated I became. Why had she done that? Had she caught my uncle doing something to Mia? But that made no sense. If so, she'd have acted immediately. Inside the cabin, during the night. Instead, without a single blink, she placed the blame for his injuries—his death—on the tiny shoulders of her daughter.

I stood up and, with the tip of my toe, kicked my yoga mat so it buckled and flopped in a very unsatisfying way. My rage required redirection. I needed time to process. To plan.

I checked the time. In ten minutes, I was to continue my interrupted session with my crap psychiatrist. I was sorely tempted to ghost his ass. Let him wait in his virtual world for his virtual client until the allotted time elapsed. He would never know the end of my story. My story, and Mia's.

But what if I told him the truth instead? As the clock ticked down the minutes, I considered the benefits of sharing my new insight. I'd provide no spoilers that the murderer in question was his mother-in-law, but when everything was illuminated (as eventually it would be), the knowledge would be such a delightful sucker punch. I would have to ensure I could witness it.

"Lainey," he practically whispered after I joined the meeting, "it's so very good to see you."

"Because I'm your favorite?"

"Well, you didn't hear that from me." Cheshire Cat grin. "We were at an important juncture. Wouldn't you agree?"

"Perhaps, Dr. Morrison. How did that make you feel?"

He caught my not-so-subtle volley and laughed. "Keen to continue our good work. And of course, concerned for you after the breakthrough."

Hardly a breakthrough. More like an abscessed tooth I'd been running my tongue over for decades.

"I joined the session today to let you know. I need to tell you I was wrong."

"Wrong? About what?" His eyebrows knitted together.

"I made a serious misclassification."

"I'm not following. During our previous session, you described that last night with your uncle. Before his death. We should discuss what led you to—"

"It wasn't me."

"I'm sorry?"

I figured it was best to just spill it. "It wasn't me who killed him."

He half smiled, half shook his head. As though my admission was nothing more than a ticklish breeze over his ear. "Yet during our many, many hours at Albethey, you never wavered. Your narrative was consistent. So I'm struggling here to grasp—"

"I thought I was protecting her."

"Who? Your friend? From?"

I had to pause, control the sensation ballooning in my chest. He was a man unable to connect two very obvious dots. Even when the path between them was already grooved.

"I was certain it was her, Dr. Morrison. That she'd lashed out at my uncle. And I knew it was my fault, you see. So all I could do was keep her from being prosecuted."

"Ah," he announced. *Bing* of a (very dim) light bulb. "So it was your belief that your friend in fact committed the murder of your uncle, and even though you were innocent, you gave up years of your youth so she'd avoid any repercussions. That was your stance?"

"Correct." *Incorrect.* It was so much more complicated. I loved her. I loved my uncle. I had tried, but I'd been unable to manage the requirements of both relationships. I fully understood that I was to blame for all of it. Same as I was with that girl who drowned in the pool. I was a terrible friend and a terrible niece. I deserved death and had even found solace there. In being absolutely nothing. "But I was mistaken, you see. About everything. I realize that now."

"Okay? And in what way were you wrong?"

"It wasn't her." I don't know how I could've thought she had that in her. The capacity to swing a board at a man. To stick a nail in his neck.

His mouth adopted a peculiar pout. Like a parent disappointed by an unmade bed. "And when did you have this . . . this new revelation?"

"I reconnected with my best friend. We put the pieces together."

"Recently? You found her?"

"Uh-huh. Now that's a crazy story."

"Well, I'd love to hear it," he said, his tone much less therapist, much more info whore.

"Thank you for offering me space," I said, making no effort to disguise my sarcasm, "but I'm not ready to delve into it."

"Your choice, of course. All in good time. But if you didn't kill your uncle, and now you say your friend—"

"It was her mother."

"Her mother . . ."

"Who murdered my uncle. She ruined my life back then. Still ruining her daughter's life today." And I was ferociously mulling over how I was going to address that.

"If I might be blunt, you've made another U-turn, Lainey. Just this morning, I reread the police report and the interview with the cabin's owner. And as I've already said, nowhere is there ever a mention of guests. I have to ask myself . . ."

"Ask yourself what, Dr. Morrison?"

"There are significant inconsistencies. During our first session, you said you were ready to tell the truth. You've hinted that a young girl was important to your story. And now, there's yet another flip to the girl's mother. I have to pose the question: Could these all be deflections?"

"And what am I deflecting?"

"Your responsibility. For your actions."

Oh, I hated him. *Hated him.* That feeling was coming through with crystalline clarity. "It's simple, Dr. Morrison. All I wanted was to keep my friend."

"And also keep your uncle."

"What else do you want me to say?" Even if I put every vile act on one side of a scale and all his nurturing on the other, it still tilted toward love. Didn't it?

"We should keep moving forward. Investigate what led you to—"

"I told you. I didn't do it."

"Lainey."

"That heinous woman did. And then abandoned me in the woods." I stayed beside him. Black flies came, landing on his wound, on him. Landing on me. At some point, I lay down. Time passed, and I left myself. I wanted to find him. It hurt too much to be alone. I drifted upward until we were together. Uncle James and his puppet.

Dr. Morrison's lips parted but before he could utter another word, I clicked Leave Meeting. I got up from Andrew's desk and walked out onto the balcony for fresh air. When the sun struck my eyes, the world became a blur. I reached up, felt moisture along the sides of my cheeks. Perhaps that meant I'd been crying.

CHAPTER THIRTY-NINE

Mia

AS SHE SLID onto the bar stool, Mia's skin erupted in goosebumps. The air-conditioning was cranked to the max. That or her skin was covered with a sheen of nervous sweat.

An hour earlier, she'd called her mother and said, "We need to talk."

"Well, hello, daughter. Finally ready to apologize?"

With each click of her mother's tongue, Mia wanted to shrink. Compress all the questions, which were swirling like a tornado inside her head. But she couldn't shy away from the conversation. Perhaps there were other factors, something she was missing. Perhaps she was being misled by a volatile and possibly violent woman she hadn't seen in a lifetime.

"Not that."

"You sound awfully serious, dear." A single drop of silence. Then, "Is this about Ian? Have you finally decided to leave him?"

"I'm not going to talk about that man. It's something else. I need to understand."

"Well, if cryptic were a sport, you'd be on the podium."

Faye had suggested a "stiff drink" and chosen the swankiest cocktail bar in Callow. The one above the restaurant where they'd celebrated Ian's birthday dinner. When she finally sauntered in, twenty minutes late, she slid onto the stool beside Mia and immediately ordered two boulevardiers. Then said to Mia, "Don't worry. You'll like it."

They watched the bartender in awkward silence, and a few minutes later, amber beverages appeared in front of them. Single ice cubes and twists of orange peel. Mia sipped and involuntarily shuddered. The drink was pure alcohol.

"So what's all this about? You may as well say your piece."

"I don't have a piece, Mom. I just want you to be honest with me."

"Can you provide an old woman a little context?"

"About . . . when I was a teenager."

A leaden sigh. "Why didn't you say so over the phone. You had my mind going in a hundred directions."

"I want to know about—"

"Those terrible years. You were always so moody and depressed." She took a large sip of her drink. "My word, you were absolutely pitiful company. What didn't I have to endure. But I did, as you well know. Endure it all, as that's what a good mother does."

Mia ignored the insults. The insensitivity. "I want to talk about Lainey."

"Who? I'm not familiar with anyone by that name."

"You are entirely familiar. Stop pretending."

She took a sharp breath through her nostrils. "Fine then. I figured something might resurface, what with Ian's little project. You know, I tried to be supportive back then. You finally managed to make a friend. I tolerated an entire year of you trailing behind that reprobate."

"She wasn't a reprobate."

"Oh, dear." She gave Mia a pitying glance. "You never could judge character. She was troubled from the get-go. But I allowed you your moment of rebellion. I knew it would fizzle out."

"*Fizzle* is a weird word to use, isn't it? Considering how our friendship ended." A man dying in a brutal way. A vulnerable girl separating from reality.

"Forgive me if I'm not a linguist."

Mia wrapped her hand around the glass, the icy coldness penetrating her palm. "We never discussed it, Mom. What happened that summer. In fact, we never spoke about it at all. Don't you think that's strange?"

"Like I've already told you, I've made a concerted effort to leave the past in the past. I don't want to be dragged down. But you seem intent on doing just that." Faye finished her drink and tapped her knuckle on the smooth wood of the bar. A flirty nod to the bartender, and not long after, another appeared. "What can I say? We enjoyed a mediocre week. I recall the girl's father was handsome, though a tad arrogant. There was a brief romance. And I mean very brief. I can't even recall his name. So that's how much it meant to me."

"His name was James Kemper."

"There you go. I can assure you he was nothing extraordinary. The visit with them was so mundane, you and I decided to head home."

"That's simply not true, Mom." They'd decided nothing. "What happened was devastating. She was my best friend."

"Puh-leeze. You had your head so far up her ass, you couldn't even think straight. And where did that leave me?"

"I don't know. Where did that leave you?"

Faye's demeanor instantly changed. She grinned and wiggled her torso. "Well, seeing as you're asking." Her hand dove into her purse, and she pulled out her phone. "I've met someone, you see. Well, not met-met, but I am bursting with excitement. Positively giddy." Pressing reading glasses to her face, she poked at the screen.

"I'm not interested, okay? We're having an important conversation here."

"Yes, but this is time-sensitive, darling. Not some drivel from an eon ago."

"It's not driv—"

"He and I have communicated extensively, and I'm completely head over heels for my amour." Faye tapped an app and showed Mia. "Meet my new love."

"Mom. You can't be serious."

"Entirely! Look at his profile."

With the phone in her face, Mia couldn't help but glance at the images. A young man at a farmers' market. On a couch reading a novel. Dressed in sporty gear on a mountain bike.

"Isn't he a dream though? A total package."

"I'm not going to talk to you about some man who's half your age."

"Why do you have to be so negative? We get along like a house on fire. It's not just his looks; the conversations are stimulating too. I've learned a great deal, Mia. He's an educator. Voracious gardener. And an ENFJ, to boot. Those are the most spiritual Myers-Briggs, you know."

Frustration was bubbling up inside her. "Mom, I'm trying to talk to you about something really important. And you start on about some guy from the internet who's probably not even real."

"Oh, that's not a worry. We've exchanged . . . well, some photos. Of an intimate nature. Let's just say he's very real."

"I don't care," she said. "I don't care about that . . . that . . . that man. Whatever he is."

Faye tut-tutted. "Mia, you must really think I'm daft. I'm not going to be taken in by some F-boy."

"Why can't you ever listen to me?"

She leaned in close and whispered, "It means fuckboy. That's the term the kids are using these days."

"Just stop."

Eyes narrowed, Faye said, "I'm sensing a judgy vibe. Don't I deserve this? I've given up most of my life to be there for you, and it's time I had some fun."

Given up most of her life? That wasn't true either. Mia closed her eyes for a moment. Even though she'd only consumed half the cocktail, she could feel her empty stomach absorbing the alcohol. Though instead of soothing her nerves, it amplified her outrage. "Just tell me this—did you kill that man?"

Faye's head lolled backward. "What is wrong with you?" She clicked the button on the side of her phone, making the app disappear. "We had—if anything—a minor dustup. Practically nothing. After he insulted me."

"Insulted you how?"

"I remember every detail vividly. Gave me a pinch of post-traumatic stress, I might add."

"Tell me then."

After wiping the corners of her mouth with a serviette, she said, "H-he informed me I was too old to be acting like a . . . like a hussy. Can you believe that? What woman wouldn't be a little reactive?"

"And that was it?"

"Isn't that enough?"

"I don't know, Mom. You tell me."

"If you must know, there was one more thing. He said I should take a note." She rolled the ice cube around in her near-empty glass. "Take a note from my daughter. That you, of all people, could give me a lesson."

"What does that mean? A lesson on what?"

"Oh." She threw up her hands. "This is all so ludicrous. I don't know why you're pressuring me. He just said you could teach me how to be beautiful."

Mia shook her head. "Why would he say that? I was just a dumpy kid." She'd already scoured every memory of James Kemper, trying to identify any uncomfortable comment, glance, or touch that was directed at her. She'd come up empty.

"Exactly. Rude, at the very least. I'm not ashamed to admit I threw my coffee at him."

"But both of his front teeth were broken. He'd inhaled one of them."

Quick shake of her head. "The mug may have slipped. The entire incident's quite hazy."

"And then you struck him with a board?"

Faye clutched her chest. "What? Where's all this coming from? I can't believe you'd even say such an atrocious thing to your own mother."

It was painfully obvious to Mia that Faye was lying. Lying to her, but maybe also lying to herself.

"You said it was me, Mom. That's what you told Lainey. That I attacked her uncle. How could you do that?"

Faye's cheeks went white. "Do not tell me you've spoken to that woman, Mia. Do not tell me you've done something so stupid."

"And then police came to our house. And you told them I hardly even knew her. We weren't even friends. Do you remember that part?"

"Of course I don't. You know my memory's pathetic. I'm not young anymore."

"I had absolutely no clue what was going on. Why you dragged me away from that cabin. Why I never heard from Lainey again. Why we packed up and moved almost overnight. My entire life. Just gone. Do you know how confusing and scary that was?"

"Mia, come on, it's all—"

"Not to mention you left a teenager in the woods with a dead body. Alone for days. It's uncon—"

Faye's closed fist came down on the bar. "Now you listen to me, miss. I need to stop you right there. Can't you see? I didn't care about some girl in the woods. Every single thing I did was for you. My primary focus was caring for my daughter."

Mia stared at her mother. For a fleeting second, she wondered if Faye *had* been trying to protect her. If, on some level, her mother had sensed James Kemper's deviant intentions. If it were Elise in such a situation, Mia might have done the same. Lashed out violently. Until the threat was eliminated. But Faye was refusing to be honest. Her reaction to Lainey's trauma was so casual. So cold. With no awareness of the irreparable damage she'd caused an innocent girl. Creating a debt that Mia could never repay.

"I-I don't believe you, Mom."

"Mia! You're twisting everything. Almost like you're reveling in this, actually. That's my sense of things. It honestly is. And you know what? I blame Ian. Reconnecting with her. She's got in your head again and made you feel vulnerable. Made *us* feel vulnerable. If she starts saying all these asinine things, you know what we stand to lose, right?" She was so close, Mia could smell the alcohol on her breath. "I knew from the get-go you never should have married that man."

Then it dawned on Mia—the reason for their estrangement. After she and Ian began dating, Faye had vanished from her life. All those years, she'd assumed she'd been a terrible daughter. Not worth the effort. But Faye had created distance because of her own fears. What if Lainey had told Ian the truth? What if she had given him names? What if she did now? Perhaps it was due to the horror Mia felt over her mother's actions, but that possibility didn't scare her.

"I don't know who you are, Mom. I've seen so many sides of you, but this is beyond."

“Oh, you’re being dramatic. How about a Reiki session for the two of us? To get some balance. I’ll find a spot and text you the link. Okay?”

“No.” Mia stood up and pushed in the stool. “I don’t wait a Reiki session. I need some space from you.”

“Space for what? Don’t do anything rash, Mia.” Faye tapped her knuckles on the bar. “Let’s stay for another drink. Switch up the vibe.”

“Don’t text me. Don’t call me. I have to think all this through.”

•

Gripping her wrist, Faye dragged her daughter and the oversized suitcase toward the car.

“We’re done here. Hundred percent done.”

“Why, Mom? What happened?”

“You will never see her again. Do you hear me? Your little friendship with that twit is over.”

“But—”

Faye yanked open the car door and hissed, “Move your backside.”

The undersides of Mia’s bare thighs stuck to the scorching seats. The hot vinyl releasing its smells. Cigarettes. Spilled yogurt. Old perfume.

“Mom, you’re scaring me.”

Nothing but hard, angry breaths.

Spinning the car around, they tore down the brush-lined driveway, the cabin shrinking in the side mirror.

“I’m getting you away from your flunkee friend and that deadbeat loser.”

“But h-he was nice to me.”

“H-he was nice to me,” she mocked.

Mia started to cry. “I don’t understand.”

“He wanted you, that’s what. My boyfriend wanted you.”

CHAPTER FORTY

Lainey

I WAS TAKING my task seriously and working hard to establish a connection. While I waited for Andrew to return from the kitchen, I kept my phone on vibrate. Each text message a thrilling buzz in my palm. With luck on my side, I'd managed to snag the catch of my dreams.

Contrary to what many believed, our sort of sexual adventure did not materialize out of thin air. Each encounter took time and consideration. The first step involved weeding through countless profiles to find a potential match. Then the inevitable screening. Neither Andrew nor I craved trashy, so participants needed to embody that special combo of kinkiness and respectability. All in all, the effort was no small feat.

If things went ahead as planned, it would be a first for us. A sizzly scenario we'd never explored before. Since the idea sprouted, I'd been thinking about it continuously. I guess "the heart wants what it wants, or else it does not care." That woman knew exactly what I was going through.

Andrew was wholly unaware of my actions. Or my desires. Which was stretching our clearly defined rules, but I didn't consider it cheating. Not technically. The groundwork was as delicate as a spiderweb. I wanted both of us to have a good experience.

When he reappeared, I turned my phone over. I didn't want to spoil the surprise just yet.

He handed me a full glass of Chardonnay and then plunked down beside me. "Never knew you had a green thumb," he said, gesturing toward the new plant on the coffee table.

The flowering jade was massive. Mia had given it to me as an early birthday gift that afternoon. I was touched and surprised that she'd remembered the date.

Shortly after our awkward encounter on the balcony, I'd decided to leave. But since then, I'd returned to the condo three times. She always invited me in, and we'd sit cross-legged on the wool rug. The tension had dissipated, my anger retreating, her nervousness fading.

At first we kept things light, discussing the weather and such, but eventually our own stories filled the air again. She spoke of motherhood and marriage. Uncertainties and insecurities. Her life was not picture-perfect, as I'd thought. It sounded bland. Soul-sucking even, with a fun factor at basement level. I didn't know what she made of my racier anecdotes, though I detected genuine interest and no side-eye.

We did not discuss the cabin in the woods, my uncle, or her mother. Not a peep about Albethey, the case study, or my mental health. The hours passed without any sense of expectation from each other. Eyebrows furrowed. Laughter occasionally rippled. Several times a soft and comfortable silence settled.

I'd read about that—how true-blue friends could be separated for decades, and the reunion was seamless. I couldn't fathom how such things were possible, but our connection had persisted. Only weeks ago, I'd wanted to make her suffer. Now all I wanted was her companionship.

"No green thumb, Andrew. It's a gift. From an old friend."

He made a sultry growl. "What kind of friend? How old is old? Is she single? Is she hot?"

I nudged him. Giggled even. Could the emotion be *fanciful glee*? "No, it's not like that." Not like that at all.

He put his head on my shoulder and gently bit my ear. "How about," he said, taking my glass and placing it beside the plant, "you drink that later. Let's go for a swim."

I knew what he meant.

"Sure. Why not?"

I gathered my hair into a messy bun and grabbed two towels. On our way to the elevator, Andrew shot a message to the front desk, and our amiable concierge met us at the amenities entrance. He pressed his keycard against the pad, and it turned green. "Have a good one," he said, as he turned and lumbered down the hallway. At that hour, the saltwater pool in the building was closed to residents. But Andrew and I were always allowed in.

The lights were dimmed, and darkness pressed against the outside of the glass enclosure. Standing on the cool tile, I unbuttoned my blouse, pulled down my shorts. Then unclipped my bra and shook it from my shoulders. Andrew was already treading water, watching me undress. When I shimmied out of my underwear, I could see his body reacting. No subtlety there.

Sliding into the coolness, I could feel it invading every crevice. To warm up, we swam back and forth for several lengths. Side by side, our paces matched. As I reached for the ladder, he gripped my ankle. Playfully tugged me closer. "Not so fast," he said, then turned me around so that my backside was against the rungs.

I tried to balance, and he moved toward me. Our wet bodies pressed together. He kissed my mouth. My neck. Using his thigh, he nudged my knees apart, and I reached down, gripping him, directing his position. Usually I found pool sex to be subpar, chafing almost, but tonight there no shortage of slipperiness. We moved together urgently, salt water sloshing in the gap between our chests, striking our chins. Every splash echoing off the slanted wooden ceiling.

Over Andrew's shoulder, through the windows, a full moon bobbed in the sky. He leaned his head back and closed his eyes. I was clinging to him, moaning. He was moaning too. I was certain the concierge was back at his desk, watching us on the security cameras. Most definitely recording us. Later that evening, when he was alone in the mailroom, he'd probably replay the encounter. His navy trousers, creased by his mother's hot iron, would be around his ankles. I didn't care. Perhaps it made him happy.

When we finished, Andrew hoisted an elbow on the deck of the pool to recover. I took a moment to examine his entropy tattoo. It was nearly healed, and the design pristine. Not to mention highly distinctive. Though regret rarely appeared in my emotional toolbox, I did have a twinge of it. Not related to the tattoo, but to the number of hours I put into creating my look-alike videos. All to feed some juvenile fantasy I'd clearly outgrown. Dr. Morrison was a dud. I couldn't get that time back, though I knew I wouldn't delete my efforts either.

The massive clock on the wall beside the pool ticked past midnight. "It's officially your birthday," Andrew announced. "I've been thinking about what to get you. And I've made a decision."

"What's that?"

He swiveled in the water, so we were face-to-face. "I want to put your name on the condo. We've been together so long, and I want you to know it's your home too."

My throat tightened, and an uncomfortable warmth filled my chest. Perhaps it was a physical manifestation of guilt. I'd characterized

Andrew in such vile terms to Dr. Morrison, but it was so far from reality. My partner was not a brute. Unconventional, perhaps, in his unabashed exploration of all things intimate. But that was only one part of him. A single bone. All his other bones could easily be labeled *traditional dude*.

"No. I don't want that," I replied. Someday I wanted a home, but it would belong only to me. "I mean, I appreciate it, but it's too much."

"You're a peculiar woman, Lainey Greene. Different from anyone I've ever known."

"I hope that's a compliment." I scooped a handful of water and splashed his face.

With a laugh, he wiped his eyes clear. "Tell me then. What is it you want?"

I put my hands on his shoulder and leaned forward, whispering directly into his ear. A teaser.

As I waited for him to respond, I could not look at him directly. Instead I gazed at his reflection in the glass. And noted an enthusiastic grin.

"Well, that's unusual," he said. "Bit odd but could be steamy. I'm sure it can be arranged."

Which was the response I required. As I'd already gone ahead and set it up.

CHAPTER FORTY-ONE

Mia

"YOU'RE QUIET TODAY," Lainey said.

"Am I?" They were seated side by side on the balcony, plates balanced on their laps. Mia had prepared a late lunch of grilled teriyaki salmon and cold noodle salad. Two glasses of iced tea with fresh sprigs of mint. Even though the food looked delicious on the plate, she had no appetite. "Sorry. I'm just feeling a bit . . . I don't know. Overwhelmed?"

Over the past few days, she and Lainey had been inside a bizarre sort of bubble. Their interactions calm and comfortable. Fun even. But one wrong word, and the iridescent dome would burst.

"You know you can say anything, right?"

Mia shook her head. How could they possibly talk about Faye? Though how could they not?

After that first conversation with Lainey, Mia had tried not to jump to conclusions. To give her mother the benefit of the doubt. But that interaction at the cocktail bar had been chilling. Faye had sidestepped the truth with disturbing ease. Denying her actions and taking no accountability for all the suffering she'd caused. What kind of person was like that? Her indifference only slipped when she'd realized Mia and Lainey had reconnected. *You know what we stand to lose, right?* Those were her words, and Mia did not miss the careful use of *we*. As though they had been a team then and were still a team now. And both should worry that Lainey might get the authorities involved. But there was no *we*. However Lainey chose to proceed, no matter how difficult that was, Mia respected her right to control her own story. She would not interfere.

Faye undoubtedly sensed Mia's position, as the barrage of texts had been relentless. Until last night, when they stopped. Which offered no relief, as Mia was certain Faye had only paused to gather steam.

"Eventually we should talk about . . . some things." She swallowed a dry bite. "B-but not yet, okay?"

"Totally fine." Lainey nodded. "Let's enjoy this nice lunch. Did you put sesame oil on the noodles?"

Mia sighed with relief. She was astounded by Lainey's composure. In that moment, she was also grateful for it, even if their rekindled friendship was destined to implode. It would be impossible to navigate the reality of what had happened all those years ago. To navigate Faye.

"I did, actually. A teaspoon of—"

She was interrupted by sharp banging on the condo door. Mia quickly checked her phone for a missed call. Security was supposed to alert the resident if a guest arrived.

"Are you expecting someone?" Lainey asked.

"No. You?"

"Hardly."

Lainey gathered her plate, her cutlery, and said, "I'll wait in the other room. In case."

Mia understood. In case it was Ian. With the exception of a couple of brief conversations about Elise, Mia hadn't spoken to him since she'd left the house. Last thing she wanted was for him to know she and Lainey were meeting; that would create too many questions that she did not want to answer. And didn't *have* to answer. He was entitled to nothing from her.

When she peered through the peephole, her heart started to skitter. A pair of police officers. Mia's mind immediately went to Elise, an accident or an injury. Slowly opening the door, she said, "Can I help you?"

"Mia Morrison?"

"Yes?"

"You're a difficult person to find. Your husband gave us this address."

"My husband?" Her hand gripped the knob. "He hasn't called me."

"No, we asked him to hold off, so we could speak to you first."

"Why?" The word just a breath.

"Do you know an individual named Faye Ellis?"

Mia nodded and then exhaled. She should have guessed. Since coming back to Callow, Faye had had a couple brushes with the law. Minor infractions, like when she was arrested for protesting the relocation of a bird fountain. That was during her short-lived activist stage. Or that time she was in a domestic doyenne phase and "accidentally" stole six crystal dessert bowls from an antique store.

Then a different thought. Perhaps Lainey had called the authorities after all. Mia steadied herself, then said, "Sh-she's my mother."

"We'd like to talk to you, if you have a moment? You're listed as next of kin."

A puff of cold shot through her body. This was not about the past. Something had happened. Something was terribly wrong.

She moved out of the way and pointed at the sofa. "We have this place as a rental property, but our tenant moved out. Awful tenant, if I'm honest. So I'm staying for a while. I don't know how long. I haven't decided, but there's no rush, no rush to do anything at all."

They were seated now, patiently looking at her. And words continued to spill out, filling up the room with useless noise. Preventing them from delivering their news. "Can I get you something to drink? Iced tea maybe? I have mint?"

"No, nothing at all, ma'am." In robotic unison. "If you'd like to take a seat as well?"

She lowered herself onto the very edge of a chair. Bit the inside of her cheek. Then they explained that her mother had been found deceased in a hotel room, and when Mia was able, they would need her to do a formal identification. Did she understand?

Yes.

Meanwhile, they were trying to piece together the events of Ms. Ellis's evening and could use Mia's input. Was she open to helping them?

Yes.

"Did you say evening? So yesterday?"

"Sometime late last night. She was found this morning."

With a shiver, she now realized why the texts had stopped. "And you're just letting me know now?"

They glanced at each other. "This is actually pretty decent, ma'am. Often it takes a day or two to notify family."

Mia opened her mouth, but this time, nothing emerged.

"Do you recognize this person?" They slid a printout across the coffee table.

A rapid glance, and Mia pushed it back. "No. Not at all."

"It's grainy, I know. The establishment is fairly new, and their security system is not fully up and running."

"What establishment? Where was she?"

They ignored her question.

"The guest in the room next door reported hearing a male voice."

"He indicated it was clearly a . . . a romantic encounter.'"

"Pricey place, but thin walls, so it seems."

"Sorry to be blunt. We're just trying to present the details."

Mia looked at one, then the other as their sentences melded together.

"Was Ms. Ellis dating anyone?"

"She was using those phone apps. But nothing serious. Every few days, she'd show me a different profile."

"So she was engaging with a lot of different men?"

"I don't mean it like that." *Or maybe like that?*

"But you can confirm she was having . . ."

". . . involvements, so to speak."

"Involvements?" Mia swallowed the lump in her throat. She really had no clue what her mother was doing. Who she was meeting. "This man who was there. Did he hurt her? Is that what you're trying to say?"

"No, ma'am. While we're not ruling anything out until we have the full autopsy report, at this point, there is no evidence suggesting foul play."

"The male apparently exited around 11 p.m., and the neighbor continued to hear your mother moving about the room."

"Suggesting she was fine when he departed."

"I don't understand," Mia said. "What could have happened?"

"Several possibilities. Perhaps something natural. Or"—they glanced at each other again—"was your mother known to experiment?"

Yes.

That seemed to be all she ever did. New styles, new diets. New personalities.

"With substances?"

"I-I don't think . . . I don't know."

"You don't know? So you can't say for sure."

"Did Ms. Ellis have any health conditions?"

"Not that I know of. But, I mean, maybe she wasn't telling me?" Mia closed her eyes for a moment. Everything was coming out wrong. She was making Faye sound like a sleazy impulsive woman who kept secrets from her own daughter.

"We did find unlabeled medication in her purse. We've already sent those pills for testing. Unfortunately, ma'am, this sort of incident is becoming much too common."

"B-but my mother was on a health kick. Excited about things." Exploring this latest version of herself. Believing she was a child of the universe. Tapping into some ethereal knowledge connecting colors or dates or lines on a palm. A silly phase. Practically harmless?

"Sadly, family is often the last to know."

Their tones had changed. They were no longer trying to disguise their disdain. Then they handed her a piece of paper. Notes scribbled in thin blue ink. The file number. Police division and phone number. Name of the hotel. Estimated time of death. Coroner's information. Both officers' names.

They had not even bothered to introduce themselves when she'd opened the door.

As soon as they left, Lainey emerged. "I heard bit and pieces. What's going on?"

"I don't know exactly. I think my mother did something really, really dumb. And now she's . . . she's—"

"What? What did they say?" Lainey put a hand on Mia's forearm. "I'm so sorry. What can I do?"

"I don't know," she repeated. "I was so upset with her at the bar. I walked out on her. I walked out." Mia's rib cage started to shiver. "I need Elise. I need to talk to my daughter." She picked up her phone to text her but couldn't tap the correct letters, and she passed it over to Lainey. “Tell her something has happened to her grandmother. I need to talk to her. Tell her to call me.”

“Got it.”

“Oh, and add in ‘I love you.’”

“Okay, done. It shows one check mark? Does that mean it’s sent but not delivered?”

“Maybe her phone is off. Or she still has me blocked. Shit!” Mia pressed her hand against her forehead. “This is all so crazy.”

“Can I drive you some—”

“I’ll call Ian. He can try her instead.” She grabbed her phone back.

He picked up immediately. “My god, Mia? I’ve been going crazy here, waiting to hear from you. Poor Faye! Did they tell you what happened? Are they investigating? Are you okay?” His voice was a twist of sandpaper inside her ears.

“I need to reach Elise,” she said flatly. “She’s not answering.”

“Elise? That’s because she doesn’t have her phone.”

“Of course she does. She always has her phone.”

“Yes, but she’s at a swim camp. No devices permitted.”

“What?”

“I suppose they want the kids to unplug.”

“No, I mean the camp. When was this decided?”

“Last minute, I think. She and Chloé took the week and went up north. It’s a camp for lifeguards to train. Build skills, she told me. Cost a pretty penny, I might add.”

“How do I get in touch with her?”

She could hear him breathing. Then he said, “Let her be, Mia.”

“Are you serious? She needs to know about her grandmother.”

“And she will know. But it could be days before they even release the body, and there’s nothing Elise can do. Let her have her week, and when she’s back, we can share this difficult news. We’ll do it together.”

"Together? I'll share the news about *my* mother on my own, thank you very much."

"I understand, but you need support, whether you realize it or not. I'm here for you, as I always have—"

Mia hung up, the arm that held her phone dropping to her side.

"I'm sure he only wants to help. No doubt he cared about Faye."

"Fuck him. He never even liked her."

She gazed at the balcony. The two chairs. Only minutes earlier she and Lainey were seated there having a simple lunch. Everything was mostly okay. She couldn't believe her mother was gone. Mia turned to her oldest friend—her only friend.

"They said I had to identify her, right? That means they don't know for sure. Maybe it's all a mistake."

CHAPTER FORTY-TWO

Lainey

IT'S NOT ALL *a mistake.*

I didn't see anything wrong with going along with my friend's delusional hope for a short while. People need time to process.

I made a pot of drip coffee and poured two mugs. Added extra sugar to Mia's; the news had been a shock, no doubt wreaking temporary havoc on her both emotionally and physically.

As we sat together, she told me what Faye had been up to. Using Tinder and Bumble, chatting with shifty strangers, and possibly placing herself in unsafe situations. She said her mother believed an orb of pink light surrounded her and offered protection from the ill will of others. I allowed myself an interior chuckle. That woman was both slutty and batshit crazy.

I'd admit, when Mia's grief began to rear its gnarly head, I lost the plot. Faye had not been a good mother to Mia. Not a good friend either. So why the intense wave of sorrow? Why the nonstop tears? I did my best to maintain an engaged facade, but my mind could not help drifting to the evening before. Where had I been? Enjoying my birthday surprise with my loving and pliable partner, Andrew.

The evening started in a hotel room. Initially I was there alone, seated inside a very large armoire. Tips of my toes pressing against the base of an ironing board. As I waited, I reminisced about my own mother. How she used to fold me up, like clean laundry, and slide me into a dresser drawer.

It wasn't long before I heard the beep-beep sounds of the door code being entered.

A nervous giggle. "I can't believe I'm doing this!"

Fuck. She'd arrived first, which was out of my control, though not what I'd hoped for. I'd tried to be meticulous in my planning. Visiting multiple hotel rooms. Finding the ideal setup. The bed had to be just the right height. The closet spacious and at a specific angle. The lighting suitable. The check-in frictionless.

I ended up choosing the new hotel where Andrew had a security contract. The oversized armoire even had a slatted door, which was surely meant to be. I used a computer at the library to book the room using a prepaid card. Shortly after, I received a confirmation to a fake email address. It couldn't get any better.

Through the slats, I watched her moving about the room. She placed her monstrous purse on a chair, then went to the bedside table. She plucked up the bottle of pinot noir and read the folded card my printer had spat out earlier. *With compliments from our staff.*

"Oh, how thoughtful," she whispered.

Andrew arrived only a minute later, and hearing his voice, I exhaled a controlled breath of relief.

"Hey, there. Is that you, Deborah?"

"Mm-hmm. And Tim, I presume?"

I had selected his name for my personal amusement. And clearly she'd lied about hers too.

"You got me!"

Lounging on the bed, her hand stroked the comforter. "You're better looking than your photos, Tim."

"I'll take the compliment, Deborah."

"Your texts made you sound a little full of yourself. But it's justified."

"My texts? But this is the first time we've spoken."

I immediately tensed. If he mentioned his partner, this would go south fast. But she grinned and kicked off her sandals. "Oh, that's the game, is it? I'll play along."

"Yes," he said enthusiastically, "let's play."

"Do you—do you do this often, Tim?"

"What? Find myself enchanted by an alluring woman?" Which was, in fact, quite accurate. She was undeniably attractive. I had the same impression now as when I had seen her all those years ago. Climbing out of her car, her curves overflowing from her tiny bikini.

When she gave a hearty laugh, bile burned the back of my throat. Then she gestured toward the wine. "Shall we?"

Andrew paid no attention to the damaged foil. That was my bad. Injecting a little something-something into the bottle had been quite the chore. After removing the cork, he poured a single glass. She was eager maybe. Or anxious. She downed half the contents in a couple of gulps. "Someone's thirsty," he joked, and then gave her a generous refill.

This was even better than I'd dreamed.

"You don't want any?"

"I don't drink."

"No worries," she said. "I'll just take a drop more."

While she was sipping a third glass, he undressed. A slow pulling over his head, unbuttoning, unzipping. He dug both thumbs into either side of his underwear and lowered them. I watched her licking her lips, and then she said, "Oh hello," reaching out to touch.

He took a small step back. "First, I need to hear you say it. You're cool with this?" He gestured about the room. "I think it's important to make sure."

She pulled him close to her. "I'm cool with everything. And you? Consent goes both ways, you know."

How fucking enlightened.

"Oh yeah. I'm cool too." With his fingertip, he traced her jawline, then helped her slip out of her own clothes. A basic cotton dress, but a lacy bra-and-panties set beneath. Some glittery material no less.

I was startled when she started to dim the lights, but Andrew gripped her breast and said, "Let's keep them on. I want to see every part of you."

The dance between them was grotesque but also fascinating. Andrew performed like a pro, and to her credit, she genuinely seemed to extract pleasure from his efforts. Usually the women he slept with faked arousal, but perhaps that was due to the observer effect. This old goat was unaware of any third-party participation, and I detected two genuine orgasms.

My primary goal was never to watch them screw. I simply wanted to orchestrate a reunion between the two of us, in a way that had a little flair. After learning the truth about my uncle's death, I needed to find a resolution to assuage the pressure inside my head. And it took some work to get there. I had to sift through thousands of dating profiles to locate her (thank you Elise for the tip!). A few blurry photos of Andrew, my usual texting charm, and Faye Ellis was open to anything. If she enjoyed a pregame frolic? Call it a kindness.

Once the shagging checklist was complete, Andrew dressed and then put on the brand-new cap I'd purchased just for this purpose. Royal blue with an iconic yellow swoosh across the front panel.

"You're not staying?" she slurred.

"Can't. But you're welcome to. Checkout's 11 a.m. tomorrow."

"Don't mind if you do." She yawned and ran her fingers down her torso. Pausing at the dampness between her legs.

After Andrew left, I watched her from my hiding spot. She went straight for the wine and poured herself the remainder. The empty bottle slipped from her grip, striking the side table and clattering to the floor. Pulling back the top sheet, she climbed back into bed. With a wobbly arm, she placed the glass on the night table and emitted a satisfied sigh. Finally she closed her eyes.

Several minutes of waiting, and I emerged from the wardrobe. I tiptoed to the door and engaged the deadbolt. Then I went to the bed and stood over her.

Darling Faye was out cold. Snoring softly. I had miscalculated either her nerves or her greediness; she'd consumed more than I anticipated. Andrew would be waiting, eager for me to return home. I'd told him I'd need a few minutes to say goodbye to the woman. A quirky and adventurous lady from the yoga studio. But I couldn't loiter long. Of course, I'd hoped to see the realization in Faye's eyes, but I had to be okay without it.

I picked up a pillow. And held it above her head. Ready to capture her last breath inside the downy feathers.

But then I faltered.

I'd been so engrossed with the thrill of planning, I hadn't fully contemplated the weightiness of the act. Since I was a teenager, I'd carried the label of killer. It didn't matter that so few people were aware of it. I still knew. I mistakenly assumed it would be easy to finally slip into my designated role. To transform the falsehood into truth.

Edges of the pillow gripped in my fists, I gazed down at my best friend's mother. What was I doing? Why was I doing it? To extract revenge for what she'd done to my uncle? To free Mia from her toxic bond with her mother? Or to have a back-pocket tidbit to use against Dr. Morrison? No. It was much simpler than that. With Faye Ellis alive, there was no way my friendship with Mia could continue.

I lowered the pillow, and with my feet planted firmly on the low-pile carpet, I applied a gentle but consistent pressure. Once the requisite four minutes had passed, I took a peek. Only evidence was a smudge of mascara on the pillowcase, which could have been there all along. I replaced the empty wine bottle and glasses, then slipped a few questionable pills into her ugly crocheted bag.

As I quietly left the room, I tucked away the indefinable feeling that sloshed through my guts. My emotional indigestion.

I'd done what I needed to do.

CHAPTER FORTY-THREE

Mia

"I'M SORRY, I can't comment on that. We don't divulge information about our guests."

Mia was standing at the check-in desk of Callow's newest boutique hotel. Behind her, the lobby gleamed with marble flooring, sleek leather seating, sisal rugs, and towering leafy plants. According to the police, this was the place where her mother had died.

"But it was two days ago. What does it matter?"

"Past or present, our policy is the same."

The girl was youngish with wavy blond hair and layers of makeup. She was wearing a uniform: a starched navy blouse and bright white blazer.

"I'm not asking you to break your policies. I'm only trying to understand what happened to my mother."

The police were not investigating. Mia had called that morning, but instead of an update, the officer's tone was abrupt. "What can I do for you, Mrs. Morrison?" He repeated what he'd said earlier. That Faye was an adult and she'd made choices. "But the apps?" Mia insisted. "The man she was with? The pills?" He'd taken time to yawn, then said, "I'm going to be straight with you. Even if we did pursue access to her data, we don't have the resources to chase down every . . ."—he cleared his throat—"date that's ended poorly. She was not there against her will. No one shoved anything down her throat. And if we located the guy, we could never prove intent."

When Mia hung up, she wanted to scream. She felt as though she was stuck in an endless and frustrating maze. No directions, no exit. Her muscles were tender, and her eyes felt grainy. She'd barely slept, but somehow she'd been able to inch forward. Viewing the body. Talking to the coroner. Planning a funeral. Her mind had disconnected from the pain, so she could do what needed to be done.

She was even able to manage Ian. While he kept reaching out every couple of hours, she found it easy to ignore him. Swipe to voicemail, swipe to archive. She would, however, reluctantly admit he'd been right about Elise. Having their daughter safe and content at a swim camp while Mia navigated all the horribleness was the best possible scenario.

"Though I can appreciate what you're saying, our focus is on protecting our clientele."

"Come on," Mia said, turning around. Lainey was waiting close by. "This is pointless. Let's leave."

"Not so fast." She stepped past Mia and then addressed the girl. "Did you actually have the audacity to say you protect your clients?"

"That's—I mean, every hotel has the same rules."

"One of your guests died here two nights ago. Did you protect her?"

"Um, I'm not allow—I can't—"

"Listen up"—Lainey squinted at the nameplate pinned to the girl's lapel—"Madison. Let me tell you what's going to happen as soon as my friend and I leave. A multitude of horrendous reviews are going to pop up on Google, Tripadvisor. Even Reddit. A full discussion about the treatment we've received. Then a scathing article will be published in Callow's lifestyle magazine. You know the one, I'm sure. I'm head editor, and we've got over ninety thousand followers on Instagram. This place is lovely on the surface, but I'll be compelled to detail the alleged drug use that occurs here. How you're failing to protect vulnerable women."

"We have no control over what our guests do in their own rooms."

"An excellent quote, Madison. Thank you very much for going on the record."

Her face paled, leaving behind an unnatural peachy shimmer. "Would you please give me a moment?"

When she disappeared through a wooden door behind the front desk, Mia whispered, "Do you actually write for that magazine?"

"Hell no," Lainey replied with a one-sided smirk.

Not sixty seconds later, the girl returned with a sticky note attached to the back of her hand. "My manager says to assist in any way possible. I apologize for the confusion, and we are deeply sorry for your loss." With orange acrylic fingernails, she started clicking on her keyboard, glancing twice at the note. "Faye Ellis, correct?"

"Yes." Mia nodded. "Faye with an E."

"Okay. I see she's stayed as a guest on two separate occasions." More click-clicking. "Yes, the first time was two weeks ago. But the room was booked in the name of Mia Morrison?"

"That's me. I won a free night in your contest. Somehow my email was in your database, and I gave her my prize."

"I don't believe we've set up our database yet. And an email contest? I'm unaware, but I can inquire with our marketing team?"

Mia shook her head. "No, it doesn't matter."

After stabbing Enter several more times, the girl bit her lip, then looked at Mia. "And we have her with us again two nights ago."

"She booked the room?"

"No, but there's video of her entering the lobby. Police wanted a copy, and of course we provided everything they asked. She used the door code to join another guest."

"This other guest? Who was that?"

The girl ran her finger down over the screen. "The reservation was under a Mr. Tim Smith."

Lainey touched Mia's arm. "Does that sound familiar to you?"

"Not at all. I've never heard her mention him." Mia couldn't recall the name on that last profile. The reader or gardener. Maybe he was a student? She'd barely paid attention. But it didn't matter now. How likely was it that Tim Smith was his real name? And if it was, he'd be one of about a million.

"I can bring you to the room. If you'd like to see it?"

Mia hesitated, then nodded.

She and Lainey followed the girl to the elevator and then up to the eighteenth floor. Making their way down a long hallway, they eventually stopped in front of a dark wood door. There was no yellow tape across the frame. No paper notice pasted below the peep hole. It looked indistinguishable from every other doorway they'd already passed. As though nothing had happened there.

With the tip of her nail, the girl entered a code into the keypad. A triple beep, a tiny light turned green, and she pushed it open. Mia and Lainey brushed past her, and she said, "If there's anything else you need, I'll be at the front desk. Please take your time."

Mia took slow, steady steps into the main section of the suite. This was the last room her mother saw. What would possess her to go to a random hotel room and meet a random man? Was she oblivious to the dangers? Mia pressed her hand into her sternum, trying to quell the sorrow.

As she moved about the space, she had an intense sensation of déjà vu. Though the hotel had only recently opened, she felt as though she'd been there before. The desk, the chair, the headboard. The abstract floral artwork and the pattern of thin stripes in the carpet.

She pulled out the drawer of the night table. It was empty. Then she opened the double doors of the armoire. Folded neatly on the top shelf was a pile of extra bedding. A plumped-up pillow. Mia pulled down a throw blanket and shook it open.

Suddenly her limbs felt wobbly, and she moved to the edge of the bed.

"Are you okay?" Lainey asked, sitting beside her. "What is it?"

"The blanket. I recognize it." A blue octagonal pattern. She was not experiencing déjà vu at all. She'd seen the room. Or one identical to it. It was all captured in the images on the USB drive she'd found in Ian's shirt pocket.

CHAPTER FORTY-FOUR

Lainey

THE USB DRIVE. That was also my doing. But zero regrets, even though the result was not what I'd intended.

After I realized Mia was so close, my knee-jerk reaction was to arrange a meetup with my former bestie. Still thinking, of course, she was to blame for everything. I wanted her to understand what had happened to me at Albethey. How they'd shrunk my thoughts, corroded my brain, polluted my blood with pharmaceuticals. How, through all of that, I'd done everything to shield her from harm.

As the years had passed, the silence eroded my desire to protect her, and an oily resentment burbled up to eclipse it. I determined it was within my rights to call her out on her behavior. Privately, of course. So I booked a room at the newly opened hotel using a fake business account. I sent out an "exciting prize" message to several random email addresses with variations on Mia's married name. Most of them bounced back, but I was sincerely surprised that my first attempt ended up with a bite. Whom I crowned the winner.

I wasn't even sure it was her, but as was my nature, I remained optimistic. I set up surveillance gear in the room so I could record our interaction. I had all kinds of ideas on how things would transpire, what I was going to say to her face, but while I discretely loitered in the lobby, I noticed an eerily familiar face. It took a beat or two before I realized it was her mother. And then, to my absolute dismay, Dr. Morrison appeared shortly thereafter. Needless to say, I did not interrupt their playdate and eagerly anticipated reviewing the footage.

Their encounter commenced with a heated argument.

"It was a mistake," he said. "Don't you get that? It was poor judgment. And as you well know, it was very short-lived."

"You didn't seem to mind at the time, Ian."

"And you can't resist holding it over my head, Faye."

"That's not fair." An exaggerated pout. "It's been difficult for me too. I didn't expect my son-in-law to seduce me. To take advantage of my loneliness."

"What?" He shook his head. "That's not what happened, and you damn well know it. You pursued me."

The remainder of their conversation was inaudible, but at one point, she straddled him on the desk chair. Tried to kiss him, but he twisted his face to the side. Finally he leaned his head back and sternly said, "You exasperate me, you know."

It was the dullest romp I'd ever witnessed. Though they managed several positions, there was no biting, hair-pulling, or ecstatic rutting. While Faye appeared to enjoy the exercise, Dr. Morrison's heart clearly was not in it. The poor boo.

After they finished, he said, "Can we agree this was a bad idea? And it won't happen again? We don't want anyone getting hurt, do we?"

"Yes, and yes. And of course we don't." Then she started peppering him with questions about his work. About the case study and reconnecting with his former client.

My ears immediately perked up.

"How's that going?"

"All fine, Faye."

"But you're talking to her? That sick woman?"

"As I said, nothing I can discuss."

"No? Well, if there's ever anything we *should* discuss, you've got my number."

He gave her a puzzled look and then drifted out the door.

I extracted stills from the video, did a little editing, and created an artful collage. After saving copies to a USB drive, I casually popped by their residence that evening and deposited the tiny drive in a laundry basket of soiled shirts and underwear. I was confident Dr. Morrison did not wash his own clothing, and Mia would find it there.

Afterward, I spent considerable time pondering the affair between son-in-law and mother-in-law. His actions? No great mystery. Most men were invariably guided by their penis and fully believed they could get away with anything. But the mother? Why would she do that to her daughter? I initially concluded that Faye Ellis must have hated Mia. Or else wanted to be Mia. But a hotel bump-n-grind? Where she was so pushy to start the action? It took a little distance for clarity to arrive, but her motive eventually became obvious. It wasn't about sex at all. She was threatened and creating leverage. Just in case I told the truth.

•

Over the past two days, my psychiatrist had reached out multiple times. I labeled it *shades of relentless hounding*. Made me feel like a high school boy was crushing on me. No doubt that degree of pursuit was against patient-doctor guidelines. But I didn't mind. I made notes and had a tickly feeling my collection of ephemera would come in handy at some point.

"Lainey, finally! I've been concerned. Are you okay?"

"Totally. Just incredibly busy."

The wood paneling of his college office filled his background, and as he shifted, his leather chair creaked. "I do believe I was overly abrupt during our last session, and I wanted to apologize."

"Abrupt? I don't recall." I did recall.

"I failed to express myself properly. Perhaps we can frame it that way. I do recognize how difficult this is, and the progress we've made together. But . . ."

"You think I'm delusional." Or, better put, "making shit up."

"No, not at all." He coughed into his hand and closed his fingers around the lie. "Let me say that I was reminded that navigating trauma is not a linear process. No one is a perfect witness. Not even to their own experiences."

"I disagree."

"How so?"

"We are perfect witnesses. Maybe not to describe the minutiae of a scene, but our bodies remember."

I was tempted to ask about his mother-in-law. If his skin remembered her skin.

He ran his fingers through his beard, then said, "Have you continued to interact with your childhood friend?"

"I have."

"Anything you'd like to talk about?"

"Not so much, really. I was certain she'd forgotten about me, but turns out she missed me as much as I missed her." I sighed with a little theatricality. "Our lives are so different, but she's essentially the same person. Shy. A bit naive. In need of a helping hand." I sounded like a boy scout prepping for a merit badge, but I was being sincere.

"Do you think it's wise to explore that 'relationship' at this time?"

I did not appreciate his air quotes. "Wise? How could showing kindness be unwise? Especially when she's going through a challenging time. I'm sure even you appreciate a soft shoulder." No double entendre intended.

"I see." He was clicking his pen, as he often did when mildly annoyed.

"Have you experienced grief, Dr. Morrison?"

"Well, yes. I'd assume most people my age have been touched by it."

"How? A parent? Sibling?"

"Odd you should ask. It's been a particularly hard couple of days."

"Oh dear. A recent loss, I'm gathering?"

"Yes, Lainey. A recent loss."

"What about personal?"

"I would say family members are personal, no?"

"I mean you. Your own life. Where you thought you'd be and are not. All your failures. They must feel like tiny deaths, of a sort. I'm curious if you grieve yourself."

His mouth tightened. "I'm not sure where you're trying to go with this, but let's bring our attention back where it belongs. On your experiences. And not my multitude of shortcomings." He grinned then. But I could tell he was feigning humility.

"Sure."

"Your uncle. That was undoubtedly complex grief. Given the dynamics of your connection."

"I'm sure it was. Have you ever heard the idea that grief is the persistence of love?" I saw it on an Instagram reel. Figured my phone was listening in on my sessions, and the algorithm took it upon itself to offer a salve.

He nodded. "Yes, I'd say that has merit."

"Someone dies, but the love doesn't. So it's lodged in your chest. Love can swell up and destroy you."

"That makes sense. Love can be joyful, but also the most painful emotion."

"Right? Last night I was googling stuff, trying to get some information on the soul. Sounds wacky, I know."

"Not wacky at all. People often turn to research as a coping mechanism when things are beyond their control. Did you discover anything interesting?"

More pen-clicking. I knew he was bored, but I didn't care.

"I ended up down this rabbit hole about energies. Probably just pseudoscience, but I came across this theory that we're all unstable."

"Unstable how? Mentally?"

"No. Physically. We blink in and out of existence a million times a second. And it's the electromagnetic field around us that brings us back together. Some people think that's evidence of the soul."

"I'm not sure how valid—"

"It doesn't matter if it's valid or total trash. It resonated with me. The idea that we're not solid. That we . . . we flicker."

"Okay then."

"I wanted to tell you all this."

"Is there a particular reason? Forgive me, but it all seems somewhat . . . out there."

"To give you a heads-up, I suppose." While I'd already taken steps to excise some of the damaging elements from Mia's life, there was more work to be done. Her husband was a problem. My decisions might cause her immediate pain, but she wouldn't have to walk through those dark woods alone. She'd have me by her side.

"A heads-up?"

"It's just basic decency. Seeing as we've spent all this time chatting, I figured you deserved that."

"I'm sorry, Lainey. I'm unsure if this is a productive use of our time."

I stared at him. Counted the seconds until he blinked first. "It's not complicated, Dr. Morrison. Soon you're going to recognize your own instability." I tossed him a heartfelt smile. "You might even feel your soul flicker."

CHAPTER FORTY-FIVE

Mia

WEARING A SIMPLE black dress, Mia sat on a wooden pew. She knotted her fingers together and squeezed until her knuckles turned white. The arrangements she'd made were a mistake. A generic gathering in a damp building, followed by a traditional burial. Her mother would never have wanted that. If Faye had any say, a final goodbye would be a twilight garden party, fairy lights, wind chimes, and energy healers. Light and unconventional, instead of this forgettable series of conventional steps.

She scanned the near-empty church. Ian had assured her that Elise would be back in plenty of time to attend the service. Sandy had told him the girls were taking the camp bus, which would bring them directly into the city. Ian would collect Elise at the drop-off point and explain everything. Yes, it would be a shock. Yes, it would be a rush. But he could handle the situation in a sensitive and age-appropriate way. "I'm trained for that," he reminded her.

Just before the service was about to begin, Ian strode down the aisle toward her. Mirrored sunglasses covering his eyes. The sight of him filled her with revulsion. How could she ever have found him charming and attractive?

When he reached her, he yanked the sunglasses from his face. His expression was a knot of seriousness. "The bus is delayed," he whispered. "There's construction on the highway. Traffic is down to one lane."

"And?"

"I apologize, Mia. I totally miscalculated the duration of their return trip."

"So she's going to miss this? Miss it all?"

"I truly hope not. As soon as the bus arrives, I'll go straight away."

Mia pushed a fist into her abdomen to sooth the wave of nausea. "I should have waited. I knew I should have waited."

"Hey," he said, touching her shoulder. "There's nothing we can do right now but work together. Let's put our disconnect on a shelf for today. We share this grief, Mia."

As he spoke, images from the USB drive flashed through her mind. His fingertips indenting another woman's flesh. His bare back shimmering with sweat. His open mouth twisted, upper gum on ridiculous display.

He pointed at the empty spot beside her. "May I?"

"No, you may not."

Angling herself away from him, Mia stiffened her back. It occurred to her then that he'd done it on purpose. Encouraged her to make immediate arrangements, only to "miscalculate" a bus ride. Without Elise, he probably assumed she'd lean on him. In her sadness, she'd draw him close. He'd made it clear they could address her "obvious confusion" later, and he was willing and available to help. Even at the thought of it, her disgust was thick and heavy.

The minister stood before the lectern and tapped the microphone. *Shall we begin*, he mouthed to Mia, and she nodded. "A warm welcome," he said. "To all who have come together to support this grieving family. Faye . . ." Then thirty minutes blurred past, and the service was over. She vaguely recalled a reading from a leather-bound book. Organ music, and a few faint voices singing hymns. Mia did not have the capacity to prepare a eulogy and forbade Ian from doing so. When the minister had offered up the microphone, not a single person stepped forward to recount lively or amusing memories of Faye.

After the attendees left the building, a few headed to the parking lot, while others went to the cemetery on the south side of the property. As Mia stood beside the gaping hole that was ready for the casket, random people approached to offer condolences. She recognized two of her mother's neighbors, as well as the cashier from the local convenience store. The man who'd sold Faye her last car. There was also a woman in a tailored suit, her tote bag stamped with the name of a realty company. Was that the extent of Faye's social circle? Were these the only people to mourn her mother?

Ian kept his distance. He was standing beneath a massive oak tree near the road, phone gripped in his fist. Once everyone finally dispersed, he lifted his hand to wave and then climbed into his car. She did not wave back but instead felt a warm flush of embarrassment over the custom paint color he'd chosen. Seafoam green. Then behind that, shame. She shouldn't be bothered by something so inconsequential.

Mia was not the only person monitoring Ian. In a high window of the church, a tall figure was also following his movements. Her face was concealed beneath a wide-brimmed hat, but Mia knew immediately it was Lainey. They'd agreed she could attend, if she remained unseen. Which she'd done successfully, hidden in the back corner of the upper level. Knowing she was close by was the only thing bringing Mia comfort.

"Um. Hi there. How are you holding up?"

Floral perfume wafted beneath Mia's nose, and she turned toward the hesitant voice. "Sandy. I'm surprised to see you."

"I just wanted to tell you how sorry I am for your loss."

As she took a step backward, Mia's heels sank into the soft grass. "Thank you," she replied curtly.

"If you need anything, don't hesitate."

A brittle twig snapped inside her chest. "If I need anything?"

"I know. I'm sure everyone says the same thing." She gestured behind her at the now-empty cemetery. "It all starts to sound insincere, doesn't it?"

"Not all." Mia sniffed. "But you do."

"Excuse me?"

Perhaps it was grief that prompted the sudden bluntness. "We were friends, Sandy. At least I thought so. But you turned your back on me."

"What?"

"That really bothered me, you know."

"*I* bothered *you*?" Sandy folded her arms across her chest. "I came to pay my respects because our girls are close. That's all. If you want a conversation about anything else, we can have it later."

"How about we have it now?"

"You really want to do that?"

"Why not?"

"Fine then." She threw her hands up in the air. "I thought we were friends, too, you know. And I couldn't believe you'd send your mother to deliver such a cruel message."

"My mother? I don't recall you even meeting her."

"Nope. That's right. Just that one unforgettable time."

"What are you talking about?"

Sandy gazed up at the sky and then back at Mia. "She wanted me to know that you found me tiresome. And shallow. Oh yes, classless too. You could barely tolerate my company. But the final kicker? You didn't trust me around your husband. You thought I was trying to sleep with him."

"You can't be serious." Though she'd wondered recently if Ian and Sandy had had an affair, she never once entertained that thought while they were friends.

"But I backed off, you know. Respected your wishes. Anyway, I figured it was more about your husband's behavior than it was about me. Ian made it quite clear he was available, but I ignored him." She scowled. "Because I cared about you. I never even liked him. Still don't. He's pompous and entitled and small-minded."

"I-I can't believe that." Mia's heels sank deeper into the grass.

"Why not tell me to my face? Didn't I deserve that? At least I wasn't the only one. I bumped into your old neighbor. You sent your mom her way too. She said the exact same thing, and then I realized you really aren't well."

Mia skimmed the history of her adult friendships. Over the past few years, each one had invariably ended with an impenetrable wall. Occasionally, total silence. And when she'd given up hope for reconciliation, her mother always swooped in with reassurance. Rinsing away the sting of rejection. "If a friend treats you that way, Mia, she's not worth a moment's bother."

As Sandy turned and stormed away, Lainey arrived at Mia's side. "What was that about? You okay?"

"Nothing. I'll tell you later." Sandy's unsettling story was yet another prickly item to add to the pile of things to think about another day.

"Have you arranged anything for afterward? Tea and such?"

"No, I didn't bother." She didn't see the point. Who would attend? What would they possibly talk about? No one even seemed to know her mother.

"Let's go somewhere then. Have a coffee."

"I don't think I can sit still." She was both exhausted and full of energy. She worried if she stopped moving, she might crumple. "Maybe I should head to my mother's? Not that anything has to be done immediately. But to get a sense of the tasks ahead?"

Lainey nodded. "If you're up for it. I can take you."

Following Mia's directions, Lainey drove to Faye's home. A historic bungalow with a mustard-yellow door. As they pulled in, Mia noticed somebody crouched on the bottom step. A girl in an oversized hoodie, arms wrapped around bent knees.

Mia shoved open the passenger door and sprinted from the car. "Elise?"

But when the girl lifted her head, the hood fell away, and she realized it was Chloé.

"Mia?" She jumped up. "Finally!"

"What are you doing here?"

"I got home and saw the note from my mom."

"Did Elise see it? I thought Ian was picking you two up? Did he talk to her?"

"I never saw him there. I went home by myself. And I've been trying to find you. I called and I went to your house and then came here. I banged on the door, but no one answered."

"What's going on? Where's Elise?"

Chloé's chin began to quiver. "I've tried a bunch of times, but she won't text me back."

A sudden pain erupted behind Mia's eyes. "What does that mean? Why would you need to text when you're together?"

"I-I went to swim camp by myself."

"Then where's my daughter?"

"I don't know, Mia." Chloé started to bawl. "I don't know where she is. She was staying with her grandmother."

CHAPTER FORTY-SIX

Lainey

THE CHEAP LAWN ornaments jumped out at me first, before I even noticed the teary-eyed kid on the bottom step. I knew immediately I'd been to Faye Ellis's house before. It was the afternoon I'd followed Dr. Morrison for the first time. He'd stopped there on his way home, banging on that ugly yellow door with such obvious irritation. I'd sensed the occupant was a woman. Also sensed she was his lover. Bonus points for me on both fronts.

When I approached, the girl did a double take. Of course she recognized my face. I narrowed my eyes, and she quickly looked away. Smartly saying nothing.

Digging a key from her purse, Mia unlocked the front door. "Elise?" she cried, as she bolted inside. "Elise!"

I trailed behind her. But there was only silence.

The home's interior was, in a word, objectionable. Low ceilings, weak lighting, cramped rooms. A mishmash of personal belongings and random furnishings, with no cohesiveness. Multiple shelves and curios were jammed with kitsch. On the wall above her sofa, an enormous garish macramé of beads and wool. Directly across from that, prints of Warhol's soup cans.

"She was here," Mia said. "For certain."

While I would've preferred waiting outside, I understood that friendship required effort. Clearly, some days more than others. Taking light steps, I moved deeper into the house. All the windows were shut, and the place smelled earthy and stagnant. I tried not to breathe too deeply. I didn't want that woman's filthy air touching my lungs.

Mia was standing in the middle of a closet-sized bedroom at the back of the house. The floor was scattered with typical teen girl possessions. Mounds of fast fashion, a makeup bag turned on its side. Foundation and eyeliner and tubes of whatnot spilling out. A laptop sat on the night table, the lid dotted with stickers of a smiling lemon, a dancing avocado, a bullhorn with the phrase "Good vibes only!"

"This is her stuff. She must've snuck home. Brought things over."

Mia plucked up a hoodie, lifted it to her nose to inhale. And then she called the police.

I remained close at hand, catching her side of the conversation.

"Fifteen, she's fifteen, I said.

"Yes, I've contacted her friends.

"I don't know. She was staying at her grandmother's.

"No, I can't reach her. She's not even answering her friends.

"I don't know how long she's been missing.

"Like I said, I don't know. She was supposed to be at summer camp.

"Of course she didn't . . . I am calm." She held her phone in front of her face and yelled at the bottom of her screen. "I'm extremely calm!

"Thank you. Could you at least hurry? Please."

When Mia disconnected, her hands curled into fists. "They're useless. They're asking if she ran away. Why won't they do their jobs?"

"Mia?" A faint whisper from the annoying friend, who'd been loitering on the porch.

"What it is, Chloé?"

"This girl at camp snuck in a phone, and I texted with Elise."

"When?"

"Like, maybe the first day? Only a couple of messages. She said she was going to see her gran's new place?"

Mia shook her head. "What new place? You must've misunderstood. There's no way she'd take Elise on a trip without permission."

As I was listening to their tête-à-tête, I realized how little Mia knew of her mother's true nature. Though my interactions had been limited, I had a firm grasp. I'd witnessed what she did in the dark. And also knew what she'd done in broad daylight.

The oversight was not Mia's fault though. Most women likely believed their mothers cared about them. Accepted that premise without question. But in reality, the dynamic was more complicated. Few mothers were saints. Most probably had a taste of venom on their teeth.

I touched her arm. "What can we do to help? Your daughter hasn't disappeared. She's got to be somewhere, right?"

Mia rubbed her palm over her forehead. Her shoulders were slumped, and her eyes sunken and dark. I took a moment to acknowledge some gratitude for my personal situation. Childless, husbandless. Spinsterish women were statistically proven to be happier. Lived longer too.

"Yes," she said. "Let's scour everything. If my mother was planning a change, there's got to be information here somewhere." Then to the girl, "And Chloé? You watch the road, okay? Wouldn't put it past the police to miss the house."

As the teeny bopper skedaddled, Mia and I set to the task. Poking through every corner of the whore's house. First the bookshelves, then those dusty cabinets. I searched her kitchen. Balanced on the sill above the sink were several polished stones. I was tempted to touch them but resisted. I even peered inside the refrigerator. Nothing much but wrinkled grapes and an uncovered bowl of mac and cheese.

"Oh my god. What on . . ."

I followed Mia's cry of distress. The heavy odor in the main bedroom was the absolute worst. It reminded me of when Faye and I had hung out in the hotel room. Citrus and patchouli, so cloying, my nostrils burned. I was not a fan.

"Have you found something?"

"This. I don't even know what to make of it."

She thrust a thin black notebook toward me. I skimmed a few pages. It contained line after line of specific dates and events. Concise descriptions of evenings. Dinners out. Movie nights. Gifts like flowers or lingerie.

"Your mother's social calendar?" It appeared Faye had been quite active.

"No, that's not about her. It's all me. Me and Ian. She's been recording my life. Keeping notes on my marriage. Some of it, she was there. Like that bistro dinner?" Mia pointed at a recent entry. "But other stuff, I told her about. A nightdress, for instance." Which was detailed about a dozen lines lower. "She even wrote down the color. Cocoon."

"This is really weird, no?"

Though I was itching to reveal Faye's most putrid tidbits, I suspected an intervention was unnecessary. When a clearer mind prevailed, Mia would connect mother and husband all on her own. I figured allowing the truth to naturally unspool would produce the sharpest sting. Which, in the grand scheme, was better. Leaving no possibility of waffling. No chance of reconciliation.

"I don't even know what to say. Why would she do that?"

I knew why.

Mia abruptly strode toward the door. "Where are the police? What's taking them so long?"

Placing the notebook on the dresser, I said, "Let's keep searching, okay?"

I took another pass through the main area of the house and then ventured into the spare bedroom again. The closet offered no hints, just a pile of plaid shirts and farmhand overalls. In the corner, there was an ornamental desk. I assumed it would be empty, but when I opened the middle drawer, I found a purple folder.

As I scanned the paperwork, sweat instantly sprang from my pores. The floor rippled, and I pressed my hand against the wall to steady myself. Out of nowhere, I was dizzy, unwell. Like a heat lamp was above me, crackling on full blast. What was happening? I tried to count my fingers, one, two, three, but they were fading. My skin, the painted wall, both gray. The color of deadness.

Don't, Lainey. Don't drift away from yourself.

Go and show her.

I forced myself to take a step. In the living room, I clutched the folder in my fist. A realtor's business card stapled to the upper front corner. With my free hand, I dabbed sweat from my upper lip. Then pushed the words from my mouth. "Stone the fucking crows, Mia. Look what I've found."

CHAPTER FORTY-SEVEN

Mia

INSIDE THE PURPLE folder, Mia found the deed to a piece of real estate. An aging cabin in a remote location, about two hours east of Callow. She didn't recognize the address, the site survey, or name of the nearby lake. But then Lainey said, "It's the same place. Where we were."

Several seconds passed before she processed those words. "As teenagers?"

"Yup."

Mia was stunned. It was the property where Lainey's uncle had died. Where Faye had swung a board, and a nail had pierced James Kemper's throat. Whether or not it was an uncontrolled reaction to an insult was neither here nor there. Her mother had violently killed a man and pretended otherwise for years. And now she apparently owned the place where she had done it.

Suddenly some of Faye's outlandish comments made sense. She had spoken of taking charge of her destiny. Said that part of her was stuck in the past, and she was refusing to allow old energy to continue to dominate her. Mia had dismissed it at the time, assuming it was due to Faye's preoccupation with the so-called mystical arts. But it was all about purchasing the cabin.

She had so many questions. Had her mother always kept an eye on the property? Or did she track it down after Mia mentioned the republication of the case study? Had it been for sale? Or had she reached out to the owners with an offer? And what could she possibly have planned on doing with it?

Quickly flipping through the remaining pages, Mia found two financial documents outlining the payments. Faye had withdrawn money from the equity in her bungalow. And in addition to that, there was a supplementary payment in the sum of thirty-eight thousand dollars. Mia stared at the number, and a tingly wave of awareness spread through her bones. Ian. It was Ian. Her husband had provided that amount.

Only days ago she'd confronted him about the line of credit, and he'd offered a vague explanation about cryptocurrencies. Saying he'd chosen not to bring it to her attention, as she had no grasp of such a complex investment. She'd accepted yet another lie so easily.

Mia rushed outside. "Chloé! We know where she is. We're going to . . ." She was suddenly breathless. Her vision sparkly. Elise had to be there. There was no other possibility. "We're going to go get her."

Without waiting for police, Mia and Lainey climbed into the car. She entered the coordinates into Google Maps, and together they sped off. As Lainey drove, Mia continuously checked her phone. Expanding then contracting the map. The slow progress was agony.

Leaning forward in her seat, she planted her hands on the dashboard. "Can we go any faster?"

Lainey was speeding, swerving in and out of traffic. "Not if we want to arrive in one piece."

"Okay, okay."

After what felt like forever, they exited the highway and drove through a single-street town. Most of the shops were vacant, and several buildings were boarded up. When that street ended, an old logging trail began. For twenty minutes or more, they bumbled along an unpaved stretch of road. The car dipping left and right, wheels disappearing into enormous potholes. Eventually, the road narrowed into a driveway, and Lainey drove straight through the overgrown greenery.

When they finally pulled into the yard, Mia peered through the windshield. The cabin and surrounding area were not at all how she remembered. In the center of the property was a dilapidated structure with graying clapboard. The wraparound deck had a broken railing, and the sloping roof had a marked slump in the center, shingles missing all over. The place was obviously neglected. Possibly abandoned.

Before the car had come to a full stop, Mia leapt out, calling her daughter's name, but there was no reply. She hurried into the cabin, and finding it empty, tore back into the yard. She raced through overgrown grass, and when she'd nearly reached the dock, a sparkle of light caught her eye. Squinting, she saw a small figure about fifty yards up the shoreline seated on a large rock by the lake's edge. The water was lapping over the girl's toes, and she was holding something reflective in her hands. A spoon perhaps. Maybe a tin can.

"Hey!" Mia yelled, running toward her. "Elise!"

Head jerking around, Elise scrambled to her feet and rushed along the sandy beach. As soon as they reached each other, Mia grabbed Elise and hugged her tightly.

"Mom. Oh my god. You're here! Finally!"

"I am." Mia pressed her face into Elise's mess of greasy hair. "I'm here."

"I knew you'd come get me. I totally knew it."

Now holding Elise at arm's length, Mia surveyed her daughter's face and limbs. Elise's shoulders were blistered, nose and lips peeling, but she had no obvious injuries. "Are you okay?"

"Yeah, mostly. Just, it's been a lot."

"I'm sorry this happened," Mia whispered. She had to compress her emotions, otherwise tears might start and never stop. "I'm sorry you were left here. I'm so sorry I didn't come faster. I thought you were at camp."

"The camp." Elise blew out a stream of air and grimaced. "Yeah, that was a bad idea. I was so pissed off, Mom. I figured you expect me to do awful stuff, so why not do awful stuff, right? I wish I hadn't done it. I'll give the money back. I'll give it all back."

"We can talk about that later. What matters now is you're safe."

"It sucks here, but I'm not hurt or anything. Gran totally oversold this dump. I thought it'd be fun."

"I know." Mia shivered. What if Chloé hadn't gotten that text? What if Lainey hadn't opened that drawer? Elise would still be there. Waiting as the sun went down again.

"Then we got into a fight. She said she was going to turn this place into a wellness retreat, and it was her life's work, blah, blah. I told her no one'd ever go. Let alone pay. I wasn't trying to insult her, but it's, like, totally true."

"I know. You didn't mean any harm. It's okay."

"And then Gran said she'd be gone a day. I told her I wanted to go home, but she had some stupid date and was going to come back afterward. But she didn't. She took my phone too. And I was like, *What the hell?* She probably did that because I made her mad. There's no phone here. I walked for hours, but then I turned around. Figured it was better to stay put. That's the rule, isn't it? If you're lost, don't wander off?"

"Yes, that's the right thing." She squeezed Elise again. "You're very smart to do that."

"Yeah, and whatever freaks owned this place had to be preppers. Every cupboard's full of canned food."

"That's lucky. And you're okay. You're really okay?"

"Mom, where's Gran? Why would she just leave me here?"

Mia gently rubbed Elise's arms. The feel of her daughter's warm skin was soothing. "I'll explain later." News of Faye's death could wait.

While they were talking, Lainey had remained close to the car. Mia waved her over.

"Elise, this is an old friend. Lainey Kem— Lainey Greene. From when I was young."

"Hey." Lainey waved her hand.

"Um. Hey?" Then, "Can we get out of here, Mom? I seriously need a shower. This has been the worst trip ever. I have to tell Chloé everything."

"Absolutely, my darling. As soon as you're ready, we'll leave."

When Elise disappeared inside the cabin, Mia turned toward Lainey, but she was no longer there. She was standing at the very end of the dock gazing out over the still black water.

"No major trauma?" Lainey said, when Mia approached.

"Doesn't seem so. She's shaken up, but she managed."

"I'm glad we found her."

"Yeah. I was losing it."

"Oh, you were not. You were just being a mom."

"And you?" Mia said, locking her elbow with Lainey's. "Being here. It's got to be triggering. I didn't even think."

Lainey kicked a pebble, and it plopped into the water. "You know, I never could forget this place. It always loomed large in my dreams. Haunting me."

"That makes sense. Given . . . well, everything."

"But you know what? There's nothing of my uncle here. Nothing of me. It's basically just a shithole, isn't it?"

As Mia was about to respond, Elise reappeared. She was wearing her backpack and tugging a clear garbage bag full of recyclables. "I hate to say it, Mom. But Faye is such a flake. I really despise her. You can't rely on her for anything."

"No, you can't," Mia said. As they headed toward the car, she wrapped an arm around Elise's shoulder. "Were you scared?"

"Of what?"

"This place. Being alone."

"Not really. There's no one around. Like, literally no one." Elise rolled her eyes. "But if I ever eat beans again, I'm totally going to die."

CHAPTER FORTY-EIGHT

Lainey

THE MEETING PLACE was perfect. Located in a sleepy town a pleasant drive from Callow. Generic street, generic customers, generic eats. But the reason for my selection? The name: Karma Kafé.

I decided to wait on the park bench directly across the street. Exactly two minutes before our scheduled appointment, Dr. Morrison appeared on the sidewalk. Then strode inside. Through the front window, I could see him scanning the patrons, and realizing I wasn't there, he selected a table off to the side.

Even from that distance, his agitation was visible. He rolled up the sleeves of his lemon-yellow shirt and repeatedly checked his expensive watch. Then gnawed the side of his thumb, caveman style. I cringed, recalling my nights at Albethey, imagining him sneaking into my room. Climbing under the white sheet with me while I opened my legs. *Christ. Young people are so dumb.*

I decided to wait. Nothing wrong with allowing the doctor to simmer on a burner of his own making.

I'd spent hours fantasizing about how to eliminate him from our lives. Reasonable ideas like being trapped in a car on a sweltering day.

Or falling overboard on a lake and a propeller clipping his skull. Some implausible ideas too. Choking during a rousing game of chubby bunny, or inhaling psyllium powder. Oh, and an old standard: tossing a toaster into his bathtub. I'd admit, electrocution was enticing. Watching his spine arc, muscles convulse, eyes bulge. Just as mine had all those years ago.

Though tempting, I never mentioned any of those potential solutions to Mia. I'd decided it wasn't worth the emotional fallout. Dr. Morrison's demise would cost Mia and Elise too much. Especially Elise. Losing her father, even in an elegant way, would damage her. Perhaps permanently. Besides that, the man wasn't the devil. He was just a really shitty human being.

I'd opted to be direct. I planned to outline some strict boundaries. Clear rules for moving forward.

When he started to become extra antsy, I marched into the café, ordered an iced latte, and then sidled toward him. As I approached, he rose abruptly, leg jostling the table. With a sweep of his palm, he directed me toward a seat. That simple motion made me bristle, and I ignored it, dragged over a third chair.

Sitting again, he said, "I do apologize, Lainey. I haven't been available these past few days."

He was gazing at me with a pleasing degree of naivete.

"Something personal, Ian?"

He chuckled when I used his first name. "Keeping it informal in public, I see. I get it." Then a single deep breath, no doubt to straighten the mask. "It's all good. Nothing I can't handle."

"Ah, okay. Care for a beverage? A calming tea, perhaps? My treat."

"Very thoughtful, Lainey, but no thank you. Happy to sit and talk while you enjoy yours though."

I loudly slurped my iced coffee. "Cool spot, no?"

"Uh-huh," he said, glancing around. Then he turned his gaze toward me. "Meeting like this is a little unconventional, but I do like to accommodate. Give each patient leeway."

Why did he insist on using the term *patient*? I hated that. "Leeway for me? I'm not so sure that's necessary, Ian."

"I'm sorry?"

"All week, I've been mulling over how to handle our issues. It's a heady feeling when the power shifts."

A fluttery blink. "Apologies if I'm a little slow today. Power shifting? Did you consider there to be a power imbalance between us?"

"What kind of inane question is that?" I said with a hearty laugh. "Of course there was."

"We should discuss that, no? My goal is to support you, be a guide as you explore your traumas."

"And help me, you have. But first, let me preface things by saying I started out with good intentions. Truly wanting to deal with the past and get to a better place. You know that, right?"

"Yes, I do." Encouraging nods. "Absolutely I do."

"I should also clarify that you were the budget option, Ian. I don't have health insurance, and therapy is way too fucking expensive for regular folks."

"Oof, okay." He chuckled. "Unfortunately, that's accurate. It's out of reach for so many who desperately need it."

"But good intentions are, like, seriously difficult to maintain. Too tough for this lowly patient, at least. Somewhere along the way, I slipped."

"Hardly lowly. And I'm sorry that's been your experience. I understand the struggle, and I'm confident we'll get back on track."

"Hey, don't get me wrong. It hasn't been all bad. I've had some illuminating moments. And you've given me quite a lot."

"Glad you see it that way. Sometimes painful—"

"Like that video I have of you screwing your mother-in-law. That was pure entertainment. I mean, by the time she started mewling, my ribs were sore from laughing. She played quite the kitten. I'm sure that wasn't the first encounter. But perhaps the last?"

Even with his thick beard, he could not hide his face blanching. "Wh-what?"

"I do have a question though. Was she satisfied with your performance? As a medical doctor, you must know hormones have shifted by the time a woman reaches that age. I thought you could have been more attentive. I'd give you four for effort. Seven for agility. Extra point for the stamina."

"I don't know how you came up with such an outlan—"

"Don't be coy, Ian. We're adults here."

"Lainey, let's dis—"

"Did you know the police are still trying to identify the man from the night Faye died?" That was a teensy lie. The police couldn't be bothered. "He was caught on camera." I'd heard Andrew's endless complaints about the security contract for the new hotel. Issues with the software. All the hallway cameras still nonfunctional, and the ones at the elevator were producing only grainy images. That information helped. When he left, my boyfriend took the elevator. When I left, I took the stairs. "Oddly enough," I continued, "his height and gait were an uncanny match to yours. And the beard too. Even the same ball cap that you wear."

That was a regret of mine—besides the stupid hat, I did not have a single keepsake of the birthday shag-a-thon. I would have loved some video snippets. An evening of amour with Andrew and Faye. Or Tim and Deborah. But I accepted not every plan could be perfect. Those memories still existed within my fabric. It would have to do.

"Lainey, I'm worried you're having a break with re—"

"I wonder what they'd say if I sent them some stills of you two lovebirds. Anonymously, of course."

His paleness was replaced with a bright flush of anger. "What exactly are you after?" The prickliness was immensely satisfying.

"Do you miss her, Ian? Your wife's mom. Or is it a relief to have her gone?"

"You read about that in the news, right? That's how you know." He flared his nostrils. "And what you're suggesting is entirely preposterous. I had nothing to do with her death. It was an accident."

"Oh, really?"

"Yes, it was. Misadventure. That's been confirmed."

"Oh, dear. That's tragic, isn't it?"

He shrugged. Cool exterior reinstated. I needed to launch my next bomb.

"And then there is one more small item on the agenda. You and me, Ian. The scope of our . . . well, entanglement."

"Entanglement? Our interactions have been entirely professional. Ignoring these egregious breeches of my personal privacy."

Personal privacy? For someone educated, that was quite the redundant phrase.

"Has it though?" I said softly. "Didn't you leave me a set of keys to your condo? I'm certain that's all documented."

"You know I did, Lainey. To assist you. Get you to immediate safety."

In a conspiratorial whisper, I said, "And also to fuck me in a convenient location, right?"

A sharp and sudden shake of his head. "This has gone way beyond. These . . . these delusions." Even though he was incensed, he remained glued to his seat. Same as he'd done for Faye. Like a good boy.

"There's no need to insult me, Ian. I do have a series of snapshots to mark those occasions. They're kind of sizzly, actually. You from behind. Full display of that cute little entropy tattoo on your shoulder."

Andrew had enjoyed those impromptu evenings. When he helped me check on a condo for a client from the yoga studio. He never questioned why the furnishings were so spartan and assumed I'd been tasked with watering the few potted plants I'd scattered around.

"I don't know what you're trying to accomplish, but these behaviors, these blatant lies, will have repercussions."

"Not all actions have equal and opposite reactions, you know. Some shit goes unchecked."

"Mark my wor—"

I put up my hand to interrupt him, and he fell silent. "Look around, Ian. We're not at Albethey anymore."

After a moment, he said, "I don't understand why you're doing this. We were making progress, were we not?"

It was exhilarating to watch him flail. Could joy pulse?

Unzipping my sling bag, I wriggled my fingers inside and withdrew an old Polaroid photo. The image was faded, colors bleeding, but still recognizable. Two teenaged girls cheek to cheek. I slid it across the table toward him.

He resisted for two seconds and then plucked it up, brought it closer to his face. As he examined it, I could practically see recognition jumping from neuron to neuron.

"You wonder why? For my friend, Mia. And her daughter, Elise."

He dropped the photograph as though it'd burned his fingers. "This is fake. I don't know how you made it, but it's not real."

"Come on. Now you're just being ludicrous. You're not the only one capable of deceit, you know. Mia sought you out because she missed me." I frowned. "Sorry if that hurts your feelings."

He flumped back into his seat, his gaze darting left to right. "This nonsense is getting old."

"I know, it's a lot to absorb. Emotions can be tiring." Then I said, "To be clear, I'm withdrawing from our sessions. You do not have my permission to use anything I've said. Any of our conversations, past or present. I can't stop them from republishing your case study. But there will be no addendum. I'm not giving you anything else, Ian. I'm done."

I'd come to realize that therapy was simply not for me. I was not a talk-talk girlie; I was an action girlie. And all I really needed to feel better was a refresh. A reconnect. With my best friend.

"This is—"

"You must realize by now the pile of dirt on you is overflowing. Can you imagine the fallout? Full destruction of your reputation. Career implosion. If the police knew about your special bond with Faye, that might spark an investigation. Which could snowball, you know. How would you look in orange?"

"What do you want?"

"Nothing unreasonable." I took another noisy slurp from my latte. "Just some space. Do whatever Mia asks and then stay out of her way. She doesn't need you. Neither does Elise."

He positioned thumb and forefinger on his chin. With an icy tone, he said, "You're a very troubled woman, Lainey."

"Am I though? Didn't we concur I was making strides?" I slid the Polaroid back into my purse and stood up, mildly disappointed with his negative assessment. It was time to wrap things, and I decided to conclude with politeness. "I do worry about you, Ian. I care what happens, you know. How things will end."

CHAPTER FORTY-NINE

Mia

MIA RAN HER usual route, along the sidewalks in her neighborhood, traversing Main Street, past a parkette, and then turning onto the wooded trail.

In the month since the cabin, she and Ian had officially separated. While at first he'd argued against it, that abruptly changed, and he told her he'd do whatever she wanted. He agreed to move out, and Mia returned to the house with Elise. The new arrangement was causing the least disruption to Elise's life, and for the most part, she seemed unfazed by the shift.

Mia's conversations with Ian remained tense. Initially she'd interrogated him. Repeatedly asking why he'd given her mother that much money. Why had he kept it a secret? But his response gave her no satisfaction. "I thought it'd get her out of our hair. She said she was opening a business."

While Mia didn't buy his lies for a second, she couldn't see beyond them either. She had this niggling sense that the reason was obvious, but it was too close to her face. Perhaps in time, she'd inch backward, and the haze would lift. Though she was working to let it go and not torment herself.

She was also trying to forgive her mother. She'd begun to see Faye as a woman who was mentally unwell. How else to frame the neurotic recording of Mia's life? Or how her mother had inserted herself into every relationship Mia ever had? Viewing Faye through a lens of empathy did not soften the grief or confusion, but it did help her to process Faye's pathological behaviors.

To Mia's surprise, Elise did not appear traumatized by her experience at the cabin, though she was distraught over her grandmother's death. Mia and Ian had arranged weekly therapy for her, and their daughter was accepting the support.

Mia was also striving to be a better mother. To learn ways to lift Elise up, instead of trying to anticipate and control all outcomes. She started by telling Elise she was genuinely sorry for tracking her movements. That even though the girls' actions were incredibly scary, the monitoring was entirely about her own insecurities, and nothing to do with Elise's character as a person.

Mia had realized that with a teenager, there would always be elements of risk. And as a mother, always elements of fear. But trust between parent and child was paramount. She now understood that if she'd been less of a wall and more of a springboard, Elise might have come to her before making such dangerous choices.

Mia and Lainey continued to talk and meet, almost daily. They were getting reacquainted with each other. Rediscovering the power of their friendship. Though their history contained a dark tangle, their connection was still there. Their conversations and their laughter were still unbelievably easy.

While she'd gained a deeper understanding of Lainey's past, Mia would never admit to watching her therapy sessions. She'd only accessed Ian's laptop one more time, and that was to delete the spy software. Lainey had lost so much, and it wasn't right for Mia to take her story without permission. If Lainey wanted to share, she would.

On a very basic level, Mia could relate to what Lainey had experienced. Most women likely could, especially those who did exactly what was expected of them. Allowing the needs of others to continually supersede their own. The delirium of negation, as Cotard's syndrome was described. At every stage of life, parts of women were dying. Or already dead.

If she didn't want her daughter to have that experience, Mia needed to set a better example. She had to genuinely invest in her own well-being. To discover who she was.

"Somewhere along the way I lost myself," she'd said to Elise that morning. "Though I know that's probably hard to understand at your age."

"No, I get it, Mom." Elise had grabbed her swim bag and then hugged her. "It's never too late, you know. To be you."

As Mia ran along the trail, she smiled at the little memory. Her daughter's words were simple and innocent, and entirely true. In the past, she could not see herself beyond her family. Ian. Elise. Faye. But those fears were melting and being replaced by something else. Perhaps it was the glow of excitement. Of future possibility. The care and support she'd always desired were there now, and a huge part of that was Lainey. Mia had this soothing sense things would be fine. She would find her way.

CHAPTER FIFTY

Lainey

WITH A THIN blade, I slit open the tape on a long cardboard box. I'd purchased a shelving unit, four wooden dining chairs, and a pair of night tables. Last week, Mia had graciously offered the use of the condo, which now belonged exclusively to her. She'd used funds from her mother's estate sale to buy Dr. Morrison out. Of course, I'd immediately said yes and brought over my meager belongings. That afternoon, Mia and Elise were helping me assemble flat-pack furniture.

Mia assumed I'd broken up with Andrew, and I failed to correct her. Though I was "taking some space," he and I continued to date and frolic. Common sense told me it was prudent to keep him at a distance. At least for a while. I had no clue what that bitch, Faye, had shared with Mia. Even though the photos I'd uploaded to the dating apps were poor quality, I couldn't risk my friend recognizing my partner. I'd wait until those memories dulled.

"Should we lay it all out first?" I asked Elise. She and I were working on the shelves. "Maybe put the screws and stuff in a bowl?"

"On it!" she chirped.

I loved the youthful enthusiasm. We'd developed a close connection. Cool-aunt-cool-niece kind of vibe. At first she was leery and justifiably so. Earlier in the summer, we were strangers, clubbing together, boozing together, late-night dining together. When she realized I wasn't going to rat on her and her twit friend, she saw me for what I was. The most curious of coincidences.

Mia pulled chair legs from a box and placed them side by side on the floor. Her loose hair was catching the sunshine that poured through the oversized windows. I once saw an Instagram reel that said something about darkness being attracted to darkness. But my darkness wasn't that way. It only craved light.

My best friend hadn't changed at all. The person she was as a teenager was still inside her. Same as me. (Mostly.) When we met again, we were both flimsy and weak at our edges. Molting animals. Together, we would find strength to grow that next shell. And I firmly believed our decades-old vow continued to bind us to each other. She would protect me. I would protect her.

As the sun lowered in the sky, I thought of my uncle. The love he'd given me. The extraordinary damage he'd caused. When I asked Mia about that night, she remembered very little. Neither did I. Both hot chocolates had been spiked. We'd crawled into the cabin and up the steep stairs to the attic. Mia and I had curled together on the wooden floor and woken in the same position. Had my uncle carried her away and returned her? Or had he realized how vital she was to my well-being and let me keep her after all? I thought about those questions for hours and hours. Would sharing any of that benefit Mia? Would it benefit me? I decided the answer to both questions was no.

I'd spent enough time lingering in the past. Though I'd changed my perspective on the value of my therapy sessions with Dr. Morrison. At first I thought reliving the awfulness had done nothing to alleviate my discomfort. But I'd been wrong. Telling him some portion of the truth had cut through the murkiness. I'd given my trauma shape and color and power. Now that I could practically touch it, I was able to let it go.

"Can you hold this?"

"No prob," I said.

Elise handed me two lengths of wood, their ends touching. As she twisted the bolt with a hex wrench, I tried to identify my emotions. Pinpointing the hints my body was offering. Heart thumping at a slower speed. Breath gliding in and out of my lungs with ease. Muscles loose and limber. I decided I was feeling content. I decided I was feeling safe.

I made a promise to myself, then and there: I'd allow nothing and no one to take that away from me. I sincerely hoped Ian would stay in his little corner.

"Looking great," Mia said. "We'll turn this place into a home before you know it."

As she spoke those words, I felt lightheaded, and bent slightly at the waist. Everything I'd gone through had carried me to that moment. I realized now there was beauty in delirium. Wholly detaching and vibrating inside a pocket of emptiness. In that place, I discovered the brink of myself. And maybe that was what it took. I had to die to come alive. To understand. To understand love.

ACKNOWLEDGMENTS

I was uncertain about writing an acknowledgments section. How could I possibly express the depth of my gratitude for the support and kindness I've received these past couple of years? And if I'm honest, I barely remember writing this book. A string of moments in the haze, and somehow these pages appeared.

So I'm going to keep it very simple.

For my agent, Danielle Egan-Miller, you've been a steady source of guidance, and so incredibly generous with your time and enthusiasm. Thank you.

For Lara Hinchberger, your excellent editing truly transformed this book. Thank you always for your careful eye.

For all the others on the team behind this snazzy final product—I appreciate it all.

For my friends in the writer community, who kept checking in and cheering the small steps. I am deeply grateful.

For the friends who have walked beside me, no matter my pace, thank you. It has meant so much.

For my partner and love, Simon Archer. Gosh. What to even say? You are good, through and through.

Finally, for my three children. The enduring love . . . the words, the whispers, and now, the dreams. I am forever thankful. You're my heart. Still, and always.

NICOLE LUNDRIGAN is the Canadian bestselling author of several critically acclaimed novels, including *A Man Downstairs*, *An Unthinkable Thing*, and *Hideaway*. Her fiction has twice been shortlisted for the Crime Writers of Canada Award for Best Crime Novel and has appeared on "best of" selections from *The Globe and Mail*, the CBC, Amazon, *Chatelaine*, and more. She grew up in Newfoundland, and now lives in Toronto.